PICTURES ON
THE WALL

PICTURES ON THE WALL

by

HUGO CHARTERIS

introduced by

DAVID LODGE

SANDNESS
MICHAEL WALMER
2024

Pictures on the Wall first published 1963
© The Estate of Hugo Charteris

Introduction first published in this edition
© David Lodge 2024

Published by

Michael Walmer
North House
Melby
Sandness
Shetland, ZE2 9PL

ISBN 978-0-6457519-3-2 paperback

ERRATA

This edition has been created utilizing a previous edition; thus errors have been reproduced. On page 247, line 10, for *he done* please read *he had done;* on page 255, line 17, for *gratiude* please read *gratitude*; line 23, for *remember* please read *remembered*; line 29, for *to* please read *too.*

INTRODUCTION

Note: Some readers may prefer to read the novel first and the introduction afterwards. Indeed, I recommend that procedure, since an introduction inevitably gives away too much about the story as it unfolds, and deprives the reader of enjoyable and thought-provoking surprises. DL

Pictures on the Wall, a novel by Hugo Charteris first published in 1963, is what is sometimes called "a period piece" — that is, an item of literature or other work of art whose special interest lies in its evocation of a historical period. The period which Charteris evokes, and describes with convincing authenticity, is the one which followed the end of World War II, which I remember well, as I was a schoolboy living at home in London at the time. I did not read any of Charteris's books then, probably because no adult had suggested to me that I should. But for some years he was recognized as a novelist of exceptional skill and sensitivity, highly praised by critics and fellow practitioners — *"essentially a writer of our day,"* one of them declared.

Hugo Charteris was upper class, with aristocratic connections and a life-style to match. But *Pictures on the Wall* appears on first acquaintance to be a novel drawing on a period of his life spent in managing a "Detention Centre" — a Borstal type of institution for delinquent youths, situated in a dull part of the English Midlands not far from Birmingham. The main character, Philip Ayrton, is its Warden and administrator. This milieu is evoked convincingly, and I was astonished when I looked up the scanty facts of Charteris's life which were accessible, and found no mention of his being employed at any time in charge of an institution of that kind. How, I wondered, had he created such a credible impression of what it would be like to manage a Detention Centre, without experiencing such a responsibility himself?

Perhaps he did experience it, without admitting it publicly. But he was such a clever and imaginative writer that, like many great novelists, he could create a totally convincing picture of a given milieu from a limited acquaintance with it, or out of his own imagination.

The central character, Ayrton, through whose eyes and thoughts we obtain an idea of the community in which the story unfolds, is a family man in his mid-forties, with a wife, Ella, two children of well-spaced ages, and a dog. But he is much more interesting than that description suggests. He is sensitive, idealistic and altruistic — committed to helping the youths who are confined in the Detention Centre. In the past he had left his public school to become a monk in a Catholic religious order, and later found his vocation in trying to make the D.C. a place where its young inmates might improve their characters and the quality of their lives.

In the early part of the novel Ayrton appears as a humane and dedicated man whose management of the Detention Centre is admirable. He coaxes the youths in his care to behave decently, helps them in their appointed tasks, and encourages them to make the most of their limited opportunities. But there is a fatal flaw in his character. There are women as well as men in the local community, and Ayrton becomes infatuated with one of them, an attractive young woman known as "Minty". Infatuated, and then obsessed.

Charteris describes this development subtly. Ayrton knows very well that as a married man with a family he should not get romantically involved with a young woman barely twenty years old. But Minty fancies Ayrton, teases him, and casts an erotic spell on him. He convinces himself that he is deeply in love with her. One day they go for a walk into the nearby village, and as his wife Ella is conveniently away for two days, Ayrton offers to show Minty the inside of his home. It isn't long before the couple are "making out" as American teenagers say, on the marital bed.

The story has a second level which includes an inmate of the Detention Centre called Goole, who, unknown to Ayrton, is in a relationship with Minty. Goole is a gifted musician and singer, whose favourite instrument is the guitar, and Ayrton envies his skill with it. Smoking is banned in the D.C., but Goole smuggles a quantity of tobacco into the place which causes great concern to the senior staff when discovered. Ayrton however is too obsessed with his desire for Minty to take a grip on this issue. He writes a long love letter to her, but *"[h]e then did something which next morning he could not really believe he had done. He posted the letter."*

Ayrton is terrified that it will go astray, be discovered, and ruin his reputation, so he recklessly tries to get it back by stealthily entering Minty's home to recover it. When she finds him there rummaging among her papers, she struggles with him, is hurt by Ayrton's grip on her neck and exclaims, *"Go away! Don't you know* yet — *you're* mad.*"* Her reaction is understandable, but does not weaken Ayrton's obsession with her. He is also disturbed by domestic issues in his own family. His young son John is suspected of having pocketed his mother's diamond ring, which had always fascinated him, and in fact has hidden it in a locker, simply so he could handle it and play with it. The ring is soon recovered, but the episode is a blow to Ayrton's pride in his family.

Goole has almost "done his time" and is awaiting the date of his release from the Detention Centre. When he reports to Ayrton for a "Last Interview", Ayrton tells him to sit down but avoids meeting his eyes: *"Would Goole go straight? Yes. Would he keep up his reading lessons with the help of the After-*

Care Associations? Yes. Would he marry this girl who had stood by him? Yes, he thought he would. And was she the right kind of girl for him? Yes, he thought she was." This is an artful combination of the suppressed thoughts of the unfaithful married man, which we can guess at, and the evasive replies of the youth to his probing questions. To represent these thoughts in explicit dialogue or authorial description, as in most novels, would have been much less effective. Hugo Charteris was an innovative master of his medium, prose narrative.

The novel ends on a positive note of hope and reconciliation. Ayrton's daughter Christine, a pianist, announces that she is engaged to be married, much to her mother's delight. Christine is happy, and *"[t]he reflected glory of that single fact shone now on Ella's face, making her look happy too."* To Ayrton *"[i]t was as though the two women had escaped from something. But from what …. what else but the tyranny of his aspirations and of his own point of view? Well, he too was glad. […] In remorse he felt delivered. But by whom? Paradoxically it was Minty who seemed like some sort of optical illusion, to have lured him not, as he hoped, to herself, but to where he was better off; and to have demoralised him only to strengthen him."*

There is a religious subtext in this conclusion to the novel, of the "Amazing Grace" type: *"I once was lost, but now I'm found, was blind, but now I see."* It comes from Ayrton's — and Charteris's — social and moral principles, acquired from their upbringing: the experience of Eton, Oxford, and having personally had what was called "a good war". That was World War II, in the course of which Charteris was decorated for valour in Italy, after holding off a number of enemy soldiers with a single machine gun. He was the complete English gentleman hero.

DAVID LODGE

Edgbaston, November 2021.

I

PHILIP AYRTON, a man in his middle forties and Warden
of Edgecliffe Detention Centre, was reading the correspondence column of the *Daily Telegraph* where protests
were being made against the failure of pre-war army pensions
to keep pace with the cost of living. The opinions ran so
true to form that he got very little stimulus from what he
read. Nevertheless he was lured on by reluctant sympathy
and partial identification.

From upstairs came the sound of advanced piano scales
and finger exercises.

What hurts them most, he thought, is the fashionable
valuation of a man by the amount he earns *regardless of how
he earns it.*

There was comfort in this thought.

He puffed his pipe and glanced at his watch. Five
minutes more.

Addiction to conversations with himself stemmed from
the absence of any alternative. Ella seldom had a clue what
he was talking about: abstractions held no meaning
for her.

Yes: to-day any means of gaining a living tends to be
that and nothing more, neither better nor worse than any
other means. Technical excellence in a given function has
obviously always brought high rewards, but to-day even if
this function happens to be crime then along with high

rewards goes *ipso facto* a certain public esteem. The big-time gangsters are like Cabinet Ministers, " at the top." Only bishops, officers, headmasters and governors of prisons prove the exception to the rule for they, although " at the top," and fairly well paid, stand low in public esteem. To *these* professions moral valuation does seem to be applied—but upside down. In other words: two of the dominants in British life to-day are teen-agers and crooks !

Many of the letter-writers, he noticed, had been serving abroad, and this was perhaps why some of their opinions struck a particular chord of sympathy in his own heart.

For in a way, he thought, we too have been living abroad, out of touch. Although the Prison Service has altered in the last twenty years, we are as chained to its conditions as any family attached, say, to the Gambian Constabulary. Ella and I are all right: we're getting on. But it has been hard on the children, on Christine at least: moved from pillar to post as much as any army daughter. Worse still, she has been up to a point kept in quarantine by me when at home (from the inmates when we were in a Borstal), and put in quarantine by others at school and in the neighbourhood because of her associations with a prison. She has been brought up in a world apart.

The trouble with Christine was she " buried " things. You never knew what affected her and what didn't. The only time she " came out " was in her music and that was why, as soon as he discovered she had some aptitude, he had encouraged her to take it seriously and lately to make it her life.

He raised his eyes from the paper, put his pipe tip in his lips and listened. It was possibly disappointment, half an hour ago, that had driven him so deeply into the paper.

For it was the first time he had heard her since she had gone to Birmingham to study and though her technique seemed to have made progress, it was all somehow laboured.

Well, he was paying through the nose for every pang. He listened rather wistfully, remembering what he had felt years and years ago when he'd heard her pick out that Brahms cradle song by ear when she was scarcely more than a toddler. Others had noticed her, too. So it hadn't been just his idea. But in those days she had made the instrument *sing*. . . . Well, now she was studying for her L.R.A.M., was within reach perhaps of producing sounds that would justify everything, the arguments with Ella and the Education people, the expense and the work. Strange how Ella couldn't see that Christine was not attractive to boys. He had tried to explain that to have a vocation as opposed to a job would be a substitute for a husband and family—should these fail to materialise. Besides, he still longed, really longed for her to become a good pianist.

Against Ayrton's ankles lay the warm comfortable weight of Peter, his black Labrador. Gradually his thoughts drifted away from his hopes of Christine's talent to his affiliated hopes for Morgans Garages which he had bought low in January. In the last month the shares had gone up twenty per cent, and this gave him a small pleasure.

Although the windows were shut, the curtains occasionally stirred in draughts from the rough wind which could be heard rustling outside. Compromise between these draughts and a rather cheerless fire in an Economy grate, gnawing its way through poor quality coal, kept the temperature just too low for comfort, a condition which was reflected in the thick jersey visible on either side of the Warden's dark-blue, emblem-spotted college tie.

Pictures on the Wall

The pipe in his hand, sometimes between and sometimes at the threshold of his lips, the settled position in his chair, his rather motionless face and another casual glance at his watch (as though time, if not his friend, was at least not his master)—all this was proof of business as usual.

One day at Edgecliffe was very like another: and there had been a lot of them.

Ayrton was in his prime, but the dowdy, thin cotton covers on which he was sitting, the two vases like fairground trophies on the dresser, a few dog-eared Penguins and old *Observers* in the rotating half-empty book-shelf, and the four pavement-artist oils beside the Van Gogh reproduction were all suggestive of stagnation. The events of his life, he knew, had by now imposed on him a scene, props, and to a certain extent a part. Like those strange (they *ought* to have been familiar!) drab, television documentary plays this room reflected an utterly hybrid background: neither bourgeois nor working-class, comfortable nor poor, traditional nor modern, private nor public. . . . It was simply muddled and fated. The very furniture looked as if it were on loan from the Home Office, the books were those he could lend to Borstal boys and one of the pictures on the wall was by a former inmate.

Considered either as a barometer of social standing or even of psychological health he was reluctantly aware that the reading of this interior must be round about the " W " of *Wet*. Certainly it scarcely fitted his Borstal nickname— " The Squire."

He could of course make the excuse that the house was Ella's province. He could even cheer himself up with the thought that compared with the packaged neatness and impersonal tidiness of many middle-class living-rooms there was something almost hopeful about the scruffiness of this

one. Ella's wild ineptitude when she tried to ape her
neighbours' furnishings sometimes had original results.
Three ascending china duck, for instance, on the wall by
the fire had needed a special invisible pin to fix them in
flight to the wall. Losing the third pin and patience, Ella
had used some sort of nail, missed her aim and decapitated
the leading duck. Any of her neighbours would then have
got a new set of ascending china duck. But Ella's hunger
for ascending duck wasn't strong enough: the leader was
left decapitated which made the whole group slightly less
ugly and commonplace as though a healthy tendency
towards complete disintegration had set in—through the
leader losing his head. And then there was her reluctance
to change the name of the house from Shang-ri-la. He had
been fastidious and would have preferred a number.
Shang-ri-la was either too heavily ironical or absurd. But
she had said she didn't know what he was talking about,
having never heard of Shang-ri-la, but if that was the
house's name she didn't see why he couldn't leave it.
" You and your names," she said. " Remember the fuss
you made about ' Christine ' ? " He remembered. Sometimes he was grateful for the gulf that so often divided
their points of view, felt rescued by it from what he admitted
was a tendency to stiffness, priggishness and ready-made
class or highbrow attitudes which he of all people should
by now have shed—living as he did with convicted men in
the middle of nowhere.

It was 5.45. He did not really want to see the News but
it would fill in time till Receptions and there was always
the possibility of something unexpected having happened.
He was about to get up when he heard Ella's steps on the
stairs. " Ella," he called, but she didn't hear and for a
moment his eyes strayed back to share prices. Then she

came past, outside the door, and he called her again, so that she stopped, heard his third call and came in with a pair of John's shorts in one hand. " Want to see the News ? " he said.

She turned on the machine saying, " The way Christine works ! "

He raised his eyes dishonestly as though listening for the first time.

But he said nothing.

When Christine failed her scholarship last year, he had felt an almost personal sense of defeat as though some aspiration, inside himself to which he could hardly give a name, had, not for the first time, been reduced by the verdict of an insensitive world to the dimensions of a trivial illusion. A secretarial course, her headmistress had advised, would fit Christine for a number of jobs. He had reacted strongly. The idea that education was mainly to fit young people for a function seemed entirely wrong. Education was there to make the most of what was *in* a person. And *in* Christine there was music. So he had raised the banner of his meagre private means against the arbitration of bureaucrats. Christine should study on. . . .

Had she " leapt at the chance " ? Christine wasn't a leaper. She had said she was glad to be able to go on but Ella couldn't leave the subject alone, was always insinuating that Christine found it all " too much."

But surely that was much better now ! She was playing Scarlatti, probably because she knew he liked it. Paying him back ! (How touching was an adolescent's consideration, particularly your own child's.)

People sometimes complained of Scarlatti being jangly, fidgety and cerebral. This just made him smile—the smile which had once made Ella blurt, " You don't smile, Phil :

your lips get leaf-curl." (It must have been quite a maddening smile to have moved Ella to metaphor!) But contempt had its place: he was quite happy to be maddening when people dismissed Scarlatti as "jangly"—Scarlatti, formally exquisite as a humming-bird, yet torrential, powered by all the forces of chaos without abandonment to them. Tension just, only just, resolved. And what tension! To-day tension in art was not . . . resolved!

He smiled and replaced the tip of his pipe which he had moved outwards a quarter of an inch as a substitute for answering because answering would have meant discussing the music Ella didn't like or the intensity of Christine's work which she also didn't like, not only because it was "too much," but because according to her it stopped Christine "seeing a bit of life now and again"—"life" being any activity that might lead to boy-friends and marriage. In fact Christine had plenty of spare time. But there! he did not wish to revive an old argument, particularly as Ella had lately been in no state to argue.

They had been five years at Edgecliffe. At first she had agreed the place was peaceful after Borstals—not having the boys on top of you—but in fact she had soon begun to miss the company of a staff which had been big enough to include "people like ourselves," the bus service at the door and shops you could walk to. Now that Christine was out of the house she seemed to comfort herself with John, more perhaps than was healthy for either. It was true she had been left a lot on her own . . . and then there was her age. . . . "Change of life," the doctor had said at first but how long could such an explanation be valid? For three years now she had been different. Moods, listlessness, going to fat—to say nothing of subjection to all kinds of imaginary fears.

He blamed Edgecliffe largely. Well, he had applied for one of the new open prisons . . . ten minutes in a bus from a Marks and Spencer's.

Not that she had ever made a fuss about Edgecliffe, not directly. She knew the probable alternative, if he were promoted, would be governorship of a big prison and hangings. She knew he did not want that and she knew too that he had wanted to be his own master as soon as possible. All of which had added up to Edgecliffe—an honour, he had liked to think, and a prestige appointment. So she had never grumbled. Just once or twice she had ended a conversation by silence and dabbed her tears with her apron, a trick she seemed to have inherited direct from her peasant grandmother. So, lately they had come to regard Edgecliffe as their last post for it was probable that if he turned down the next offer of promotion there would be no other.

It's a funny thing to look at your wife after twenty-two years and try and really *see* her—freshly, as a stranger might. You can't. Even when we disagree, he thought, it's like a single body with two heads. And yet it shouldn't be like that. Marriage, if it was to be healthy, should be free and all the time re-creating its freedom. To let it stick in a rut is a sort of servitude. Yet Ella's sole ambition seemed to be to re-create that same servitude for Christine as quickly as possible: marriage, children and so on.

All his life he had wanted to "break the circuit," do "something more," transcend at first in his own life and now vicariously through Christine's. Yet Ella couldn't see that it was desirable.

He held out his hand to her invitingly.

She sat down nearby as though perhaps if she sat near

him and adopted the same position she might come nearer to enjoying Christine's music.

Her large " soulful " brown eyes turned to the ceiling. Untidy hair and big beads made her look rather like a medium. She was three years older than he.

" Well, she has come on, hasn't she ? " he said.

" I don't know, Phil. If you say so."

" Nor do I know," he said.

Now a voice out of the grey set suddenly said : " B.B.C. Television, Fife-Forty-Five . . ." and a few seconds later images appeared in the middle of the panel, shivered, raced backwards, expanded, vanished and then flickered into a picture of a bland-faced young man sitting half-way on. He had the unused look of a chick out of an egg or something that was sold in Cellophane.

Ella went out with the shorts.

The newscaster smiled like something electric turned on: there were possibilities of a Summit Meeting, Mr. Macmillan had been to see President de Gaulle informally, the floods had done a million pounds' worth of damage in Devon, the French had exploded a bomb in the Sahara, a new split had developed in the Labour Party and the hunt for missing Valerie was still unsuccessful. The items, like the ·announcer, were all familiar and somehow in Cellophane, hygienic. Even the posse of citizens lined up with sticks looking for Valerie did not suggest anything upsetting or out of the ordinary any more than did the mushroom of smoke against the Atlas Mountains. It was all wallpaper : and less affecting, less felt, than the familiar weather which greeted him, sometimes fine, usually grey, on the hundred yard walk to the office.

" I'm going now, dear," he called, switching off.

" All right, dear."

Taking his duffel-coat from the peg by the oval mirror, he put it over his arm and opened one of the doors leading into the hall and looked in at John, who was playing with his model train. Ayrton often looked in like this before going out but having done so had lately felt diffident and tongue-tied. John was such a silent child.

" Done your home-work ? " he said in a kindly, almost conspiratorial tone as though together they would fight and easily overcome this dreary enemy—work.

But John said nothing and looked down, placing his engine on the rails as he did so.

" Yes, he's done it," came Ella's voice.

" How was school to-day," Ayrton said. Then, when John still did not answer, he said, " No news good news ? " and for a moment delayed shutting the door in case there might be an answer. But there was none.

In the passage, for some reason, he suddenly had a qualm, suddenly thought, oh, God ! If it could all be better, livelier : Christine, Ella, John . . . Edgecliffe. There was no freedom to manœuvre : margins were tyrannically small. Life seemed to be almost over before it had ever begun.

The only article of furniture in the house which he had bought with any satisfaction was the case of three humming-birds in the hall. They were inside a big cloche, grouped round a tree stump, imitation creepers, leaves and insects. One was perched and two suspended. Their wings, which in life would have been invisible with speed, giving them the mysterious power of hover and nimble flight, were fixed wide open, and their eyes were beads. They were very dead. Yet in the past from these gaudy husks he had sometimes got a feeling of life, not of life as it was at Edgecliffe but of life as it might be. Vivid, exuberant, finding joy in mere existence, a world in which even the cruelty was innocent and part of the beauty. In fact there had been moments when a glance at these birds had helped him to ascend a ladder of light—out of and away from his grey profession. They had been (he told himself) to his starved eyes what Scarlatti had been to his ears, an earnest of something quite different, though what that something was he could hardly have said.

But it was a long time since he had had the feeling, except as a sort of memory, second hand. Indeed the feeling now, like the humming-birds, was somehow stuffed.

He went out and at once looked up. At least the stars still lived. Yes, lived! There they were shining in a brilliant maze, some low and coloured, some familiar. . . . And the night air was bracing, sharp and slightly fouled with coal smoke. From the curtained amber-coloured window came the sounds now of a Chopin prelude. It was all like a certain kind of Christmas card. Cosy, traditional, " good." In his heart he suddenly thanked demure Christine for her humour and courage. But why " courage " ? and why had he once said to Ella, " It's hard to know what to tell them " ?

In wishing that they should find vocations, instead of just functions, he was no doubt trying to live his own life over again. Not that he hadn't at last found a sort of vocation. He had. Once he had realised the religious life was not for him, he had at least been lucky enough to find an alternative vocation in this job which he had now done for twenty years. And so perhaps after all " nothing was ever wasted." The previous disciplines, first of his novitiate and then briefly as a teacher had surely helped him deal both with sin (plus hypocrisy!) and with youth. In his heart of hearts he could not help feeling that in the Prison Service Philip Ayrtons didn't grow on every bush. Society had many bulwarks against the criminal, but most of them were blind, mindless, merely suppressive or defensive (however necessary)—police, prison officers and so on. Only here and there were men, favoured by education, experience and natural gifts, who could, provided they reached positions of authority, now and again do something positive in this " ever more significant field."

Why should it be " ever more significant " ? (He had read the words in a report and felt them to be somehow true though not in the way intended.)

He walked on, towards his cheerless destination, pursued by the sensuous, introvert beckonings of the Chopin prelude.

I've never lost sight of beauty, he thought—or of personal usefulness. But in the world to-day what has happened to beauty? The word is never used. Why? Is it because we cannot bear the pain of mentioning something we cannot analyse, nor produce—nor do without? Because it really is true, we cannot live without some redeeming factor, something that will raise us from the world of appearances and statistical truth. That's why my inmates love advertisements.

They are redeemed by them—but to damnation.

2

REACHING THE LIGHTED PORCH of the red brick building, Ayrton took out his bunch of keys. Liversey, a new member of the Disciplinary Staff, was on duty at the door, and came out of the windowed enclosure which contained the switchboard. Although in mufti, Liversey saluted and said, " All correct, sir. Three Receptions."

" Don't worry too much about the saluting here, Liversey."

" Yes, sir," Liversey said, and remained rooted to attention.

Ayrton looked at him. He had a birthmark over his face and neck like a map of the British empire before 1945. South of Singapore, so to speak, it was obscured by his collar. His weak, sensitive face seemed to verge on apathy and increased Ayrton's fears that Detention Centres, far from getting the best available officers, were now getting —volunteers certainly—but volunteers for the wrong reasons. Well—who wouldn't " volunteer " to serve in a D.C. rather than a prison ! No one. In which case why weren't the best chosen ? Because the prisons needed the best in order to function at all.

" How are we going to fit in another three ? " Ayrton said, hoping to bring the man out. He wanted people to talk openly about penal problems, particularly staff and sometimes on very special occasions even prisoners. But the shyness of other men in his presence had convinced him over the years that they mostly found his voice and smile not encouraging at all, but wintry, wistful, fastidious, tentative, sardonic, perhaps even complacent. Often when he smiled they didn't see anything to smile about and vice versa. Still, he persevered with discussion in order to make work more tolerable and occasionally, he had to admit, for exercising a superiority that had nothing to do with rank.

Liversey, still at attention, clicked his tongue.

Ayrton raised his little finger and thumb and made an octave-span adjustment of his glasses. He could not converse with anyone standing at attention.

" We'll be taking them into our own houses as lodgers soon," he said and he moved on, slowly, a little hunched, pulling out his keys and beginning the ceaseless jingle which accompanied his movement in that place as certainly as the noise of harness accompanied a trap horse. The leaf of each key, smooth as St. Peter's toe, brilliant as dented lead, engaged and turned as though in soft mud. Practice makes perfect.

After penetrating four doors he reached the red linoleum passage which shone like a liquid. There was a line of offices on the right and his Deputy, " Big Jefferies," was standing by a hot fire in the first with the door open. He always seemed to be standing by that fire.

" Three ! " Ayrton said, pausing.

Removing his elbow from the mantelpiece, Jefferies reached over for the ledger and said, " One Taking and Driving Away, one Robbery, one G.B.H."

" We'll have to put them in the hospital."

" The hospital's full."

" Well, now it's going to be fuller," said Ayrton, smiling

to make his contradiction amiable: but Jefferies didn't smile. He was against D.C.s anyhow but particularly against them as interpreted and administered by Ayrton. Worse, he had only been sent here for the promotion, as a preliminary to retirement. Unlike Ayrton he had come up "through the ranks" and had done twenty years as Officer and Principal Officer.

The sheets of the new arrivals were pinned together opposite a manuscript entry, in the book, of their names, ages and offence.

Ayrton stayed to read the book, there where he stood, but Jefferies's elbow went back to the mantelpiece and a sibilant, muted tune broke from between his teeth, suggesting the sameness of all arrivals and the pointlessness, if not bullshit, in poring over case-sheets. Jefferies might not be far wrong but the little that he was wrong aggravated the tension which had been building up ever since he came. To take one example: when Ayrton stopped the saluting, Jefferies had seemed to make a point of talking to him from a particularly slovenly position, as now.

"A first offender!" Ayrton said.

Jefferies nodded as much as to say, "First time the bloke was caught, you mean." With his big ears, cupped outwards like the handles of a goblet, and his huge pale face, he looked like the bulldog burglar in a children's animal comic. A few inmates preferred him to Ayrton, which Ayrton was careful to remember. Jefferies adjusted his focus to a different part of the wall and began another tune through his teeth-tips. "Two more years," Ayrton had overheard him say, "and I'll be shot of this lot. Thirty years as Prison Officer, then Number 2 to a f——g children's nurse! What a fate." It had been in the passage, after a disagreement, intentionally loud.

Pictures on the Wall

Yesterday Ayrton had tried to draw Jefferies into conversation saying that with the ten per cent of First Offenders D.C.s had their best, perhaps only chance of justifying their existence. So now he said, " Let's see, what's he been up to . . . ? " as though continuing that conversation.

" Who's that then ? " Jefferies said. Speech often seemed to make Jefferies uneasy, as though as a process it was usually daft, often risky. He smoothed a few strands of pale hair back along his bald head.

" The First Offender."

After a moment Jefferies continued the soft sibilant tune which seemed to say, " Why answer when it means repeating what's written in front of his eyes ? "

" Fractured someone's skull . . . ! "

For a moment, unreasonably, the sheer intensity of the other man's general disagreement held Ayrton where he stood. Then, in the continuing silence, he gave up and turned away, taking the book with him, down the passage, down the liquid strip of cherry linoleum.

His own office, unlike Jefferies's, indeed unlike Ayrton's own home or any other room in the whole institution, was ·cheerful. He had himself chosen the curtains with the wild-duck design, the gay carpet and the British Railway's posters, one of girl skiers in Switzerland, another of bathers looking up at a B.O.A.C. Comet over the Mediterranean and the third, above the fire-place, of girls in bikinis leaning against a sailing dinghy by a blue sea under cloud-dappled skies. All this he had purposely planned as a bridge between the inmates and the outside world, a bridge to better things barred to them only by himself who had it in his power to decide the final date of release. If it made their tongues hang out, so much the better. If it " didn't make sense "—that too would be a good thing. The more remote and inscrutable he made himself, the more effect he reckoned he would have when he made one of his rare appearances—or when he became familiar in private. Indeed " remoteness " and therefore silence were his most treasured weapons. There was too much talk (with prisoners) in penal work nowadays and inmates were adept at turning it to their advantage. On the whole the less talk, the better. At First Interview he purposely kept talk to a minimum drawing his impressions from appearance, manner and the tone of the few words spoken.

Putting the book in the middle of his table, he went to the cupboard where he kept a few private belongings. Here was a mirror, on the inside of the door, and into this he looked. One of the things he insisted on was scrupulous tidiness and cleanness. His own " shooting-jacket " and grey flannels were off-the-peg stuff, nothing wonderful for fit, but as near possible the free citizen's equivalent of the lads' battledress tunics ; in the same way his own hair was not much longer than theirs. He kept the tweed spotless, the flannels creased and his hair neat with comb and water. They could do the same.

He turned his face a little in the mirror.

" The Squire " ! The nickname, he liked to think, had come largely from Lucy, his previous retriever, who had dogged his footsteps wherever he went, indoors and out, and from the gun, spouting from his crooked arm on Saturdays. Inmates must have been reminded of the pictures of gentry they saw in illustrated papers. His clothes too, off duty, had a shabbiness that proclaimed a *gentleman's* indifference to public opinion and a security in his own valuation of himself. So " The Squire " he had remained and on every other Saturday could be seen, here too, setting out squirishly with Peter at his heels.

Pictures on the Wall

How about his face? Monk, monkey, or *manqué*? It was a bit of all three: sandy-haired, long-jawed, thin-lipped, angular, intense, reserved (the reserve of dis-appointment?), and slightly weathered by the winds of Edgecliffe. No boy brought before him could fail to be daunted by his deep-set eyes. For short-sightedness had, paradoxically, given them a look of shrewd perspicacity, a look of X-ray intensity. In the middle of the thick lenses the pupils seemed to float remote but omniscient, elusive but determined, and as he looked at himself even he was impressed—and, for a moment, felt a bit omniscient, elusive and determined.

It was dark now so he pulled the wild-duck curtains and stoked up the cosy little coal-fire, the only flames the boys ever saw except when they were on boiler fatigue. Then he sat down and, flicking off some fragments of pencil-shavings from the thick W.D. blanket table cloth, he opened the big book and unscrewed his fountain-pen. He would have liked a pipe but he had made a rule that no member of the staff should smoke inside the D.C. precincts. Not even in the staff assembly room. Example, he had told them, was the only possible basis for imposing a morality. True he smoked a little at home but then this job condemned you to be just a little bit hypocritical all the time. Just a little bit. As the penologist Alexander Paterson had said: " The claim to be just is what becomes a burden."

A firm knock sounded on the door. He carefully did not reply at once and this was understood for the knock was not repeated—all part of the technique of being remote.

" Come in," at last he shouted, and with the back of his hand brushed the face of his open book.

Chief Officer Parks came in. He was No. 3 in the Centre, a slight man with fixed, stern, fanatical, grey eyes, a monk of Her Majesty's Prison Service whose confidence that an inmate was here for his own good never seemed to waver. "Ready, sir?"

Ayrton said he was ready.

Then Jefferies came in and sat down heavily and indifferently beside him just as Parks yelled, "Walk in now, sharp, hold your head up, stop there, face the Warden, state your name. . . ."

It was another evening, like any other and he would be through in an hour.

3

BUT TO-NIGHT, for some reason, how tired of it all he was! The shouting and stinging echoes in the confined space, the flurry of arms pumped up and down shoulder-high, the rigid warped positions of a boy who had only had five minutes' drastic tuition in military postures; the old questions from his mouth and the old answers from theirs. How he longed for material that offered scope for a little optimism.

The first man was a hardened product of an approved school, already a native of crime, deaf, out of reach perhaps of anybody but some woman, mate of his body and soul. The second had a stepmother who had sold his clothes to the pawnbroker every Friday till he killed his Alsatian puppy with a gear-lever on a Thursday and stole a car on Saturday. With his father it was "yutter yutter yutter." Fifty-two pounds a week were coming into the house in wages, but he was already on probation for stealing ten shillings. The owner of this record, a sturdy, short, red-headed youth with a child's face, looked puzzled. He had probably been crying. But in the middle of the watery childishness there was a choleric look that made it seem conceivable that even here he might suddenly try violence as a way out. Ayrton separated the expression in the moistened eyes from the mature body and thought: he's younger than John—five or six. After three months' emotional "deep freeze" and physical culture at Edgecliffe his biceps would be quite extraordinary. Next time he wouldn't even need a gear-lever. He would be able to take life between finger and thumb.

Presumably the puppy had been the only thing he loved. At first he said it had bitten him, but then some other memory seemed to silence him and when Ayrton murmured, " Why did you do it . . . ? " the seconds ticked away, measuring the depths of the unanswerable. At last Ayrton, lower still and without looking anywhere near the boy but just at his statistics on the page, said, " You don't know—do you ? "

Then, as though communicated with for the first time, the boy muttered back, in the infectious low tones of secrecy: " Nossa."

" Will this girl in the post office keep up with you ? "

" Nossa."

After a moment's silence Ayrton started on the bit which always reminded him of a clergyman's *And now to God the Father* . . . " Well, while you're here you'll be expected to do three simple things, try hard, keep yourself tidy and clean and do what you're told. . . . That's all then. . . ."

That's all then, Harrison, that's all. . . . It should have been a Negro spiritual, to an accompaniment of drill commands.

The shouting started. Parks managed to put sympathy into it somehow. Arms pumped wildly. Harrison had to be headed off from the wall—he was thinking so hard about where to go. " There's the door, lad—ever seen one before?" Parks shouted, as though it were all normal, sensible movement " Up up up—higher—left right left . . ."

The door slammed and the " tempo " could be heard being maintained with rhythmic shouts all the way down the passage—" up up up."

" Needs somone to take a gear-lever to him," Jefferies said.

" Certainly he needs something . . ." Ayrton said.

With Biro poised over the blank space under "Harrison" he tried to think of something to write so that this labelling system of his should not break down for want of fuel. The presence of Jefferies who was looking sideways at the book, did not help. " First impression "—the two words seemed suddenly pretentious, like something from the diary of an adolescent. How could he go on playing this game with himself? " A f——g children's nurse." Was that what he should have been? But supposing the inmates *were* children . . . as that one seemed.

Parks's shout came again in the passage and hurriedly Ayrton wrote, " Must learn to control his temper." But he could hardly get the words down. (What's the matter with me to-night? he thought.)

" Turn to your right, lad—your RIGHT—now halt, face the Warden, stand at ease . . . legs apart . . . hands behind your back. . . ."

And there was Goole—the First Offender, the absolute newcomer to the world of crime. The man for whom D.C.s were primarily intended.

Now! Ayrton thought. *Now!*

Apart from committing Grievous Bodily Harm, Goole had also been charged with Indecent Assault. The Court report suggested he would have been convicted of this too if the girl had given evidence. But she hadn't. Presumably Ayrton thought, she had been grateful.

He was not a giant as his crime suggested, but thickly built with deep shoulders that sloped to a strong barrel body. Dense black eyebrows almost joined over broad-nostrilled nose; mouth thick and sensuous; tense, yet dreamy eyes. Unlike the others he had not moved quickly and at once to where he was ordered, in front of the desk, but had seemed at a loss for what was required of him. His reactions somehow satirised the shouting without meaning to. He even seemed, meanwhile, to take things in with his eyes . . . the objects on the desk and the man behind it. The immense strangeness of his predicament was mirrored in every glance, every move he made. Occasionally he swallowed; or he took perceptible deep breaths through parted lips, and moved his feet. And until Parks ordered them behind his back his hairy hands hung slack showing fingers deeply stained with tobacco. When he answered his name his voice sounded tentative as though he were uncertain the situation could be meant to be shaping as at present.

His eyes met Ayrton's with simplicity and Ayrton's after a pause, dropped.

" First Offender ? " Ayrton said, and Parks confirmed smartly.

When there was no probation report or previous history

the only source of information was the lad himself. In all such cases the Chief Officer made a preliminary biographical note so that the Warden should have something to work on. This, along with Goole's intelligence test, was what Parks placed in front of Ayrton now.

The intelligence paper was blank.

" You can't write at all ? " Ayrton said.

" No . . . sir."

Goole's voice was deep but mild, contrasting strangely with the look of tension in his dark eyes.

Nor could he read. Parks's spidery hand told this story. Goole was twenty years old. A gipsy. Born in Kent in 1940. Mother died when he was five and father when he was nine. Stayed on the road with relations till he was fourteen. Never attended school more than a few days at a time. Fair-ground attendant. Casual labourer. Stayed in the Birmingham area. Boxer. Had earned occasional money playing in a Solihull band. Worked at the fruit in the summer and hops after. Unemployed. Began going with a girl he met fruit-picking. Met her in a pub with the farmer for whom he had been picking fruit. A fight started. Said in court he didn't remember what happened.

" Who looked after you when your parents died, Goole ? "

" My uncle."

" Now what did I tell you, Goole ! " Parks shouted.

" Sir," Goole said.

" What happened to him ? "

Goole's face seemed to see no connection between his uncle and himself.

" He's maybe—I dunno, sir," Goole said. " Worcester way."

" When did you see him last ? "

Goole's face clouded.

Ayrton suddenly said. " What year is it now? "

Goole's brows knitted even more heavily and he looked round at the wall as though following an almost invisible insect. Suddenly he smiled as though admitting it wasn't there, the insect, never had been. The suddenness and completeness of the smile embarrassed Ayrton. Parks shouted, " Look to your front."

" You don't know the year. It's 1960."

Goole was not impressed.

After staring down at the papers for a moment Ayrton said, " So you had no home really ? "

" Nossa."

" And this girl you met fruit-picking . . . she was the cause of the fight."

Goole's eyes said " yes."

" Let's hear you," Jefferies said.

Goole said, " Yes . . . sah."

" But she didn't give evidence against you. . . . Why was that ? "

Goole didn't answer.

" She was your girl ? "

" Yessah."

" Yet you assaulted her indecently ? "

Goole did not reply.

A tiny contraband thought, a cloud of irrelevance no bigger than a man's hand, loomed on the margin of Ayrton's thoughts : he wanted to know what Goole had done to the girl, wanted to watch in his mind's eye, the doing of it. And he suddenly heard himself say: " What in fact did you do to her ? "

Moments passed.

Pictures on the Wall

And then, " Can't you remember ? "

Ayrton looked down at his papers : Jefferies stirred. Ayrton felt thwarted. He said sharply, " While you're here you had better answer when you're asked a simple question. Where was this fight ? "

" At the Three Musketeers. Hotel like . . ."

" What were you doing there ? "

" I was waitin' for 'em to come out, sir, see. I was in the car park, I knew his car. It was blue. A Jaguar, it was. I'd seen it before. I just waited beside it."

" Then ? "

Goole's face clouded. It was like the date again, confused by possibilities.

His girl ? · His honour ?

Suppose Goole had merely done what the heroes of westerns did every night, administered private justice where official justice could not or would not do anything ? Because Goole couldn't call the police or a lawyer. Goole could not read or write—(a state of exclusion and isolation in the modern world which was as hard to imagine as the mentality of a savage) ; and Goole belonged to no massive body, union or firm. He did not even belong to a class or a street. He was not even any longer a gipsy in the corporate sense, only a gipsy in the sense of being a misfit and as such likely to get suspicion rather than justice wherever he went.

Ayrton was interested in Goole.

Conscious that moments, perhaps minutes had passed without a word, he felt required to speak. But his thoughts played truant again, strayed to memories of himself as a young man when he emerged from his exhausting novitiate —neither a monk nor a member of the class and set-up to which he had once belonged, a professional nonentity,

29

without connections, older by four years. A displaced person indeed though not to the extent of being illiterate.

"You have been sent here to learn that you can't take the law into your own hands ..." he murmured, talking low and coming to his own rescue with words that needed no thought. "Here: you'll have to do what you're told. Now ... you say you can't remember what you did. But I can tell you: you did something pretty savage or you wouldn't be here ... I see you've applied for permission to receive letters from a girl. Is this another girl?"

Goole hesitated. "Nossir ..."

"Well ..." Ayrton pondered, looking sideways at the report. "Miss Heidi Roberts. She wouldn't give evidence because she didn't want to get you into worse trouble."

"Nossir."

"And you think she'll be writing to you?"

"Yessir."

Silence. Perhaps they were all thinking about Miss Roberts.

He said at last, "We've no objection. But how are you going to read her letters or answer them?"

"Blokes read 'em out to me," Goole said.

"You mean you have had letters from her in the past?"

"Yessir." Surprise imposed another moment's silence. Then Ayrton said, "What does she work at?"

"She's in ... a factory."

"Do you expect her to try and visit you while you're here?"

"Yessir."

Ayrton wondered. When he looked up Goole was looking about him inquisitively, as though still free.

"What do you like doing best, Goole?"

" I'm a good singer," Goole said indifferently but apparently ready to prove it.

Ayrton looked down, disappointed. So many men said that.

Now Ayrton made his usual speech about effort and cleanliness.

Goole smiled, not cheekily, not in any way offensively; just resignedly—at the programme. All the officers saw that smile. Even Jefferies must almost have pitied it.

Within a few hours such a man would be either broken or ripe for one of those explosions which would earn him a few hours in the " cooler " a square of stone space in which the only piece of furniture would be himself. After that he would " fit in."

Ayrton told Goole he'd get lessons, while he was at Edgecliffe, in reading, and the day he'd come out if he behaved would be 20th December.

Then Parks's voice tore viciously, without a grain of sympathy, at the fabric of Goole's composure. " LEFT TURN—QUICK MARCH, SWING YOUR ARMS—up up UP," and Goole marched out in a way that no one could take exception to.

Jefferies breathed eloquently.

" Curious case," Ayrton said evasively. " The gipsy and the factory girl . . . and the farmer."

Jefferies said, " The girl—the one who's going to write to him. She's a tart, isn't she ? "

Ayrton recognised the objection in the Deputy's tone: " If she's bad," he said, " she won't stand by him. There won't be any letters."

" She's got him three months already," Jefferies said.

" He's got no one else," Ayrton said, then affably: " he's the kind I was talking about. First Offender. The kind this place could help—or harm. He's the kind we'd like to know something more about," and as he spoke he wrote (perhaps for Jefferies's benefit) the name " Goole " on his memo-pad to remind him to do what neither he nor anyone else had time to do : find out more. One had to take these opportunities. After all the official line was : D.C.s are not just punitive sausage machines.

Jefferies said, " That's it then. . . ."

As he walked out Ayrton's Biro shifted to the blank space opposite Goole's name, then descended as follows : " Gipsy. A blunt, formidable man. Care, while he is here, to avoid provocation or injustice in case there has already been some of both. Interesting face. No. I.Q. given as he cannot read."

The entry at least looked tidy and professional. It brought Goole into the picture.

But he closed the book quickly, snapped it shut.

4

It was disappointing to see Christine's head beside John's, silhouetted against the screen of the television. Her ears, he thought, should have rejected the sodden familiarity of drumming hoof-beats and fists on faces like packets of rice dropped on tin.

" Bang, bang, bang," he said. " Let's eat in here to-night at a civilised hour."

Pictures on the Wall

Without moving her eyes from the set Christine said, "Mum's got it ready in the kitchen," then as though conscious of her father's reaction to seeing her sitting there she got up slowly and stretched, leaving John behind her hypnotised. She was wearing tight trousers which ended half-way down the calf, and a blue jersey that cut across the thickest part of her bottom with a scarlet turn-up. The whole effect was unexpected in this room, particularly on Christine. Ayrton did not know if he was pleased or put out. The garments were brave on Christine, like battle flags on a ship with slight armament. They were even poignant.

Ella came in and Ayrton said, "How about eating in here to-night ? "

" But it's ready Phil. . . ."

" Well, that's that, isn't it ? "

In the kitchen they sat down to fish-fingers, pickled beetroot and tea. "We had an unusual case to-day," he said.

The quality of his family's silence was more eloquent than words.

Christine obliged at last, " A murderer ? "

" Why d'you say murderer ? "

" Well, you always used to say murderers were ' un-usual ': not really criminals at all."

" No. Not a murderer."

Ella said, " We haven't seen Christine for two months and you want to talk about criminals." A moment later she said, " I'm sure the Fawcetts *are* expecting you to call, dear."

" That's the second time to-day I've heard you talking about the Fawcetts," Ayrton said. " Why can't I talk about criminals if you talk about the Fawcetts ? "

" The Fawcetts live in Birmingham, Phil," Ella said, with a touch of exasperation.

" But we met them for ten minutes in a hotel last summer ! "

" They're nice people."

Christine said, " Dad wants to talk about eating in the kitchen ' at a civilised hour '."

" Let's hear about Birmingham and the Fawcetts then. How's it going, Christine ? "

The upper-rims of her spectacles were tortoise-shell decorated with gilt, and behind them her eyes, usually rather sharp and defensive, took on an alert almost apprehensive look. After a moment she said, " Mr. Cramer says I've got a long ' pool ' ahead." Having said this she smiled as though she had made a poor joke which someone had better appreciate.

" You see, dear ! " Ella said.

" Hasn't anyone who ever got anywhere had a long ' pool '? " he said.

Ella said, " Tell us more about the hostel. Is it near anywhere ? "

Ayrton thought, it isn't really the Fawcetts she's talking about : she's trying to personalise the vast, anonymous city in which Christine is now living alone, with seven free hours a day to fill. The Fawcetts are merely a symbol, a handle with which to grasp what is otherwise shapeless, inconceivable. Home, identity, a permanent relationship.

And then Ella went on to Katie Howden, Christine's friend at the hostel. She too was a landmark. Ella asked where Katie came from, what her parents did. Christine wasn't sure.

In time the sound of their knives and forks took the place of speech.

" D'you meet many other people ? " Ella said at last. She had spoken with difficulty as though the question had cost her something.

" Now and again."

" There's plenty of boys in Birmingham," Ayrton said.

Christine flushed. " I thought you wanted me to work hard, Dad."

" There's time for both," Ella said.

" You'll make it," Ayrton said.

" Make what ? " Ella asked.

" Make the grade. With her music."

" Sometimes I don't understand you, Phil," Ella said miserably.

If I knew how to teach her myself, he thought, she would do it. If I could only teach her, she would. He thought of what he felt when he heard Scarlatti and smiled to conceal the unsmiling nature of his thoughts. " Do what you can. No one can do more. Isn't that what they say ? "

He mocked his words with his tone to save their sententiousness from being mocked by the others. Then he said to Ella, " She's going to show me the atonal scale."

Because if I don't look out, he thought in the subsequent silence, that's what I'll soon hear, even in Schubert.

5

In fact he had sought an opportunity to be alone with her not so much to hear about the " atonal " scale and to watch her playing but to talk to her about her mother, perhaps even about life in general, in fact have with her the kind of talk they might all have had downstairs, when Ella interrupted his allusion to Goole. It wasn't often he got the chance to have a general talk with anyone. Jack Beasley, D.C. chaplain and Buxton vicar, saw only Christian hope in every subject and Dr. Ames liked whisky, fishing and the notions of the Boer War. The subjects which roused Ayrton to warm conjecture left them both speechless.

The room where the piano stood had been given over to John as a playroom since Christine went to Birmingham. Bricks littered the floor and a cowboy hat hung on the edge of an old pedal sewing-machine which had been a wedding present from Ella's grandmother in Caernarvon.

Christine slumped down in the chair with a hint of aggression as though she were a taxi-driver called out late : well, where do I go ?

Wanting to make a familiar if not coeval approach, Ayrton sank backwards across the arm of a big chair nearby and propping himself against the far arm in such a position that he overlooked the keyboard, he said, " Tell me,

Christine, before you explain. How d'you find your mother ? "

" Mum ? " Christine said nervously and seemed to get suddenly smaller. Then she played a loud chord. Before adding to this sound she said, " She's O.K., isn't she ? What do you want to know ? " and she suddenly started a monotonous finger exercise. " About music ? "

" I think John misses you," Ayrton persevered.

" Mum spoils him, doesn't she ? D'you like this ? " Smiling, she played a chord which sounded like a flat-iron dropped on the ivories.

" What d'you want to know," she said, dropping three more flat-irons. " It's merely a question of what your ear is accustomed to. This consisting of a third and a pure fifth sounds O.K. to you, doesn't it ? it's consonant. But this (another flat-iron) is dissonant. In fact there's no such thing as dissonance or consonance. It's merely a matter of degree and what you're accustomed to. Listen to this new kind of music horizontally (she smiled teasingly) for contrasting 'lines' of melody all on the same twelve notes. Listen vertically for the chromatic content only, not for connected progression of harmonies as in Chopin. It's really very strict and disciplined and the very opposite of 'chaotic.' " Christine was talking fast and edgily as though repeating fragments of statements she had heard. She sounded as though on the verge of losing her temper either with him or the music. " It's the new classicism. You surely see it's more like Bach—even more like your Scarlatti—than it is like Beethoven or worse still Richard Strauss."

" Worse ? "

" Well, there was a lot of gas, wasn't there ? They were getting away with murder, weren't they ? Wagner, Delius

—you couldn't go on from there: it was soup already. Like Bergson in philosophy."

"Soup? I don't understand, Christine. What is the point of music if it doesn't engage one's feelings? What's the good of telling me to listen ' horizontally ' and ' chromatically '? I can't. I didn't need a musical education to enjoy the old stuff but it seems I do for this. You talk about a new ' classicism ' and I do see what you mean. There is a search for a form here, but a search for form just for the sake of form. Surely that's wrong: form should be secondary to content. Where there is no content I well understand people becoming obsessed with form. Perhaps that's what has happened here! No content!"

"Oh, well . . ." she suddenly smiled and played another stretch of noises which did not seem to lead into each other. "It's interesting, isn't it . . . I thought it was your ambition for me. . . ."

"Yes, it's very interesting," he said hastily. He watched her pale hands deftly at work on the keyboard and could not help thinking sadly that in some ways this modern music probably suited her better than the old because when she played Schubert she never, so to speak, became airborne, presumably because the feeling expressed in the music found no echo in her. *Why?* In this music where there was no feeling to express (except perhaps for cerebral distinctions) she should be on firm ground.

She ceased, whipped over five pages, peered up at tiers of pencil marks like a child's addition sums and explored her way aggressively through more sounds which he found it difficult to believe any ear could have readily differentiated one from the other, certainly not at speed.

"What are those figures?"

"Fingering."

" What I don't understand is how it can be possible to like the old and the new as well at the same time; how can the revolution in sensibility allow any surviving part of the old to live on terms with the new: these sounds aren't a development, they're simply different, more different from the old than Indian or Chinese music. They suggest an audience of Martians or men with enormous heads and no bodies or limbs like eastern beggars, shrivelled from disuse. It seems to me that someone like you should only be able to listen to the old now, not for pleasure, but for technical interest in derivations ... musical archæology."

" But that's just *you*! Dad ..."

" No, dear, it isn't." His voice rose and he felt pressure behind his words, so that they came out like penned-up animals and went a bit wild from a sense of release. Perhaps it had been inconsiderate to expect Christine to talk about criminals, her mother or John. But she could talk about music. It wasn't often he had a chance of being understood. The back of her slightly downcast head was not exactly encouraging but she had asked for it. " Those sounds," he said, " in relation to traditional music reflect not a development of feeling or even a revolution in feeling—but an *alienation* of feeling. . . . You may say, ' Speak for yourself.' I do but I also speak for others and in time this will be admitted. Jazz, that's different. Indeed that *is* a revolution in feeling—revolution against that noise there . . . that, that deformed child of classical music, in which feeling has become impacted, abused, suppressed, over-cerebralised. In jazz, feeling, however crude and un-differentiated, bursts through but pays a price in being held together only by such basic disciplines and conventions as make for monotony if you listen for long. Jazz is the journalism of primitive feeling, not the poetry of contemporary feeling. Jazz is the music of escape. Perhaps there can be no sublimation, no domestication of contemporary feeling—of the feeling, that is, which is pertinent to our moment of history. The special is too powerful for the whole. And split from it. Harmony impossible. . . . The very existence of jazz alongside tape-recorder music points that we are living in an age when feeling in art is divorced from intellect, content from form, to such an extreme extent that both are dangerously deprived."

At that moment Ella came in.

Christine said, " Hallo, Mum."

Ayrton adjusted his spectacles.

Ella said, " Having a nice time ? "

She had been washing-up, she said, and had thought somebody was going to come and help her.

Christine got up saying, " Sorry, Mum . . ." She shut the keyboard, in a way that was unconvincingly reluctant.

Ayrton smiled as she went.

Then he was alone.

I was more boring than washing-up, he thought.

Peter seemed to have been waiting for this situation for he picked up a brick and brought it to Ayrton's leg. When Ayrton moved, Peter's whole body was shaken and twisted by the frenzied activity of his tail ; when he was still, Peter became suddenly subdued by doubt : was there going to be a walk or not ? Surely there was.

The young don't want familiarity and intimacy because they don't want to feel, he thought. They don't want subjectivity and subtleties because their only hope is simplification. They appear to have no *Weltschmerz* simply because really they have so much that to let in a little would be to risk drowning.

It was nine o'clock.

Neither the *Daily Telegraph* nor television held any charms for him and a serious book, if there was such a thing in the house, would, like Christine, like Jefferies, like Ella merely increase his sense of frustration and isolation. In my own home, he thought, it's sometimes as though I were staying with strangers. I might have more in common with Goole!

6

PETER'S ENJOYMENT of liberty and exercise was infectious and soon Ayrton was striding over Marshal's field with a feeling of astringence for the fate of his intellectual overtures to his own daughter. Now and again he caught glimpses of the dog tacking along at a canter, nose to ground, or urinating lop-sided or scratching provocatively as though daring some rival to approach; then off he went again, nose to ground, vanishing and reappearing in the moonlight far away, moving like a shadow in fast orbit round his master. We should all be more like that, he thought. Each one of us is alone, anyhow, whatever.

A hundred yards to the left he could see the porch light of the Detention Centre and lights in some of its rooms including, on the first floor, lights in the three cells where new arrivals slept for a week till they had " settled down." Goole, he thought, Goole.

Pictures on the Wall

In moonlit mist Marshal's hen-houses looked like a vast aerial convoy of Noah's arks drifting through high cloud. Their sloping tops gleamed but below them the dark soil showed grey, blank as empty space.

Suddenly, away to one side, Ayrton heard the long low, hypnotised, terrified growl which usually meant Peter had " seen " something in a clairvoyant's sense. As usual too, the noise ended in a sudden carillon of panic-stricken barks.

Furtive muttering broke out nearby in one of the long hen-houses, a regular clucking sound like the machinery of panic being slowly wound up. Ayrton called harshly. Sometimes lovers, unearthed by Peter, took offence.

Again that wild, panic-stricken barking, warning the whole world that here was something to beware of, a human being with six legs and two heads and no arms crawling about at night. . . .

Ayrton went back.

Peter was near a hedge. The torch-beam showed his coat bristling and his whole body frozen in a position of recoil. For a second the dog dared look round and his amber eyes flared briefly. Then he turned back, gave tongue again, this time with more authority and aggression and even took two steps forward.

A pollarded willow in front was certainly threatening: a club-headed giant it seemed leaning forward with seven whips, but Peter raised his snout and delicately, sceptically nodded the end of it, taking the very smallest sniffs such as he reserved for subtlest dilemmas, not for trees. Slowly his head worked round to the left, from where the wind was blowing.

Ayrton swung his torch.

A figure !

He could see that it was a young woman—one of Marshal's landgirls or whatever they were now called— the corduroyed huskies in wellingtons who tended the chickens as well and for less money than men. " Good evening," he said.

He switched off his torch thinking there was probably a man in the offing, perhaps one of his own staff.

Now that it was dark he could see that the girl had positioned herself carefully in the shadow of the tree. Not a gleam of moonlight touched her and her stillness was strange.

" I hope he didn't frighten you."

" No—he didn't."

Something about her tone suggested she knew who he was.

" It's not Shirley, is it ? " (He knew it wasn't.)

" No."

" You haven't . . . lost your way ? "

" I thought you might have lost yours."

He smiled at the rudeness of her tone—and at the possible justice of her point. It might be Marshal's niece.

" Well, you seem to have cast a spell on my dog," he said, and using Peter's threatening proximity to the girl as an excuse he walked straight forward, switching on his torch, and slipped a lead through his collar. The light dodged and flickered here and there and in the course of its wanderings paused on her face.

She was no one he knew, but beautiful; in fact in that place incredible, a mirage.

" You're not from round here, are you ? " he said, hearing his voice changed.

Antagonism was implicit in every second of the silence which followed.

"Who are *you*?" she said at last.

Marshal's niece was an actress. "Philip Ayrton," he said, and then did not feel like describing himself further.

He touched his spectacles, smiling into the dark. "I'm sorry if my dog gave you a fright. I hope I . . ." His voice petered out: he couldn't say "didn't interrupt you."

The possibility that the girl was in fact a complete stranger to this field, and despite her tone, frightened, unprotected and longing for him to go away delayed him for a few extraordinary seconds.

Perhaps it was some hangover from his conversation with Christine and from the day's work in the Centre, perhaps it was the sheer shock and suddenness of such an apparition in the surrounding dark, as though, like the hermits of old in their grey uncomfortable caves, the very absence of what he most desired had taken shape before his eyes. He stayed where he stood unable to move away. After all, why not? But why not *what* . . .? Talk. Just for a few minutes. She was in no position to refuse and he was used to being obeyed by the young.

With every second that passed he felt more and more bewildered as though he were drifting away from himself; as though iron hawsers of habit which he had supposed to be unbreakable had simply fallen apart like old web, of their own accord. At the same time he realised what he might be doing to the girl simply by standing there, silent and still. Memory of newspaper headlines and towpath murders might already be coursing like ice through her veins. She would be thinking that no one would hear if she screamed. The wind was too high. . . .

At that moment he himself became frightened.

A sort of giddiness, as though some other identity were

becoming his, recalled him to elementary courtesy, rescued
him from the temptations of anonymity.

" Good night," he said, moving.

She replied with the same word—spoken faintly.

He turned away.

Well, it happens, he thought, doesn't it, often enough?
For most men it's in streets and undergrounds, at " En-
quiries " *guichets*, in cinemas when the lights go up, at
parties, during visits to or periods in hospital or wherever
you're likely to see a young woman—a face is glimpsed
and a spear of divine softness penetrates instantly, the head,
the heart, the loins. For me it happens in a hen-field. In
either case she vanishes—and the moment flakes away
from life as though it had to return to the place it came
from, some sort of inexhaustible infinity, unknown, leaving
you only with an image which blurs and then in a few
minutes, perhaps a few days, dissolves utterly, never to be
recaptured except, so to speak as a harmonic, in another
face, another time. For someone who lives at Edgecliffe,
getting more forehead and less gum every day, the rarity
of such an experience and the dimensions of contrast it
affords raised it to the level of the supernatural. He was
able to smile at his recent sense of power in the dark.
Could fantasy go further! I have no option, he thought,
but to " kiss the joy as it flies."

Who, he wondered, would soon be kissing the girl?
Hexley, the rubber-faced P.T. instructor, had an inexplicable undertow for pretty girls? Hexley probably.
But completing his circuit and passing not very far from
where Peter had run the girl to ground he met Liversey—of
all people, quite unaccountably returning down the
road from Marshal's farm. Liversey and a girl like that!
Ayrton greeted him in an almost congratulatory fashion

tainted with irony; but nothing could be learned from his reply.

When he got in there was a message on the humming-birds: would he mend the strap on John's satchel.

7

THE EYE rests naturally on a single island in an expanse of level water and Ayrton, in the days that followed, often thought of that exceptional apparition in Marshal's field.

Christine went back to Birmingham. There was his work, Ella, the newspapers, television. . . . He could feel no surprise that that improbable face, depicted by the beam of his torch as an old medallion embedded in black velvet, should nag memory.

Liversey's girl? Every time he looked at Liversey he thought it less likely. But then who had she been? No clue offered itself. It was as though, switching off his torch that night, he had switched her out of existence. Only her image persisted.

One morning he woke up having dreamt about her—(it had become " her "—just like that). But he couldn't remember *what* he had dreamt about her. She was just somehow " there " like something left behind by a tide.

Ella had already left the bed in her old towel-type dressing-gown and the remains of her seven o'clock tea stood under the bedside light with a library edition of the

Memoirs of Lady Diana Cooper, on which a few crumbs of biscuit had settled.

The noises of the awakening house came up to him with a clockwork familiarity which for some reason he noticed. This morning it was as though each of those clinkings, flushings and creakings were trying to tell him something.

Soon the customary sight of his own slightly enlarged face in the round shaving-mirror engaged his attention so that he paused with a clean frontier of skin neighbouring the creamy edge, paused and peered closer as though in the course of the night another face had been substituted for his own, a face different only by virtue of some appalling increase in sameness. Suddenly he felt: this, for better or worse is what I am.

Some people might have drawn satisfaction and a sense of achievement from such a crystallising moment. But Ayrton felt stranded by it, as though within sight of some unspecified but important objective he had been denied all further chance of movement. It came over him then that for months, perhaps years, he had been living without looking forward and that this was virtually a contradiction in terms. Anticipation, of course, belonged particularly to youth—was the very core of youth, but it should never disappear altogether. Even during his last moment alive a man should somehow be able to look forward.

He could see the main building from where he shaved and the inch-mesh wire gleaming, like a web, after rain, in the low sun. The sight of this vaulted experiment in penal reform which had often, on other mornings, revived in him some glimmering sense of vocation, this morning merely increased his depression.

What was the good of pretending? As far as a Warden was concerned Edgecliffe offered less opportunity for reform than a prison governorship. True, there was more personal contact than in a prison but it was so brief as to be scarcely worthy of the name. At interviews he some-times got a glimpse, or thought he did, of the root of a boy's trouble. A moment later, in a flurry of pumping arms and a bedlam of shouting, the delicacy of a special situation was swept away in the undifferentiating current of official " tempo." At such moments the greater frustration was probably his. After all, in a few weeks the boy would be out. But he would not. And as the years went by the thirst to exercise justice (since that was his function), or even just the desire to help, was ever more sharply mocked by mirages. How could the delinquents have been closer —how possibly could they have been more hopelessly out of reach.

Tempo! An R.S.M. could do his job better than he and lately he had begun to wonder if that might not be what the Commissioners saw him as—an R.S.M.! Why else should they have appointed him to implement the " short sharp shock."

The possibility that the Commissioners regarded him as an unimaginative martinet, a fit instrument for inflicting a " mental flogging," contrasted so strongly with Jefferies's view of him as a " f——g children's nurse " that he suddenly felt a sense of complete bewilderment. What hope had the moderate point of view, nowadays, when secretly (oh, always so secretly) both extremes wished to destroy it. Confusion was increased fourfold when the two opposite extremes (Jefferies and the so-called progressives in this world, communism and big business in the larger world) so often seemed to be on the same side—particularly when opposed by liberal humanism. It was three years now since he had drawn up a strongly worded recommendation that money should be spent on providing every boy in the Detention Centre with a room to himself. Quarantine for the young criminal, he pointed out, had been one of the main objects in creating Detention Centres. The dormitory system merely defeated this object. Cells would not only lessen chances of contagion, they would also provide, in rudimentary form, a chance for wardens and officers to develop therapeutic relationships with their charges. He had worked out that with an hour's " visiting " every night he could give each boy three half-hour periods in a three-month sentence; ludicrously inadequate—but at least something with which to balance the violent emphasis on physical activity and extrovertion which could only result in a mere " deep freeze " of the " basic psychological malady."

There had been a number of letters to and fro. Pike it had been then. Sir George Pike now. Absolutely nothing happened. After a year a new gymnasium was put in at the cost of about two thousand pounds. He had only been asking for plaster-board partitions. . . . The former monk!—they had probably thought—is getting nostalgic.

Ayrton looked at the surrounding country.

The siting of Detention Centres is one of the deterrents to escape.

People talked about rural England having vanished, but here was an area not a hundred miles from Bristol where an escaper would have to walk twelve miles before he ceased to feel conspicuous. The result was a sort of exile for everyone at Edgecliffe: criminals got three to six months, Prison Officers three to six years. . . .

Downstairs he avoided looking at Ella. This morning, to live at all seemed to require the benefit of an illusion and this was more easily obtained by reading news-papers.

John came in to say good-bye. Ella said, " Will you be all right, John ? "

When he had gone Ayrton said, " Why shouldn't he be all right ? "

" He's young yet, Phil. He still doesn't like going to the bus stop alone. He's just eight."

She raised her cup to her lips, sipped and swallowed with a sort of mild physical thankfulness which suggested that as long as there was something warm and wet she could be content, and others could be, too.

She was looking at the mail-order page with a look of disappointment, as though the items depicted in little squares were already in her possession and not living up to the qualities claimed for them.

There were moments when he despised her capacity for acceptance. Yet it was possibly her very capacity for acceptance (usually he had called it her " loving nature ") which had been responsible for the whole shape of his life —the Prison Service, their marriage, and the children. You could put it that way. You could put things almost any way, but that particular thing you could certainly put that way. Particularly this morning.

But he said, " How about going out to-night, Ella ? "

" *Out*," she said. " Where to ? "

" We could go into Bristol—anywhere . . ."

" What's come over you ? "

" Well . . . think about it." He rose.

" You've got the Youth Club."

" I can give it a miss," he said, moving.

" Jack depends on you."

He smiled then and for some reason did something he

didn't often do, stopped behind her and kissed the top of her hair. Between the pepper-and-salt strands he saw pale skin and a few tiny flecks of scurf, lower—the almost wrinkled flesh of her bosom, like a material that is beginning to " go " and the long cleft between her soft heavy breasts. In recent years her skin, which had once been his delight, seemed to have paid a penalty for its extreme softness. Like broken elastic it let everything sag and spread. Sometimes she gave an impression of dissolving absolutely, for instance when she was in warm soapy water or in pillows ; then her assimilation, with the water or linen, struck him as a form of flight, one moreover in which she seemed bent on involving John. He had sometimes had to make an effort not to be disgusted by so much softness. It exacerbated the disadvantages of anyhow knowing her flesh too well. Such ubiquitous compliance, along with the inevitable familiarity, had lately seemed to constitute a form of mild taboo as though it were all *his* flesh and enjoyment of it a form of masturbation, so private as to be " wrong."

Such qualms he imagined came to most marriages, if nothing worse. What made them worse, in his case, was having to deal for hour after hour with the abnormal and the sub-normal: he went home at night in need of compensations, contrast, which Ella had become increasingly powerless to provide. Physically in particular, he had felt a need for intercourse of a quite exuberant normality. After ten hours in the Centre his body sometimes craved sex as a sacramental recreation—something to renew him, as prayer renewed priests. Instead, for years now, he had had to rest content with Ella's pretence at participation and sometimes not even that. She had sharpened rather than assuaged his hunger for health, driven it to fantasy and

ambition. But who was he to talk, he the former monk?
There were moments when Edgecliffe seemed a limbo of
sickness in which the guardians (having come there of
their own accord) were thereby sicker than the guarded,
and health, pure health, the prerogative of none but Peter,
his dog, Tabby, the Deputy's cat and one or two inmates
whose background had been such that " integration " for
them had meant crime.

He gave her shoulder a slight, and as it were transcen-
dental, squeeze as though encouraging her to like Edgecliffe
and life a little better, to keep new by keeping interested.
He would write again to the Prison Commissioners about
the Open Prison.

" Found your ring yet ? "

She said Gwen (who cleaned for them) thought it might
be behind the chest of drawers which together they were
going to move that morning.

Her engagement ring had been missing for a month now.
It had cost £80 in 1946 and had not been insured. He
was rather irritated by her indifference to its fate but was
reluctant to seem merely financially concerned. As a
symbol the ring had depreciated, though nostalgia still
came when he thought of it.

" We'd better try and find it," he said.

" That's what we're doing, dear."

She took another sip.

Pretending to be struck by a thought on a completely
different tack he said, " Did you ever think again about
the driving lessons ? "

" Oh, Phil, we've been through all that."

He stood there for a moment behind her.

" Or the part-time nursing, Ella," he said, coming out

into the open with a tone of challenge, " up at the hospital."

" I've got work enough part-time nursing two men in this house," she said, and she got up and began clearing. " Besides I'm not going back to that, thank you very much ! "

After a moment she added, " What's come over you ? After all the things you've said about mothers going out to work when they've got young children ! "

" I meant merely while John's away at school. Part. time. . . ."

" I'm all right, Phil. You get on with your boys."

" Well, think about to-night. . . . We could take the car."

Then he went off.

Most days the sensation of their being in a rut did not disturb him but to-day, for some reason, it certainly kept him ferreting about as though lost.

People, he thought, look back when they can't find their way or come to the end of it ; or when they can't face things as they are. How dead the humming-birds looked. " No, Peter," he said at the door and shutting the dog in he set out down the stretch of blue tarmac towards the Detention Centre.

8

STEEPED AS AYRTON WAS in psychological reports, he often found himself applying their jargon and yard-sticks. In some cases the result was ludicrously inadequate, in others light was shed. This morning, as he turned from his wife and began walking towards the main building, he found himself thinking that youth for him had been a sort of illness from which Ella had saved him by supplying him with the kind of love and emotional security he should have had much earlier. However corny such an explanation may have been and however irrelevant the lapse of years should by now have made it, he could not, in his present state of mind avoid dwelling on it, any more than an engineer might dwell on the nature of the steel, forged long ago, which had gone into the making of a now suddenly wilting bridge. If a man marries to be cured of something, what happens when he is cured? Can he live indefinitely on the medicine?

Only child of an ageing pedant whose dog-collar evoked Latin, flogging and class-distinctions, it seemed to him now that the main home influence in his life had been a tall pale relentless sister called Duty, stern daughter of the voice of God. Such a person would have explained the absence of his mother who could never have lived under the same roof as Duty and his father. No mother could have done that. Still, she had died, his mother, she hadn't run away. And there had been no sister, only a parlourmaid and his father or rather the closed door of his " study."

Those long lines of uniformed adolescents, crashing out the words of " Eternal Father Strong to Save " under the Gothic vaults, now seemed incredibly far away like something seen through the wrong end of a historical telescope. The Dickensian fancy dress, lexicons, parades, semi-ecclesiastical militance of rituals for a class that was *au fond* more dedicated to ruling (*vide* Tom Brown) than to the virtues it allegedly esteemed.... For him that system failed—because it succeeded too well. His inner insecurity had made him particularly gullible. Consequently, to a fanatical extent, he had " believed "—and accepted—the " front " of the system as its core. The Great War plaques in chapel he had taken at their face value and longed to lay down his life for his country. Because if he sacrificed himself, then surely the system would have no alternative but to love him ... allow him to belong.

But the system had not loved him, and the more he wooed it, the more he felt " all thumbs." Clearly he had been a prize prig.

Even now, after all these years, Ayrton could not analyse the feelings with which he had finally emerged from that home which was also school, and the school which was home. It seemed to him that he had been picked up by Pusey House at Oxford as easily as most of his contemporaries were being picked up by communism. The Catholic Church opened her arms. Perhaps she was the first female; certainly she came in the shape and long skirts of Father Lawson—who told him he could scarcely escape God's Love however hard and however long he tried. So he might as well give in early and love God, because God *minded* that he did not already do so.

God *minded.* . . . *Someone minded* . . . !

Ayrton's resistance was nominal: and soon it seemed to him that he had been waiting to give even more than to receive.

The day he made his decision to abandon Oxford and become a monk was still uncomfortably vivid. It was as though he had been allowed to become an angel on this earth. He had felt wings, giddy elevation and ecstasy. His father's style of letter-writing broke ranks, so to speak, in dismay. (God was a Protestant as well as an English gentleman; monks not conceivably either.) But the clash of wills had really been settled long ago. By then only the father was shocked. And that is an understatement. Ayrton never saw him again.

The pale chiaroscuro on the inclined face of the Virgin lured him to lonely prayers. Tears wet his cheeks.

Passionate days! He was so unworthy. He closed his eyes and promised that all his life should be given in return for the gifts he was receiving now. For it was now and again now, all the time. What separation was this that had ended? The answer came in chimes like a dance of stars joined suddenly by the shuddering volume and rhythm of earthquake and sea. (He was not alone after all: someone practising in an organ loft!) The world was full of miracles. . . . A bird on his sill, an anthem heard from a chapel window as he passed, the face of a girl who looked at him, the young pendant beech leaves glowing green in May—all, at any moment, could take on the nature of a personal message confirming him in his decision. Indeed the very simplicity of his vocation became the source of doubts and self-questionings. Could this be right, he asked Father Lawson, surely the road to God was hard and difficult, demanding sacrifice of the world ; he on the contrary had been given the world, and in the most material and sensual way at that. Tastes, sights, sounds and colours had never been more vivid.

He need not have worried. The long retreat from those ecstasies piled up in the course of years a costly payment. Raking over swiftly the cold ashes of memory one coal still glowed : an incident at Corfield where he did his novitiate. He tripped forward carrying holy wine on stone stairs. Glass was everywhere and his blood, seeping steadily from his palms mixed with the wine. After a moment of shock he had run (yes—enthusiastically) to the novice master, Father Aelred, and with bowed head and stricken mien confessed his fault, hiding only what he knew could not be hidden—his wounds—in the palms of his hands. " Father, I beg pardon and penance. . . ."

He had been twenty.

He could still see Father Aelred's bright old eyes, wearily suppressing a gleam of what ? something almost violent— repudiation not merely of his incompetence and sancti-moniousness, but of what amounted to involuntary mockery, blasphemy.

But had it been so involuntary ! *Had it ?*

Even after the passage of many years he could not think of that period without a feeling of distaste for himself —as though Ayrton the novice stood before him in the flesh, if that were not a euphemism for the shaved scarecrow he had been. Censure of others had been his ghastly hobby, though this had partly proceeded from that censure of himself which the training cultivated as carefully as athletes train muscles (and for which he had already been limbered up by his " sister " Duty).

Competition in humility—most revolting of all con-
tradictions in terms! He could see now the sidelong
glance, the chastened downcast eyes, smell the bareness,
smell stone, hassock and robe and sweat on serge, taste
bareness and see the colossal emblem of martyrdom which
was so often and unhealthily presented in terms of *suffering
sought* rather than suffering faced when necessary. To-day,
he saw Christ as a human hero, a fatalist, ironist and intellectual born out of wedlock, a most unmasochistic man
braving torture for principle and for a sleep-walker's
unfathomable sense of mission. (Yes—that too!) But in
those days how had he seen Christ? He couldn't remember.
And how would Christ have seen him? Little clinging
spy, sneak on the world's youth! Sometimes it seemed to
him that the second half of life had been allowed him only
to make up for the first—and for youth, too! But to what
end—" make up "—when now there was no end? Often
he felt sick of his " enlightenment " as though the meanest
point of all was the one he and so many others had reached:
a profoundly devalued view of life with mortal atrophy of
roots; a fatal loss of certain, usually hereditary complexes
and attitudes which gave life meaning, and a lack of anything
which he could respect, to take their place. What madness
might not men such as he clutch at to save themselves—
from that face in the mirror, that nothing, out of nothing,
towards nothing?

He did not want mansions in heaven but his heart did
crave significance *through joy*. It ought to be available, and
was—to animals, to humming-birds.... Yes—even animals
had the joy of Handel. Why not modern man? Jazz
circled round joy, round and round without ever getting
nearer.

Towards the end of his novitiate the love he still offered

had seemed to be failing under a law of diminishing returns. Once again he was experiencing rejection by a system. If his earlier troubles had been partly due to deficiency in animal spirits, the new ones seemed to spring from a warped surplus of that very commodity.

Like the other novices he had connections and relationships with the outside world which had now to be subordinated to the purposes of God. In his case family presented no problems: he had none except his father; but during his time at Oxford he had made friends of both sexes. Now he discovered that girls to whom he would probably never have written, had his life pursued an ordinary course, became objects of his religious concern. He prayed for them, and to give his prayers more solid material to work on, wrote to them and received answers. Many of them must have marvelled at the unexpectedness of this penpalship particularly as the contents of his letters were always carefully weeded of all but the most avuncular inquiries. Statements about himself were impersonal, "selfless." In other words the keynote of his correspondence had been love—but love of what kind? They at least were in no doubt. Their answers reflected in most cases a polite gratitude or indifference or a genuinely moved gratitude for being involved, gratis, in his heavenly dispatches. And so his love accumulated girl beneficiaries—and for good measure, a few men. And his prayers were studded with starlets. In this way, *it*, the offence crept in, disguised. Custody of heart, custody of eyes, custody of hands: all constant, ceaseless. The way it got in was in the form of a religious sentimentality towards women: ladies first in his prayers. If he kept their letters—it was merely to guide his prayers.

But there could be no custody of dreams. The novice

master told him they would pass. But they didn't. The most violent and shocking tended to follow the most sublime devotions. If he prayed that Jennifer, in the High Street antique shop at Oxford should enjoy God's guidance before making up her mind about going to America, then a naked Jennifer or somebody at moments like her, assaulted his sleep with actions and visions that woke him in spasms of involuntary bliss that he could not bring himself to curtail. Afterwards for hours of penance and heart-searching, the insubstantiality of Jennifer, either as an object of his spiritual concern or as intruder of his dreams, was brought home to him as nothing but signs of spiritual vulnerability, the beginnings of loss of vocation.

He prayed more and now from prayer and correspondence alike banished all girls he had known. To reward him his dreams became more violent and gradually by forcing him more and more often into involuntary sexual experiences instilled in him a craving for real experience. He wanted a woman—not a dream—a separate, talking, thinking, autonomous woman; flesh, the *mystery of the other*. There was a certain monotony about his confessions.

But he did become a monk—incredulous of that fact even while it was happening, as though he himself were looking on.

Afterwards he was sent (purposely ?) to Oxford to study. "City of dreaming spires and perspiring dreams . . ." wasn't that the saying ? How untrue that had been in his case for now the girls were not dreams . . . or visions, or memories of people to be prayed for. He saw them, heard them, smelt them, reacted to them, sometimes brushed past their bodies in libraries or on pavements.

There had been wonderful limes in the college garden. One night the air, hot and scented as flesh, had defeated him. He began to gulp it, to crave and crave, life, fullness on this the only earth. Golgotha, the place of skulls, had been *on behalf* of this life. Yet here it was all round him preserved *as* this life. Skulls: Brother Ambrose a skull, Brother Aelred a skull, Father Quaife a skull—skulls with living eyes. His jaws had locked and he had felt himself transformed into the familiar which had trailed him closer and closer for years, a creature composed of *all his opposites*.

The fathers had probably foreseen what was coming. They certainly raised less than the expected resistance; and at last gave him back to the world with helpful references. These enabled him to take a job teaching in a prep. school in Cheshire. But who was he—Brother Osbert or Philip Ayrton? Neither title now rang much of a bell. His father was dead. He had no close relations. The war was just over and he found himself emerging from shelter at the very moment when most of his generation were returning from danger. . . . It seemed to him he might just as well have had a number as a name.

Memory, of course, as well as being a censor, was also an artist, presenting things over-simplified—in crystal or sublimated form. There had almost certainly been nothing neat or sublimated about his state of mind when he emerged from the monastery. Having obeyed one blind impulse— to sign away his soul and several years of his early youth, he now, obeying another impulse equally blind, demolished the previous contract and with it the whole conscious edifice of his religious calling, the habits and disciplines of years. How could memory do justice to that experience to-day.

He became ill. Only X-ray said he wasn't.

No, the plates showed nothing even when he vomited blood. He lay as though dead and indeed felt ready to die.

This was in a Liverpool hospital. He heard footsteps and voices in plenty but discovered something he had never guessed. *There are people in the world who know nobody.* And at that moment he was one of them.

His next-of-kin, an aunt in Australia, was entered on several forms under " C. of E."

It is sometimes said by non-Catholics that " so and so ought to become a Catholic," as though this were the only known discipline and support which could save that person from absolute despair. It might well have been said of him then—exactly a month after he had ceased to be a practising Catholic.

He was, however, given the last sacraments.

But there was a lesser sacrament. More real. A nurse called Ella Rhys.

She became the person he knew—soon quite well, who called him by his name and touched him. When he first opened his eyes, in a living kind of way, she had been " there."

She bore me, Ayrton thought.

What an embarrassing, if not revolting, autobiography. That's beside the point. One goes back in order to find out where one is, and in this case where Ella is. And so he went on with it, remembering how later, when he got better, he was delighted to see that Nurse Rhys had a sort of romping gaiety. She could suddenly frisk a sheet about like a puppy with a rag when she was meant to be making a bed and then giggle helplessly when, having come to her senses, she got back to the plod of tucking in. And all this in sight of the sister. She was often in trouble but didn't seem to care, just went her way, always the same, always rather heavy, slow moving, like a beast of burden, yes *animal*—as dispassionate (he had imagined) about the functions of her own body, as about the disturbances of others.

"Come on, Lord Henry," she would say to the self-piteous docker opposite, "you aren't dead yet." (Hadn't the man proved it by going out a few days later?) But with the dying angina alongside, she had been different. Her capacity for acceptance had been contagious ... for a few indispensable. When he was discharged, he stayed on in Liverpool.

After the first week his money ran out and it was again the monks who got him a job teaching—in a school for Irish.

He found digs: 27 Londonderry Row had an aspidistra between the muslin curtains. You could see part of it in the bottom of the gap. The stairs smelt of smoke, sea, damp and old cooking. His bed crackled like someone making up a parcel whenever he turned over. But it was here he used to bring her after the pictures and here where he discovered a happiness which, once it was his, seemed the whole point of life.

Yet Ella and he (particularly he) had seldom referred to this period in later years. Perhaps there are some love stories too abject for words. The reputation of romance demands they be buried, burnt, obliterated.

Everything till then had been so pure, so ideal—so dutiful. But now conscience ceased to be a guide, indeed for a time became his worst enemy for ever standing in his way. Physical ignorance and inexperience, for a time, burdened his conversation more than usual with ideality and irrelevance. And fear anchored him at arm's length. In the end, what came to his rescue was that Ella had nursed him—intimately: there could be no shame and therefore no failure in her presence. One night they drank a lot of

Pictures on the Wall

cider. The last trams were clanking by at long intervals. The cushions reeked of dust; a drunk sang some Irish song. Too long a pauper of life he heaped her towards him. She was riches, fabulous riches. Those Italian painters who made bold to unbutton heaven and lay bare God, angels and the Elysian fields were not as illuminating as his hand when it laid bare her chubby breasts and held them. They lay down together and afterwards it seemed to him the first occasion he had ever acted without doubt —so roughly and yet she seemed to think so tenderly.

Later she wept. But why?—he needed her, he said, all the time and for ever: they would be married. She said she wasn't sure, she'd have to see. Not sure! Well, he was sure.

He took her back to the nurses' hostel with the chimneys coming out in long black ridges against the greasy, grey dawn. Then he went home and wrote her a long letter.

She hadn't taken many days to make up her mind.

It was autumn and they took the train to Caernarvon. Mr. Rhys, an R.S.P.C.C. inspector, did not seem anxious to know the details of his prospective son-in-law's previous life. Ella had somehow hooked a " gentleman " and he wanted to get back to his dahlias. Mrs. Rhys was worried. She was a good woman and very chapel. She thought Ella ought to marry someone more of her " own sort," but since the Roman Catholicism had been jettisoned, since Ayrton loved Ella, who by then had brought upon herself a suspicion she might marry nobody, resistance was nominal.

The wedding was in Caernarvon. A cousin of his dead mother came from London. (He still remembered her face, which he had never seen before—or since.) Afterwards he and Ella went to Scarborough with confetti in their clothes. It was cold but they were warm in bed. Ella wouldn't let him see her naked. It was a contradiction but he dismissed it. They went for long walks and speculated about the future. More than once Ella cried. She said he should have married someone clever. This frightened him because he did not regard himself as clever and that she should think he was, seemed to suggest they were unsuited. She could not say the right thing, she said—and cried more. It was worrying. Nevertheless, having been thin all his life, Ayrton in the following months became almost fat. In search of a better paid post and " married quarters " he wrote (with a sense of defeat and shame) to the bursar of the school which had been his home. To his surprise he was taken on. For his father's sake.

For a year he taught there, confident that he could shake off the past. But it was no good. The place was permeated with things that he had escaped, not conquered. He found he had no vocation to teach these children of wealthy homes. They made him feel either hostile and superior, or a failure. Besides Ella did not get on with the other wives or rather they did not give her much opportunity of getting on with them. She was different. And by then he was different too. He wondered how he could ever have contemplated coming back. Every stone and arch gave him claustrophobia. Sometimes he felt like a ghost haunting its old, altered home; and sometimes, literally, that he was dreaming, since one of his recurring dreams had been just this: returning to school as an adult, or as a sort of child-adult, a point which in the dream was confused and painful.

Christine was born with difficulty and christened in the school chapel.

A month later he began casting about for an alternative,

and soon he went for his interview at the Home Office. He was twenty-six. He told them he felt a mission to help delinquents, young people who were confused and who had suffered, often through no fault of their own. He explained that the teaching order to which he had been affiliated had in fact administered two approved schools to one of which he would have been sent in time. The possibility that he was running away " yet again " occurred to him but he expelled it from his thoughts and his manner—and the Home Office appointed him to a Borstal where he again took up work in which it was possible to feel a sense of dedication, self-sacrifice. This, he soon told himself, was what he had missed since leaving the monastery.

In a small way he had thrived and so had Ella. The little community which administered the Borstal at B—— would have learnt little from its daily life if it had not learnt tolerance. Ayrton's erratic past and his marriage to a girl from a completely different social background were not even noticed. It's true there were some queer customers at B——. That had been part of its charm. It is sometimes said of psychologists that a great many of them are " near-misses " themselves and quite a few of them veterans of the very disturbances they treat. Ayrton found the same true of penal work. There was a former gun-runner on the staff and a young man who had once led a gang in the East End. And to his dying day Ayrton would never believe the matron hadn't kept a brothel, though her salty reminiscences of life as a Cardiff landlady somehow avoided the direct statement. Yes, surprisingly enough B—— could do without that golden euphemistic glow which memory often, obligingly, throws over the past. It had been a happy place. Ella had been happy there. The boys had made her laugh. And he had loved her for liking them.

He could still hear the way she laughed sometimes when that Maloney came to tea. She used to die practically, wiping her eyes and covering her face and then trembling all over again as though by mistake she had shut in the very thing she had wanted to shut out and was at its mercy again. What had happened to her since then? Surely life didn't change people utterly. Edgecliffe couldn't have changed her to that extent. Ella, he thought, addressing that far away laughing figure. . . . Mother she may have been first but surely wife too, and mistress, she had become. . . .

By now Ayrton was sitting at his desk.

The sun had broken through and he noticed, as though witnessing magic, what a difference that single broad ray of brilliant sunlight worked with his mood. Yes, in the end he had found a vocation, and the version of himself which was so dear to him and which had survived so much deflation and failure, had been resurrected: he was still able to feel dedicated—a man who carried deep into the modern age the banner of an ideal, respect for every man's unique shape and significance. " What is man that Thou art mindful of him? Thou hast made him a little less than the angels." He welcomed the discrepancy, and though the mythical bathwater of Christianity could go, he would keep the baby: the importance of the individual, of each one of his charges.

This was what he thought.

9

A KNOCK CAME on the door and Jefferies appeared with the day book.

"Cigarettes," he said, and put the book down in front of Ayrton, "forty on Goole." Then he smiled as much as to say, "There's your First Offender for you!"

Needled by the tone of triumph in the deputy's voice, Ayrton began polishing his glasses. The art of silence which he practised with refined and calculated effect on inmates was also useful with the staff. It preserved a space for a manœuvre and often stimulated subordinates to a second and more exact statement of what they had already said, or, on other occasions, to an increased and therefore revealing emphasis. Silence with Jefferies, however, sprang lately from a reluctance to have any dealings with the man at all; on this occasion it also gave Ayrton a chance to come back to earth.

He breathed again on his lenses and slowly oscillated finger and thumb over the slippery surface.

Jefferies said, "I've put Hallows on a report, ' case 'e c'n tell us somethin'."

"I thought I said there was to be no more soliciting of informers."

"Soliciting!" Jefferies looked round as though for company and then scratched his head, bewildered. "'Allows grassed in the first place, otherwise we'd never've 'eard of the bloody snout. Wrote 'ome Dear Mr. Jefferies 'stead of Dear Mum—there's a gipsy bloke beside me smokes like a chimney all night. Can't get no sleep, been coughin' 'orrible. Look in his pallyarse. Always ready to 'elp yours sincerely Ted Allows."

Jefferies supported himself almost amicably on Ayrton's desk as though the sensible nature of his own point of view must now be evident even to Ayrton and so pave the way, if Ayrton wasn't proud, to a new, more familiar relationship. " That Goole's a pro., sir, I'm telling you," he said, and he breathed eloquently as though literally at the end of some exhausting new lap of experience. " We're on to a bloody ball if we let them get away with snout, aren't we ? "

Ayrton was silent, looking down.

Although in their teens, many of the inmates were habitual smokers and in one way Jefferies was right. The mere existence of cigarettes in the place could have almost any result imaginable except a good one. It could produce violence and fear, the kind of fear you could smell as you walked down corridors, hear in the silence of sleeping dormitories, see in an empty cinder path between Nissen huts. Detention Centre " tempo " could only mitigate, not prevent such a phenomenon.

Reluctantly he read the entry, written in the Deputy's unformed hand : four names charged with Untidy Bed.

He felt cornered. Jefferies had manœuvred him into a position where he could only act as Jefferies wished.

Jefferies said, " Put four others on with him. Nicked 'em all for untidy beds. Make it more convincing."

Ayrton said, " I'll take them, but we'll have to talk about this, Jim."

When the Deputy had gone Ayrton thought how Goole

had stood before him only a few days ago with that air of animal ease and, yes, of innocence. He had wanted to help Goole all he could. Now, already ... he would have to punish him more.

The "Untidy Beds" were marched in one by one, Hallows last, so there should be no one in the passage, while he was being questioned.

Stunted and facially lop-sided, his eyes squinted so acutely that each seemed to be looking for the other where it was not. Fate, in giving him life, had hit him hard on one side, leaving him warped like a bicycle after an accident. The daring psychologist's report in Hallow's file judged him to be "Disturbed."

"Your bed was in a mess, Hallows," Ayrton said in dull, mechanical tones. "I've warned the others. I'm warning you."

This lie was to help the boy lie when he got back to his mates. Now, differently Ayrton said, "About those cigarettes, what can you tell us ...?"

At that the Deputy put forty Player's on the table as though to jog Hallows's memory and remind him that it was too late to go back.

"These," Ayrton said, coaxingly. "How did they get into camp ...?"

"Dunno sa."

"How did they get in, Hallows?" he said. "We'll see you're all right. You'll be out at the end a day or two earlier."

"'E 'ad 'em affer the boiler chive."

Ayrton's eyes dropped in self-defence: the squint was infectious.

"After the boiler fatigue?" he said, looking now at Hallows's body.

" Sroitsa."

" How did you spot them ? "

" He giff me one."

There was silence. Jefferies stirred and breathed or was it sighed ? Parks looked at Ayrton. Ayrton saw Goole, and Hallows, and the shovels.

" Where ? " he said.

" On the chive."

" You mean to keep your mouth shut ? "

" Na, 'e come up, says 'ave a fag mate."

It was true, Goole, even standing where Hallows stood now, had contrived to look and behave as though he were " free." That was true.

" I see," he said. " So you didn't see how he got them ? "

" No, 'e come up wivvem."

" From which direction ? "

Hallows's face crinkled.

" 'E come up wivvem . . . in 'is 'and, see . . . ? "

" Did he give anyone else any ? "

" 'Give all the boys on the chive one."

There was silence. A boot creaked. Parks said, " Stand up, lad."

" Who was in charge ? " Ayrton said, turning to the Chief.

Hallows said: " Mr. 'Awkins, sir. He was 'avvin' a pee."

" Keep quiet except when you're spoken to. Hawkins, sir."

" And then you saw where Goole hid them ? "

" Yussor."

After a silence Ayrton said: " Have you got anything against Goole ? "

"Me, sir, no, sir. I ain't got nothing against nobody."
As though dimly aware of some dangerous possibility of
self-contradiction he said, "But 'e didn't oughter 'ave fags,
did 'e? S'dingerous. Like you said. Thoughtcher'd like
to know."

Does he simply want to please, to be approved of?
Was that what I was like with the spilt wine? Ayrton
felt a desire to efface Hallows.

"That's all," he said coldly.

When Hallows had been marched out Ayrton looked at
Jefferies and said, "He had better look out, hadn't he?"

"Goole won't suspect Hallows. We made it look as
though we'd stumbled on the fags. 'E'd put them in his
mattress—untacked the bottom. Proper pro."

Still looking at the Deputy, Ayrton said: "Goole
didn't offer you one, did he?"

Jefferies said, "Wassat?" His eyes were blazing.

Ayrton said, "Mr. Parks, I'll see Goole to-night at
five."

"Yessa." Parks went out with alacrity. Jefferies was
breathing heavily, rotating a Biro in one hand, still staring.

"A joke," Ayrton said.

"A joke, was it?" Jefferies said.

Ayrton said coldly: "In future will you please make
a point of consulting me before you engage informers.
I know . . . in prisons it may be unavoidable, if not indispensable. Here it's neither. And it puts us on their
level."

"Puts us on their level, does it?" Jefferies whispered
in an ashen voice. He smiled at Ayrton almost intelligently,
rose, muttered some inaudible obscenity and went out.
His heavy footsteps receded. Ayrton closed his eyes and
frowned. Why did I have to say that, he thought, *why?*

IO

DAMN! THERE WAS no getting away from the fact that
he had done more than merely make a bad joke. He had
suggested that Jefferies, *unlike himself*, was separated more
by good luck than good management from the people he
was guarding. The enormity of this insinuation alarmed
as well as shamed him, because in fact this was not what he
felt. Not at all. In fact it was as though some other person
inhabited his skin, as well as himself, and had on this occasion spoken for him.

He looked round. Everything he saw (including for a
moment his own reflection in the mirror) assured him that
Jefferies would find plenty of ammunition (apart from
that one remark) for thinking that he looked down on him.

In fact the gulf between this room and the Deputy's
(with its bare walls and floor, notices, files and ubiquitous
paper) followed naturally from Ayrton's policy of keeping
one office like a " happy home " for interviews and the
other like a prison nerve-centre, or an Orderly Room;
nevertheless the difference between the two rooms did
also, by chance, reflect the very real gulf in education and
background which, throughout the Prison Service still
separated Governors and Wardens on the one hand from
most of the senior Prison Officers and Disciplinary Staff
on the other. And then there was Jefferies's appearance.
He was ugly—ugly as sin.

Pictures on the Wall

Take Jefferies and—say—Goole. Put their pictures side by side and ask a thousand people which of those two was the criminal. Every one would point to Jefferies. Goole they might think was some successful . . . (Ayrton got up and went to the window) . . . no, some sort of hero, a man with a sense of mission, someone rather outstanding and " inspired."

Ayrton smiled deprecatingly at the extent of his reaction to Goole (his " projections " . . . wasn't that the jargon ?).

What could account for it ? After all, he didn't really know anything about Goole. Yet there was this sense of intimacy and sympathy with the man as though he had lived with him for years and seen him day after day.

" Typical " he decided of Goole to have offered his cigarettes round like that. And then—consider his original crime. . . .

It was summer, the sound of fast tyres on the road crisp as frying bacon, the blue tarmac clean as though swept and the line down it like a bandsman's trousers. Musky air pollinous from Hereford woods and fields. Dusk now and the imitation mullion windows glowing with warm light from the setting sun. Couples going in. Cries of women simulating the pleasure expected of them. The roadhouse remote so it had given people somewhere to go fast in the fast cars.

When they arrived they found unknown people but people mostly like themselves so that when there was contact the same small coin of conversation—always badinage—could be used several times over, in different directions, without ever seeming a repeat. But to one girl at least this is all that life has to offer, the consummation of all the suggestions, the crystallised Mecca of all the ads., since they are all here represented—on the tyres, in the sump, in the driving seat, in the bar, on the menu, on the women's bodies, in their hair, under their arms—here at

74

the Three Musketeers all the superlatives had been assembled in private possession under a Regent moon and a White Horse. Gulled to their very guts, what else could the voices do but crow. Hers too—otherwise she would have been wrong, all wrong, every day. . . .

She was " common," a low type. But sexy.

The man who brought her here has come far to find a place where neither of them will be recognised because somewhere else he has a fiancée, not so attractive but rich.

A young farmer with a Jaguar. Say Rugger-playing—but not quite a typical minor public-school type. Something smooth, of the car salesman about him, something unusual, putting sex before class, every other Saturday.

He and the girl have had dinner and their chairs are close together.

Suddenly one of the dining-room doors, the one which leads to the public bar, opens and instead of a man coming in a man stands there in clothes that amount to purposeful effrontery—dust-whitened overalls and stained battle-dress jacket. It is Goole and his bullet head moves as his eyes, under their bushy brows, take in the faces above the little tables . . . above the chromium buckets and spirit lamps, under the wooden chandeliers and coloured escutcheons and brass pans, fixing at last on the one who by then is almost the only person not to have noticed what is happening, noticed why conversation is dying out. She looks up. . . .

Anyone would think I saw a lot of films, Ayrton thought.

She begins laughing rather madly as though suddenly much drunker than she had so far appeared. " D'you see what I see ? " she says to the farmer.

And he says, " Where have I seen that chap before ? "

Does it happen then or later . . . ?

Later when they are coming out into the lounge. Then how did it happen in the car park ?

Pictures on the Wall

It was in the car park . . . with the real moon up there like the face of a petrol pump, pinned up above the cardboard replica of a girl diving over the Three Musketeers. All unreal, all cardboard, even the moon, even what happened—except that it did happen. Goole is standing there and asks to speak to the farmer. He wants to meet him, he says. Three voices in altercation, arms moving up in what at first seem gestures. Mad talk about whether or not it's a " good " evening. " I never said it wasn't," said the farmer. " Oh, yes, you did say it was a good evening." Then suddenly the girl screams while Goole says, " Well, Mr. Hewson, if you won't you won't."

Hewson says, " I don't know who the hell you are. All I know is you're standing right in our way. . . ."

The girl screams, " Jim, I'm coming with you, I'm coming now. . . ."

" Yes, you f—— are."

Hewson says, " What the . . ." But Goole interrupts:

" That's right," he says. " She is. But first I've got something I want to say to you, Mr. Hewson." There is a flurry, curiously small, limited, but intense, breathy. . . . Suddenly a solid impact and then Hewson is up as though he were a Guy Fawkes dummy held above Goole's head. He vanishes. The light from the porch catches the gaping hole in the glass and makes it look like a huge torn spider's web with the middle missing, black as ink except where two tightly gartered socks and pumps stick out, Chaplinesque —but still—still as death.

The aftermath of violence is always a gap as though time had stopped, waiting for the dream to become proved a dream. Which does not happen. The new situation, the new sights are too awful, too strange. They have not happened. But they have.

A murmur grows. People gather in the lit doorway, at the windows. Someone is shouting indoors. Goole goes up to the girl. No one can hear what she is screaming. Goole puts out a hand

and with one wrench tears down the top half of her new dress and her brassière. A breast wobbles to the light like some huge subaqueous eye. As she cowers covering it, he hits her in the face— so that she sprawls sobbing on the ground. She keeps calling his name, into the earth.

Ayrton smiled at his own cinerama—but he did not entirely disbelieve it. He even drew some thin satisfaction from it for it showed he lived a life which, however lacking in Jaguars and sexual adventure, could still comfort itself with the thought that there was much to be said for the old disciplines and decencies. Let the social sciences and industry boom, absorb the best brains and millions every year and let wage packets put easy everything within the reach of the masses, but take away the last vestiges of conventional morality, the old restraints such as proceeded most strongly from the concepts of God, Queen, Country, Work and Family and you were left with the world of fast cars, ads., the Three Musketeers—and the psychologists' report, in other words not a world at all, fragmentation, chaos, against which the whole army of economists, sociologists and psychologists and welfare officers—would prove no bulwark, not even if they came to constitute a third of the population, which they soon would unless the present trends in statistics could be reversed.

He looked at his watch. It was time for him to do his rounds.

These and Prayers were Ayrton's only regular public appearance. During rounds he whisked through the camp with the Principal Officer looking in at the various workshops, cook-houses, gym and dormitories. When he appeared at doors the instructor called the rooms to their feet and then, when there was silence, announced in clear ringing tones, " All present and correct, sir."

He never took the same route two days running and sometimes he varied his time. He liked to come through a door like a jack-in-the-box and stay in it, watching, from behind his gleaming glasses, as though held there by a spring: he liked to leave a feeling with staff and prisoners that every door and even window was a potential Warden-jack-in-the-box lid which could suddenly spring open, fixing the whole of them, their hands, feet, faces and whatever it was they were doing, beneath eyes which remained invisible but all-seeing, behind their thick lenses. On his rounds he seldom said anything, either to staff or prisoners though sometimes he would pause beside a man, particularly one who had been giving trouble, letting his gaze wander over the work as though he were looking at something which he might yet buy—one day. It was all part of his technique whereby he made himself slightly larger than life—an image.

To-day was like other days. Each door, as it was unlocked, released a flood of hot air. Then came the cry and the silence—and the eyes, everywhere, looking up at him.

And Ayrton's eyes ... on the faces and the utter drabness ... and the tension.

Next the mat-shop—where Goole would be.

Parks flung the door open and the Staff who was sitting at a desk with a big clock and a mark-book jumped to his feet.

" All present and correct, sir."

The boys continued working. Each stood in front of a tall matting-frame tugging strands into position with a sharp steel hook. There was no sound but the rustling and tugging of the steel hooks at the hemp and the occasional clacking sound of the isolated finisher, padding the wads of hemp tags into their final condensed shape.

Always at this moment, when he stood in the door of the mat-shop, the noise increased and Ayrton had once asked an officer if this was an illusion due to the door being opened, and to proximity. But no. The officer said he had often noticed it too, from the inside : as soon as anyone stood in that door the inmates just about doubled the amount of noise they made. Ayrton believed the phenomenon to be entirely unconscious, an urge, as unreflective as breathing, towards the unlocked door and the wild relief of variety. Feeling himself suddenly witnessed by an outsider, each inmate was goaded to draw attention to his shape, have an identity even though the means at his disposal was a wooden mallet and a lump of hemp. Until then the hot shuffling silence, the clock, the motionless figure at the table and the locked doors and barred windows, was a sort of death and even the officer, for the moment, a hostage from life, among the dead and buried. Then the grave opened and there was air, light, difference, an illusion of freedom. Then Me, they said with their hammers and their hooks, me Me ME NOW. . . .

But to-day, conspicuously quiet, leisurely, in the increased noise was Goole.

He looked dainty—slow even for a beginner and when he looked up at the Warden he did so openly as though in a few seconds they might be discussing matting—or anything else under the sun, even cigarettes . . . Ayrton was reminded by his eyes of the peacefulness of a gorilla in the zoo, by his hands, of the sensitive doubting touch of a chimp or infant.

Two mats down from Goole was Hallows with his crossed eyes, working quickly, often looking up and round.

The temperature was in the seventies.

Ayrton's eyes drifted from face to face while he listened to that sound as of hundreds of birds shuffling about and occasionally pecking.

Then he began walking down the frames to the end of the room. On the way back he paused behind Goole's right shoulder and watched his thick fingers at work in and out of the strands of hemp. Soon this gipsy would be in solitary confinement. Would he be relaxed there, too?

It was then that Goole looked round, *smiled* and after meeting Ayrton's eyes in silence, said, " It's easy when you get the hang, sa."

Several things happened at once. Near heads turned, near fingers slowed, the officer came from behind the alarm clock like a big cat seeing food.

Parks made a hissing sound through narrowed teeth and moved nearer Goole as though he were a thing that might catch fire; then hectically, under his breath, as though there was still a chance the Warden hadn't heard, he said: " Get on, lad, get on with your work. . . ."

Although there was no absolute rule that talking was forbidden, inmates seldom spoke except to ask for a communal tool. They knew that an officer had only to dislike someone to " nick " him for wasting time.

Ayrton was hypnotised by a feeling that the moment was important, both for Goole and for himself. Whether it was because of his recent fantasy about the man's crime or because of his argument with Jefferies about the treatment of First Offenders, he did not know—and the moment was not propitious for finding out. Possible replies schooled at his parted lips—till Parks, stepping in front of him, obscured Goole from sight.

The Duty Officer rapped out, "Reid—where's your work, in front or behind?" then looked at Ayrton inquiringly, coming closer, and Parks turned round to look at Ayrton, too. . . .

One second, two seconds. . . .

Ayrton began moving again, looking to right and left as before, as though Goole hadn't spoken.

The Duty Officer shouted, "Get on with your work!"

And then—a moment later Ayrton was out in the air again with the harness jangle of keys going on behind him as Parks sealed the class in.

"He knows he's on a charge?" Ayrton said.

"I'd be surprised if he didn't," Parks said, grimly.

In Parks's voice Ayrton detected a note of frustration as though something should have happened to Goole, there and then on the spot. Lightning perhaps. Parks was even now looking at him questioningly as though he might want to go back.

Should he have answered Goole? *Contact* had been his theme over the years. Whenever he rejected it he felt inferior to the man who offered it. But Goole's on a charge, he thought. He's a prisoner. He must *earn* contact. Think of the precedent . . . how they play up if they think you're soft. . . .

F

II

THE INCIDENT lay on his stomach. He had to think that whatever happened at the Centre, whatever happened at home there was always the stretch of earth in between. This morning he spun it out—every yard—for the second time.

No sooner had he slipped the keys on their steel leash into his pocket, than smells—fresh as spring after a cold in the head, invaded his nostrils and mocked his body with the sensual possibilities of freedom. He breathed deeply of air free from disinfectant and sweat, looked far out and all round—but had to admit that he himself was a prisoner locked up in a total of small daily tyrannies.

He had just a few minutes and two hundred yards. Often like those office workers in London, who took lunch-hour in the form of a trance, looking down at an excavator in a building site, or lying between pigeons on the Inns of Court grass, he achieved a sharp sense of happiness here on this stretch of tarmac.

To-day among the long, barge-like hen-houses on Marshal's field two or three girls in sweaters and muddy wellingtons were busy with galvanised water-cans and a small tractor. None of them was the one he had seen that night by the hedge, but big jolly Shirley who brought their eggs and went hunting on a shaggy animal once a fortnight, was in hailing distance. Giving way to an impulse he stopped and called to her.

She turned.

Her cheeks were so rosy that in cold weather the edge of the rosiness seemed a rash.

" Where's your new recruit, Shirley ? " he said.

" New recruit, Mr. Ayrton ? First I heard. Who's the new recruit, Pam ? "

Another girl, nearby, seemed glad to let her bucket down and lean against the hen-house.

" Search me," she said as though bewildered by the possibility of anyone joining Marshal's.

" Female you mean ? " Shirley said.

" Yes. Dark . . . Tall . . . Beautiful . . ."

Smiling they said, no : they had to disappoint him. And he was disappointed too, while pretending to be very much so. The sun lost some of its charm. He waved and walked on, thinking Liversey must be quite a chap to lure girls all the way from Buxton into damp fields on winter nights.

Peter welcomed him at the gate and he dawdled.

Above the porch of Shang-ri-la there was a wire contraption full of moss and soil from which nasturtiums trailed in summer. Now it was dank and blackish with a few etiolated stalks and withered blooms. He tidied it a bit, spinning out the sunshine, listening to the Hoover.

When he opened the door he heard Mrs. Merridew's voice soaring briskly and comfortingly above the drone. " She'll get her week-end, Mrs. Ayrton, now and again," and his wife in the distance answering, then the Hoover like a siren in the wind changing pitch, and then Mrs. Merridew, and then his wife.

They owed a debt for more than cleaning to Gwen Merridew. Twice she had taken John when Ella had to go to hospital. With her auburn wig, hooked nose and porridge-coloured face she was like a little old witch. Everyone else, even the people on Marshal's farm, were " new," that is, had come since the war but Gwen Merridew had been born at Edgecliffe and like the old pear tree, covered with lichen at the back of Shang-ri-la, warped to its knees with age and poor diet, she gave another dimension to the human landscape. She knew who had lived in this or that house before the war, in her father's time, and where the bomb had fallen and where the old coach road to Bristol had passed.

The strength of her character was in keeping with this " other dimension " for she had had nothing on her side. Her enlarged always slightly bloodshot eyes, tremulous mouth and wig all bore witness to a thyroid deficiency which, till National Health, had meant periodic blackouts. Walking to Buxton school from the age of five she had often fainted by the way and been left to come on by herself. Later she'd gone into service at sixteen and been got with child by an old farmer in whose house she had been working. Ayrton had heard the story in the village.

The child had been taken away from her because she could not support it. It was adopted and lost to her. For the next thirty years she had been in service. After the war an aunt had left her a cottage and she'd gone to live in it, first working in Edgecliffe Orphanage, as it then was, and later, when the Orphanage became the Detention Centre, in Buxton hotels. Two years ago she had suddenly acquired a husband—a widower, Albert Merridew, who for many years had been remarkable on Edgecliffe platforms for dour idleness. Retirement galvanised him into action, perhaps because his comfort was jeopardised, and twice a week, fortified with whisky, he made a wobbly journey up

Edgecliffe hill and courted Gwen. She winked at people in his presence, knowing he wanted someone to care for him and a house. Soon she allowed him both. She got a ring, a new name, another pension and company. Her laugh was—always had been a sort of miracle—the abandoned rills and runs of a beautiful young girl in love and the occasions for it accurate: Albert's courtship, Peter's face when he heard the butcher's van, Marshal's addiction to girls because they were cheaper. Her delight was for the way things worked yet of all people she was the least calculating. Only sometimes a sigh, like the end of life, rushed from her lips as she finished "my" (the Ayrtons') floors, and wrung out her cloth. Every child was the one she lost.

After the sunlit hedge, Gwen was the next best tonic he knew for penal depression.

"Have you ever known any gipsies, Gwen?" he said.

"Gipsies, Mr. Ayrton. They're a right pest. And lazy!" she began, laughing with her back to him. "I remember my father saying why they lived in caravans." She shook her head mutely.

Why? She wouldn't tell, then laughed and said it.

"'Cos in a caravan you can . . . do things out of the window without leaving your bed."

Bright scarlet, she turned away still laughing and covered continuation of conversation by inventing a job in the corner. "I've a new lodger, Mr. Ayrton. She's to work with Marshal."

"More cheap labour. . . ."

"Minty Bates. She's from Erdsleigh. Oh, a beautiful girl, no, really lovely."

It was absurd to feel a thrill.

"Albert (she began laughing) carried her luggage. 'Carrying luggage. What's come over you?' I said.

Couldn't get a smile out of him." Gwen dissolved at the idea of Albert's second courtship in five years. " Gave her 'is last lettuce."

" Dark or fair ? " he said with a show of mock gallantry.

" Very dark. Italian looking. The Princess I call her," Gwen laughed. " But you'll be seeing her at the Youth Club, Mr. Ayrton. I told her to get down there and meet people. I said, ' Ask for Mr. Ayrton : he won't put you in prison'."

He turned away, picking up his post. There were one or two bills, a soap circular printed like Monopoly money, and an appeal from Jack Beasley for the restoration of the porch of the church. Minty Bates ! he thought.

Ella came in and said, " You should have taken your coat this morning, Phil."

" We had a bit of a business," Ayrton said, when Gwen had gone. " Cigarettes."

" Well, it's what I've been saying, isn't it ? "

" What . . . ? "

" They ought to give you a change."

He said : " Yes. We both need a change."

After a moment he said, " Did you think about to-night?"

" But you've got the Youth Club to-night."

" I told you, dear, I don't have to go."

" Well, I don't want to leave John like he is."

" John ? "

At that moment John came in or rather was suddenly there in the room, quite silently as though a magic carpet had brought him from school to the spot where he stood by the door.

" *John!* " Ayrton said.

" He wasn't feeling quite right this morning, were you, John dear ? He was quite off-colour. Gwen said he looked a fright. I gave him Disprin and put him into bed, Phil. That'll just do the trick, I thought, and it has. He feels like a little something, don't you, dear? Run and see the pie isn't burning."

Without looking at his father, John left the room in a muted lack-lustre manner, trailing one hand languorously along a wall and sliding through the door and vanishing as quietly as he had come.

"But he never said anything at breakfast."

"I'm not surprised the way you went on at him the last time he had a cold."

"But he hasn't got a cold."

"How d'you know. The only time you notice him is when he does something unexpected. I thought he was going to be sick when he came in. Now Phil . . ." Ella's voice mounted in pitch and she began picking things up, tidying round him. "You've got troubles enough as it is of your own, cigarettes and heaven knows what next over there. Don't start troubling about here. Leave that to me. John's not like Christine. He'll take a cold that easy, for goodness' sake you've surely seen for yourself." Her tidying reached unusual intensity. He was in the way, and her voice, as often happened in moments of emotion, had taken on a Welsh see-saw inflection. "D'you want a cold lunch?"

"This sort of thing won't get him out of his difficulties at school," he said.

"What difficulties? Just because he hasn't. got your brains!"

They went in and found John had taken the meat pie out of the oven.

"He's getting quite handy in the house," Ella said hotly.

Ayrton said nothing.

Ella said, " Gwen's taking a lodger again. She won't manage to come so early in the mornings."

" She was telling me," he said.

Then, for a time, all three of them ate in silence as though they had all got what they wanted.

12

THAT EVENING the humming-birds looked more than usually dead as he took his duffel-coat from the brass hook. "All right, dear?" he said, putting his head round the living-room door. Ella, sewing, said, " Have a good dance. Don't sprain your ankle." His recent lessons in jive from the girl in the post office had become a joke between them. "Try not to," he said and then went out, leaving Peter frustrated at the front door.

Heaven knows, he thought, why I made such a fuss about trying to get her out to dinner somewhere. She's far happier on the sofa. She's O.K.

The air was sharp. He did up the nautical attachments down the front of the duffel-coat and put the hood over his head. "You must have looked a sight when you were a monk," Ella had said to him once and he had got quite a shock. The correspondence between the garments had never occurred to him.

His 1947 Wolseley always started quite well and he set off briskly down the steep hill. He enjoyed his weekly visit to the Youth Club. It balanced much that needed balancing. He mixed with young people not in trouble, danced and played with them and was even sometimes ordered about by them. Besides, he was always urging his staff to take part in local activities so as to mitigate the quarantine. "We owe it to our wives and families," he had said, "to have outside interests." Well, you've got two pubs, Ella had said.

The Rev. Jack Beasley who ran the club was a gaunt man of about thirty with dark luminous eyes and a strenuously magnanimous voice and manner. Ever since hearing Ayrton had once been a monk, he had treated him with particular warmth, the same astringent warmth in fact which he lavished, as Chaplain to the Detention Centre, on the inmates. This was irritating but in time Beasley's real kindness to all and sundry and his gratitude for Ayrton's help with the club relegated the issue to minor importance. They got on well and Ayrton suppressed an occasional temptation to smile at the desperation with which Beasley tried to put Christianity across in terms of jive, table-tennis and excursions.

Although they had met in the street only yesterday, Beasley welcomed him in the porch of the old drill-hall as though they had been separated for years. He had heard from X who had seen Christine in Birmingham and she was getting on fine, and how were Ella's legs? Hallows (who had recently developed an unexpected desire to see Beasley as often as possible after chapel) had written him a letter! They laughed and Beasley's voice rang out above the scuffling thuds of gym-shod feet and distant rock 'n' roll as though all that jolly din over there was a sort of divine service. Taking advantage of a pause, Ayrton asked after Mary Beasley and the children. Precedent prepared him for the reply. Mary was ill, she had " gone into Erdsleigh to be tidied up " and Martha had measles but Tommy and he were making out fine, Martha having gone to the Cunliffes. The full communiqué was reeled off with only a slight intensification of the glow in the dark eyes and an insertion of the pipe at a supported, upward angle as though the challenge were small indeed. And suddenly Jack Beasley showed his teeth in a tigerish grin. But it was nothing : he was only taking in air and the next moment his laugh was mild : he said, " What I say, Phil, is there's always somone worse off than Number One." (Sometimes his addiction to modern idiom betrayed him into questionable taste, but Ayrton knew what he meant : we should be thankful for any mercies whatever.)

" Quite a good turn-out to-night," Ayrton said, looking round.

" Phil," Beasley said, suddenly conspiratorial, " would you like to meet the new member. Perfectly ripping girl. Works with Marshal. I told her : Hens, I should have thought Metro-Goldwyn-Mayer had some eggs for you, Minty. Stay on, brother ! You'll double our membership."

Hearing the name Minty, Ayrton experienced another mild, absurd thrill.

They went through the first big room where badminton was being played. A few young people were watching and some smiled or cocked their heads in response to Ayrton's greeting. They were all ages—fourteen to twenty-five. Some of the girls had their skirts tucked into their knickers and others wore gym slips. Faces glowed and there were whiffs of clean sweat and an atmosphere of physical tension and release.

" There . . ." Beasley said.

It was the same girl.

She was leaning on the shut keyboard of an upright

piano with her arms folded. Her eyes were on the couples dancing but her smile was in aid of the several young men around her. It was, however, an absent smile and did them very little credit as courtiers. Nor were her eyes really taking in the dancers. She was somewhere else.

Seeing her face properly for the first time, Ayrton was more than ever struck by its moody, haunting beauty. In some curious way this beauty was separate from her—a thing on its own. You could tell it was there, in the room, just by looking at the other girls (those, that is, who were not dancing) even though their attention seemed to be engaged in other directions. It was as though Minty's mere presence had stolen something from them which they were not allowed to claim or even show they had lost.

Ayrton felt his sleeve plucked: " D'you want more lessons, Mr. Ayrton ? " It was Margaret from the post office. Several near faces turned smiling in his direction. " Perhaps later," he said, " thank you." He did not wish to commit himself now.

Beasley walked over and said, " Minty—meet some more of us : this is the local gaoler, Phil Ayrton. You're not as bad as you look, are you, Phil. Well, I've got to rush. I'm umpiring the table-tennis finals." With a friendly push on Ayrton's arm, as though putting a new popular Christian factor into play, Beasley made off.

Her green-brown eyes were cleverly ringed with shadow which made them look mysterious and " deep." Looking into them he got an absurd impression of physical danger as though they were not eyes at all but yawning pits which ought to be fenced to stop people falling in at night. But " Come on," they seemed to say, " why not fall in ? You might be happier."

Such candour of expression was a little hypnotic. Ayrton found himself staring, unable to take his eyes from her face—from the straight nose with sensitively flared nostrils, broad, sultry, slovenly almost sulky mouth (which now parted to reveal chewing-gum being slowly churned by tongue and teeth), the high cheek-bones and wonderfully graceful attachment of head to full round neck, fringed at its base with dark curls, and the straight heavy fall of hair. So many styles! Something gamine about mouth and eyes, barbaric about the carriage of her head (and the heavy silver bangle on her wrist) and classical about her nose and indeed about the whole effect. By " classical " he meant Minty's capacity to evoke legendary names, Helen, Iseult and so on, whose beauty had survived through works of art, not often therefore with any verisimilitude, but more as a constant idea cutting through all styles—the idea of Woman as seen by men, throughout the ages. Had he been a painter aspiring to add to that accumulation of physical divinity Ayrton, seeing Minty close, knew that he would have said " There ! " and wanted her for his model, or more simply —wanted her.

Ayrton had put out his hand and for some reason this brought the ghost of a smile to her lips before she responded. Hers was rather cold. She was on the thin side, a fact which she emphasised unfashionably with a distinct black belt that encircled the almost miraculously small connection between the two halves of her body. He had thought he wasn't attracted by thin women.

Still looking at him she moved her long mouth a little, sideways, and he saw the gum in it. Then she turned away and was very interested now. Smiling too. Suddenly she snorted and put her wrist to her nose as though preventing a sneeze with her mouth full of food ; at the same time she went close enough to the young man to touch his jacket with her hair. " She did it again," she said.

One of the dancers did certainly have a droll style, sticking out her bottom at unexpected moments.

Ayrton tried to get the wavelength. What was Minty doing ? Why wasn't she dancing ? There was a moment's rather uneasy silence and he said, " Good turn-out to-night ! "

No one answered. He folded his arms and looked appreciatively at the quickly moving feet, the rotating hips, and flying hair. One of the boys offered him a cigarette. After he had refused he was conscious of her looking at him attentively from a range of a few inches.

He turned and she looked back at the dancers.

He said, " I believe you've come to work up at Edgecliffe, haven't you, Miss Bates ? "

After a moment's hesitation she said, " Yes—I'm right opposite you."

She had a slight drawl, and a crack in her voice. The whole effect of this was sardonic, but not unpleasant.

" With Gwen ? " he said.

She faced him then as though he knew perfectly well and instead of answering, lowered her eyes to his college tie and suddenly smiled. He thought it a lighthearted rather inane smile. He could see no point in it. Nor in the inspection.

" Did we once meet ? " he said.

Her face became stony and she turned back to the dancers. She did not answer.

One of the boys said, " Got a good team this year, Mr. Ayrton."

" I expect we'll keep our end up," Ayrton said.

" Football's allowed, is it ? " Minty said with her eyes still on the dancers.

He looked at her curiously, " Yes, football's allowed. . . ."

" Do you have dances up at the prison."

" I must protest : it's not a prison, Miss Bates."

" Isn't it ? " she said. " What is it then ? "

" A Detention Centre."

" Can people leave when they like ? "

" No . . . But I do assure you there's a difference."

Minty's mouth settled in a mocking pout. Her jaws moved again, slowly and sluggishly as the jaws of a sleepy cow. They all watched the dance in silence. The fact she had initiated the last exchange kept him where he was. Once she looked round him, leaning forward, and shifting the gum from one side of her mouth to the other with unnecessary display of teeth, tongue and saliva as she did so. And once she closed her eyes as though a qualm of pain had passed through her head.

" Would you care to dance ? " he said.

She laughed immediately and then faced him doubtfully. Then she said, " All right," and after a moment slid from the piano as though summoned to the dentist.

They went out on to the floor and Ayrton was aware of eyes looking at them all round. He smiled convivially to one or two boys and girls he knew.

Minty turned to face him with a strange smile, expecting him no doubt to foxtrot.

He might have preferred it for he liked to have the pleasure of contact with a woman all down his front, of feeling wisps of hair on his cheek, but instead, he felt sure (as he put his hand out to set her off on her first spin) he would have the more academic pleasure of standing back and watching her possessed by the rhythm, his merest touch sufficing to whip her up faster like a top, first this way then that.

They began and one surprise followed another. She wasn't good at jive, wasn't happy on her stiletto heels, and she knew different conventions. Yet she smiled condescendingly at what she obviously considered entirely his ineptitude. They went on for several minutes. Suddenly she caught her nose as though to suffocate a sneeze and bowing her head she stopped, walked past him back to her place by the piano. He followed her and while she was asking the young man for a cigarette (by merely touching the packet in his hand) Ayrton said, "I enjoyed that. Thank you."

She smiled non-committally, and when she had lit up she looked stonily at the dancers.

He tried to place her background. She, as though aware of his curiosity, seemed to go out of her way to deny the smallest clue. Her eyes narrowed, she remained silent, expressionless and still, looking away.

People were looking in their direction.

He said, " Until I began trying to do it I always thought in jive you could get away with a sense of rhythm and a rough idea of the movements, as in rumbas and tangos. Then I found how wrong I was. The steps are formal and exact. When I danced with the young ladies of Buxton I got into awful knots until I had some lessons."

She said rantingly, " Then let that be a lesson to you, Mr. Ayrton, never to dance with 'the young ladies of Buxton'!"

There was silence. One of the young men half smiled as he smoked.

Ayrton said politely, "Where do you come from, Minty?"

" Samarkand ! "

" You've made the Golden Journey, have you ? "

This appeared to irritate her and she did not reply. For the first time now he got an impression of personal hostility as though she " knew " something to his discredit. He was puzzled. Down here he got on well with the young people and he could not imagine any of them giving him a bad name.

" Well . . ." he said and began to move, allowing himself a last long look at her face. It might be a long time before another such luxury came his way. Several people were looking at him curiously and one of the boys behind Minty was smiling at someone the other side of the room. Let him smile !

" Good night then, Minty," he said.

She appeared not to have heard so he repeated himself. After a moment he realised with a shock that she *had* heard but wasn't going to answer. Why ? Christian names were customary in the club and she was young enough to be his daughter. She surely could not object to him using her first name. Her jaws moved on her gum. It was mad but all the same rather unnerving. It had happened to him before once, when he'd been round a Birmingham Youth Club with a probation officer. He'd come up then against something absolutely *blank* and got the impression the children were struggling with the equivalent of a colour-bar : feelings which made his mere attempt to communicate an act of presumption. But why should Minty feel like this, Minty, educated and so beautiful ? Then she did say " Good night," coldly and without looking at him.

He moved away, adjusting his spectacles and smiling. He stopped at the door and had a few words with another

group. One of them said, " How's the jive, Mr. Ayrton ? "
and smiled at him knowingly.

" Don't tell my wife," he said.

He left with the sound of laughter behind him, glad of
their friendliness, even if it was, perhaps in one or two
cases, flavoured with satire. Just a little.

13

THE THING ABOUT HER that stuck in his mind, like
a bone in the throat, was the expression of tragic detach-
ment which lay in the bottom of her eyes and became
visible whenever the ripples of contempt or fatuous school-
girl laughter had blown away. She must have been about
twenty-three, he thought. Her accentless voice and laconic
diction suggested an educated well-to-do background yet
her slovenly, open-mouthed chewing and capacity for
" switching off," going blank, merely because talking to
an adult, put him in mind of working-class teenagers. Or
was she some penniless Habsburg or Bourbon ? There
was no end to the contradictory reactions she inspired.
What could have been more awkward than her jive, yet
who more devoted to the attempt ? What could have been
more gutter slipshod than her walk yet what more graceful
and *racé* than the carriage of her head, shoulders and superb
neck ? The fall of her dark hair to her shoulders and the
straightness of her back had been exactly right for the

barbaric weight of bracelets on her wrist. She might have carried a million urns from desert wells on her head, fought in battle, tortured, been tortured, shed blood for causes she had never stopped to think about but accepted as part of the life handed down to her from ages past. One moment her eyes seemed to have seen everything there was to see, the next never anything except her own wilful pleasure. And her voice, sometimes smooth and low and soft and sometimes rising to an ugly cracked drawl put you in mind of a broken wind-instrument. That too stuck in the memory. . . .

A knock came on the door and Parks put his head round:

" Goole's here now, sir. Ready ? "

Goole ! Goole . . .

Jefferies came in, and the ceiling sang as Parks shouted. Then there was Goole pumping his way across six feet of floor, swinging his arms 170 degrees for each step of eight inches.

" Halt, left TOIN."

When silence was complete Liversey put the cigarettes on the table and intoned the charge.

Ayrton touched his glasses, cleared his throat. It was some seconds before he could bring his mind to bear:

" Have you anything to say, Goole ? "

" N'sir."

Ayrton's eyes lifted. Above him was an adam's apple, moving, in the middle of a bull neck, and above that nostrils and eyes raised, unfocused, staring high. Goole would say nothing.

The large expressive face which had at first been so free and easy in this room and which, only yesterday in the mat-shop had presumed to address him in a fraternal and straightforward manner had become a fixed blank. Something had happened to him.

Ayrton frowned, placing the book more exactly in front of him and smoothing the page, concentrating.

Sometimes it happened that officers took matters into their own hands, short-circuiting the process of punishment with a fatherly clout which, done in the right manner by the right person at the right time, often did more good and left less bitterness than the creaking machinery of report, and bread and water. Indeed Ayrton had had to concede that sometimes Jefferies himself, that blunt-headed instrument of Her Majesty's displeasure, by looking like a clouter and then quite naturally behaving like one, had often soothed inmates with a feeling of fitness.

On the other hand there were times when Ayrton saw a chance with a boy, almost as a footballer sees an opening —a fleeting opportunity, particularly with First Offenders, which must be seized because it will not recur, only to find that one of his staff, one of his own side, had instantly spoiled it, by acting, usually with good intentions, as intermediary but in a way he would not have wished. Violence, extreme pressure of any kind was the last thing Goole had needed, yet looking at him now Ayrton felt that this was exactly what the man had been given. There was something shocked about him . . . cauterised. The violence might merely have been verbal and psychological, but violence there had been.

Goole didn't fit in, Ayrton could appreciate that. He didn't belong. But shouldn't this, conceivably, have worked in his favour, exempting him. . . .

Seconds ticked by. Jefferies stirred and began tapping with a reversed Biro, looking at Ayrton and then at Goole.

Ayrton suddenly thought: she'll bring the eggs sometimes, instead of Shirley. *Goole* . . .

Ayrton said, " Chief, Mr. Liversey, will you leave me alone a minute with the inmate . . ." then turning to the Deputy: " I'd like to have a moment alone with him . . .? "

For a moment they all stared without moving. Not only was it against precedent, it was probably also against regulations. Parks moved at last. Then they all went, seeming to get smaller as they moved out of their roles. " I'll give you a call," Ayrton said as the door closed, and then quietly: " Sit down, Goole."

Jefferies's voice could be heard in the passage. The tone sounded special, even for Jefferies.

Goole's eyes, for the first time that morning, lowered and met Ayrton's while his body relaxed from the mockery of the military position.

" There's a chair behind you . . . sit down."

Goole sat gingerly and uneasily and Ayrton dropped his eyes to the punishment book. What am I doing? he thought.

In a moment he would have to recall his staff. And he would probably have no startling results with which to mollify their outraged sense of propriety. What on earth had made him do it ?—something about Goole, something tantalising. Or had the thought of that girl, had love insisted . . . love . . . !

Perhaps everyone has somewhere in him a hankering for all that is orgiastic, abandoned, total and uncalculated—all that is most opposite to the common life of taboos, locks, keys, manners, ceremonials: for most the vent of newspaper crime stories and thrillers is sufficient, the impulse being subdued to a mere appendix of fantasy. But for some fantasy is not enough. They pass through life bereaved of real experience or even of full vicarious experience of their negative impulses. They never seize or even sample what secretly they most desire. . . .

" Well, Goole. . . ."

For a moment he had the illusion that the necessary words of sympathy were only just out of reach like something once known but forgotten, that the combination which would unlock Goole was " on the tip of his tongue." But it wasn't, and he had to start again:

" Goole," he said, " we never know the full story of why people get convicted and sent here. A man might get sent here who might think he had done nothing wrong . . . (and in fact done no wrong, he thought) . . . But if he was—it would make no difference. Once a man gets here, he's treated the same as everyone else. Do you follow me so far ? "

He heard a sound that might have passed for an affirmative.

Encouraged he went on :

" In other words, I must not waste time re-trying your case. It's not my job. Everyone who comes here is guilty. I can't go behind the evidence even if I want to. . . ."

Goole said nothing.

" My job is quite simple. I have to run this Centre along the lines laid down by the Prison Commissioners. One of the rules is that there shall be no smoking. I think it's a good rule. The only serious violence we have had in the last years was due to the presence in the camp of tobacco. Now you . . . Goole . . . somehow managed to get tobacco brought into the camp."

He heard himself then. It was as though Goole were a cave. His voice went out to the walls and rebounded as echo, distorted into a caricature of all that was plausible, dull and ineffective.

Silence fell; was prolonged.

Damn you, he suddenly felt, d'you think I care much if you all cut each other's throats and get extended sentences? . . . Yet . . . yet I do care a bit . . . enough to put this thing to each one of you as though we were all, I as well as you, involved in a comedy from which there is no escape. The only hope is to make it as constructive and agreeable as possible. . . .

Agreeable for you, said Goole's eyes, for your job, your record. . . . You're asking a favour, that's all, from *me*. How can you ask favours from people deprived of favour? Talk. Talk away. You'll get this from me: hands slack, half uncurled on the knees of coarse trousers, two fingers still yellow, and my eyes telling you: why should I? You'd use it against me, as you used that thing I said to you in the mat-shop. And *why* did I say it? You know, don't you! Because you had looked at me, encouragingly, as much as to say, I'd've done the same myself. Well, it's all right. I understand now. You want to be friendly but only when it suits. That's O.K. by me, by all of us. It's a wonderful let-out for you people but just give us time—and it'll be the best let-out ever. . . . For us. But don't be surprised, that's all. Don't complain if we offend your sensibilities! Expect injustice. Ayrton's voice went on, then, in the cave of Goole's silence, re-bounding:

" If you co-operate . . . if you tell me how you managed to do this and give me your word that you will not do it again I'll deal with you very leniently, very leniently indeed."

Goole's hands. One boot stirred.

Ayrton spoke lower and faster, almost hinting complicity: "I wanted to see you alone, Goole, because I thought it might give you an opportunity to talk more freely. . . . How have you been getting on with the others. Are you in bad with the staff?"

Goole said, "Nossa."

Well—he had indulged a whim and offended his staff for nothing—absolutely nothing.

Speaking mechanically, low and fast, signalling, it felt like, secretly to Goole for the last time, he said:

"We all want things we can't have. All of us. We have to learn to do without. The sooner you accept your sentence and the discipline here, the sooner you'll be out—and the sooner you'll be happy."

Ayrton waited. One of Goole's hands moved as though attempting the communication which his tongue refused. But it did not move much.

Then Ayrton went to the door and called in the officers.

Two came in looking dour, and resumed their military stations.

He said, "Where's the Deputy?"

Parks went out again, down the passage and returned. "Not in his office, sir!"

"Well . . . we'll carry on . . . I've examined the prisoner."

Had they anything to add? No. Ayrton turned to Goole:

"A week's loss of remission. Two days' restricted diet."

Parks then remained silent as though waiting for an instruction. After all, routine broken once might be broken again.

"March out," Ayrton said.

After the shouting Parks remained. His lean, bigoted, dutiful face was perplexed.

"I thought he might talk," Ayrton explained.

"But he didn't, sir?"

"No."

Parks looked knowing but made no comment.

"You see," Ayrton said, "when I first saw Goole I felt he thought he might have been wrongly convicted. I thought he might have that on his mind. . . ."

"I thought they all had that on their mind."

Ayrton said, "I meant genuinely."

The word sounded strange, almost as irrelevant as, a moment ago, he himself had suggested it should be.

"Thinks quite a lot of himself, if you ask me, sir."

Ayrton wondered what Goole thought of himself. It would have been helpful to know. He got the impression Goole had never thought of himself at all, or of anyone else either.

"He hasn't had a letter from that girl of his, has he?" Ayrton said.

Parks went to see and returned with Jefferies—carrying a letter.

Jefferies said, "Didn't know you'd started again . . . I was going to bring this through yesterday. Then we had this cigarette lark. . . ."

"I wanted to see this," Ayrton said. It was written in green ink. Although the handwriting was ragged it was easy to read.

Dearest Jim,

I don't know how long it will be before you get out—three months they told me—but I want you to know that I shall be waiting. I never could explain anything in letters. Perhaps I can't explain them any-way. All I know is I still love you and always will. Oh, Jim darling, I was just trying to help . . . ! Some-times you didn't know how difficult it was. Perhaps there was more to it than that. I tell you I don't know and probably never will. Oh, my darling, where were you ? It was two weeks at least since I heard. Then —the usual. I never really know what happens. I suppose if it had been someone else it wouldn't have mattered to you. Was that it ? I don't suppose you know either. All I know is that it *didn't* mean anything and that's how it is. I've got a job and I'm saving up and I shall be waiting. You're going to be great one day. I met a man from Blix Recordings at the Seven Wise. He said he'd heard you and wanted to sign you up, Jim—don't let it get you down. Just don't. I'm waiting and always will be however long. If they knew what I thought of them. At night I think of you. The bed's so empty it hurts. I fixed that spring—the tenor one. I think the bass would still burst out. But what was the point of mending things. I came away and got this job. Jim, darling, my arms are round you—I'm right beside you. I've kissed this. Kiss it, too. *Heidi*

Jefferies said, " Fire or part-worn stores ? "
Ayrton fastidiously raised the paper to his nose. " And she did kiss it, too—or kept it in her handbag."
Jefferies grunted.
Parks said, " It's an incitement if you ask me. All that about ' what I think of them ' ! " The circumference of his eyeballs had become fully visible.

Ayrton was looking at the letter again, incredulous, gauging the sophistication of the dots and exclamation marks after the words, " I was just trying to help . . . ! "

Jefferies said, " Kiss this ! If we're letting in that sort of letter we might as well get a copy of *Lady Chatterley's Lover*, for recreation."

That, too, might be a kindness in the circumstances, Ayrton thought. After all the Japanese had life-size india-rubber women on board their submarines in the war, one for the officers, one for the men. There might be all kinds of negatively positive approaches to the depraving factors of imprisonment. So far they were stuck with the absolutely negative ones.

Ayrton said, " Give it to him. And tell him to tell her in his next letter that if she makes another remark about ' they ' the letter will be returned."

Jefferies held the letter as though he could not believe his ears, as though the Warden had just ruled that men on restricted diet should get a ration of pornography with their glass of water at midday.

" You mean *we*'re to read *that* . . . to him ? "

Ayrton had forgotten Goole's illiteracy. He felt a qualm as though Jefferies was gradually getting the better of him.

" Yes," Ayrton said.

He was glad when the door closed. He took off his spectacles and massaged his closed eyes with the tips of his fingers. " Oh, my darling, where were you ? " Those letters often brought him into contact with fresh outspoken emotion which, now the children were growing up, he never experienced. Far cries they were. Oh that none ever loved but you and I. Years since he had even read a poem.

He supposed the letter must have reminded him of Minty

—" Oh, my darling . . . it hurts . . ."—The person out of reach. He understood. A faint self-mocking smile was born on his mouth as he pictured the extraordinary recruit to the Youth Club. Here, at Edgecliffe. But what was the good of harbouring such an image ?

The trouble was he didn't seem able to shed this as he had shed other ten-second love affairs.

He took out his keys and locked up the punishment book and papers, then stopped; suddenly thought Damn !: I should, for Goole's sake, have kept the letter back so that one of his mates could read it to him. Instead I confided the intimacy to Jefferies.

Liversey and another officer were hanging about the Deputy's room. They looked up as they saw him coming and moved and fell silent as though surprised in some illicit conversation. The Deputy himself turned away from his fire towards the desk. Shall I tell him, Ayrton thought, to keep the letter back. Then Jefferies looked up and the criticism in his expression was too much to engage with again.

Ayrton walked by and on.

Outside as he passed Marshal's field he saw three figures in the distance. One of them was Minty. The other girl beside her seemed to draw attention to him for she turned and stared. It was too far to wave. Besides he was still in view of Jefferies's office.

14

ELLA SAID SHE'D BEEN speaking to Christine on the
telephone and had decided to go to Birmingham for the
week-end with John, to see the hostel and perhaps call on
the Fawcetts. " We thought you'd be happier here," she
said. The plan was presented to him, parcelled up as it
were, sealed and stamped. He was obviously not meant
to make any alteration. " John and I thought we'd have
a look at the zoo, didn't we, dear." Somewhere on the
floor a voice said " Yes." Ventriloquist and dummy could
not have produced question and answer more smoothly.
Ella went on describing where they would stay and how it
would make a change. Ayrton said he thought it a very
good idea. . . .

Ella said, " But . . . ? "

" But nothing," Ayrton said, adjusting his spectacles.

He had in fact wondered whether he should not make
some counter move at week-ends when, as now, she
monopolised John. At times he wished he had never read
a psychological book or report or met a psychologist. The
idea of self-consciously " all doing something together "
offended his instincts and sense of fitness even more than
the continual spectacle of Ella going off with John as
though they were lovers. Or was it he who was being
silly? The change would do them good and Ella was
probably right in discouraging him from coming because

right in thinking he didn't want to come. Half-hearted he said :

"Which d'you fancy most, John—a walk on the common with me—or tea with the Fawcetts and the zoo."

"The zoo," John said with his head still turned, so quietly as to be scarcely audible.

"He never gets a chance to see anything," Ella said.

"There are fallow deer on the common."

"But in the zoo," Ella said, "you can see them." The curved back and averted head on the floor touched Ayrton with a feeling of tenderness. Why was John always so silent ? The deer had been an offer, an appeal. Like Ella's Fawcetts they had really meant something else, something it was difficult to put into words.

But that was that.

He took them to the station and waited on the platform. They got in and waved to him through the window. John was nearest and looked down at him with unusual directness as though the intervening plate glass, the proximity of his mother and impending departure gave him special confidence. Ayrton smiled cheerily and waved but could not help wondering what was going on in that pale withdrawn face. Did John see him as a praying mantis in brilliant socks ? The extraordinary thought occurred because when the boys, at his last Borstal, had put on a revue, a figure had come in carrying a gun over its arm, which looked exactly like a praying mantis—in tweed jacket and coloured socks and grey flannel trousers. A shout of recognition and laughter went up. Ella had had to help him. "That's you, dear."

When it dawned on him that it really might be like him, he had experienced a mortal qualm as though he had been killed, and come back instantly as a spectator. Surely that wasn't all, that wasn't the essential part of him. He had looked down, seen yellow socks with crimson hoops . . . *and been surprised.*

They all waved to each other and the train left.

When he got back the post had come. There was a letter from Head Office. Opening it he looked at once at the signature and saw the name of one of the Prison Commissioners, a man who was known to him personally. The letter asked him to deliver the final lecture at a special course for Prison Officers.

Although it made no mention of his application for a move, it at once made Edgecliffe seem better; and he himself clever, perspicacious and experienced. Edgecliffe even became less isolated, less forgotten. Jefferies shrank to insignificance, Goole surfaced again as material for optimism.

Ayrton's future changed, too. He would do the lecture well, his application would be well-received and he would get a governorship of an open Borstal or experimental Y.P. prison. No Victorian barrack full of stinking sluices for him, no hangings . . . Ella would get her shops and her "people like us." He was filled suddenly with a sense of once again being *able to choose.*

He put the letter down, strolled up and down in the living-room while Peter watched him hopefully. Then he went to the window which looked out towards Marshal's fields, and listened backwards into the emptiness and silence of his own house. He had never known it so empty. He looked over his shoulder. There it was: like a stage between performances, haunted with possibility and heaped with the ashes of dead emotions. The mood of alienation grew on him, magnified by the ticking, creaking silence all round. He found himself thinking of Ella and the children as though they were people he had once known long ago in different circumstances. Christine's music stand, the paintings by inmates, Ella's decapitated duck, John's Hornby engine by the gramophone all concerned him as much as relics in a museum. And Philip Ayrton also seemed unreal. It was suddenly as though the brilliant socks had become the whole of Philip Ayrton and found difficulty in believing themselves to be connected with the dun tweed jacket, off-the-peg trousers and dark-blue, emblem-spangled college tie; just as previously it had been the other way round.

Only Peter was the same, lying there with his head couched on his paws and his eyes swivelling so as to keep his master always in sight. Peter always knew when a walk was likely. A walk? It was then Ayrton thought of Minty—without shock as though really he had been thinking of her all the time, yes, even when Ella originally discussed her intention of going to Birmingham.

She'd be in one of the fields for another hour or two then, dressed up, she'd go down to the town. Or would she take an afternoon's rest perhaps with women's mags and pop records; or what?

It was a harmless and pleasant pipe-dream.

Perhaps, he thought, if I'd been to the university, to the war, if I'd sowed my wild oats like most young men or even married someone different, younger, . . . then the sudden impact of meeting someone like Minty Bates would pass unnoticed. As it is . . . I've never had an adventure, he thought. Not that kind. And coming down to brass tacks: what about the other kind of adventure which I have had, the spiritual and intellectual explorations: the monastery, God, delinquents. An enemy might say that my whole life had been a series of retreats into whatever form of consolation came handy. Who could have promised me more than Father Lawson? Who could have given me more devotion than Ella, where else could I have traded my poor qualifications for as much rank and power as in Borstals? And yet that's not the whole story. There was always something else ... Something in me that *aspired* —though at times I felt that even this was a ruse, home-made, to move me from despair and self-contempt. Now a face! And the music starts up again. To-day I could even try to write a poem.

He saw Minty's eyes, aquamarine, with several strata of markings like lucid shallow water, tiny tadpole spots, facets of agate, shadow, light and reflections and unassessable depth, her long mouth, her capacity to switch from childish triviality to tragic and mature repose; the indefinable sense of mission which attached to her person.

Something shuddered in him, with awe, with longing.

Then he remembered: he had to get eggs.

He did not expect to find anyone about but Shirley was in the sorting room.

When he asked for eggs, she said she wanted to get this lot ready for the van, could she drop some in later? Of course, he said. He looked beyond her to the passage, into the food store, and out into the yard.

"You were right about there being a new recruit, Mr. Ayrton."

Wondering if his thoughts had been ambushed, Ayrton smiled uneasily.

"I know. Where does she come from?"

"Edgbaston, is it? We always seem to get it wrong." She laughed as though at a memory.

"Wrong?" he said curiously.

" Yes, by now we're all a bit muddled. She's quite a character."

" Do the hens appreciate her ? "

" Someone will," Shirley said stoically. " Shall I ask her to drop your eggs ? She's always on about ' the prison ' as she calls it. You'd better show her round."

Shirley's smile was perspicacious enough to be embarrassing.

" You may find she'll refuse to come," Ayrton said with a smile that made light of the whole subject. " She got rather cross with me at the club for saying the D.C. wasn't a prison. I'd like my eggs in a box, not thrown ! "

But he thought: she'll ask her and she'll come. How could he be so sure ? Why was it even likely ? Well, he was sure !

He went home and watched a rugger match on television, smoking and waiting for the bell to ring, wondering if she would come. At last the bell did ring and he went to the door and there she was, in a light fawn mackintosh swinging loose, unbuttoned all the way down the front and a basket full of eggs. Seeing him she smiled as though she had guessed his sense of expectation. Round one of her wrists was the same heavy silver bangle and there too was the straightness of her back, the looseness of her hair and the wonderful carriage of her head. Her smile, so unexpected after the way she had treated him the other night, stayed on her face and she simply stood there as though waiting for him to do something more than merely accept the eggs.

" Your eggs," she said, holding them out.

The trouble was he was sick to death of ugliness. That was why he loved Gwen Merridew's laugh, Peter and the common. Not that all D.C. inmates were ugly but just as there were no windows in the Centre free of bars so there were no eyes in it free of pain. And the buildings were ugly. In a way the whole place was a reservoir of ugliness. The very tarmac which began a mile from Edgecliffe was Prison Commission tarmac and therefore ugly, his writing paper was H.M.S.O. issue and ugly. Even the reproduction of Van Gogh's cornfield in the D.C. hall was ugly. Sometimes he felt this leprosy of ugliness had infected him wholly without his knowing it and that finally he had brought it home and given it to Ella and John. And now there was nothing with which to sublimate it. No Christ, no God. No " other level." In such a place there came a time when even compassion became inimical to him simply because it always entailed pain, for him, by himself.

To all this, Minty, standing there, personified the ideal of relief.

" Come in," he said.

She looked at him hesitantly.

" Shirley often takes a cup of tea with us," he said. The " us " didn't feel dishonest. Ella was in the house, inside *him* ; he was chaperoned to the marrow of his bones. Besides, there was probably no chaperon quite like his appearance, his age.

She came in then putting the eggs on the humming-birds and looking round with frank and genial curiosity. He noticed that she was making an effort to be someone quite different from the girl he had met in the club. He wondered why. The absence of witnesses ?

" What pretty birds ! " she said.

" My wife's out, Minty."

" Yes, I know," she said and looked at him oddly.

" How did you know ? "

Without answering she went through.

In the living-room she went to the fire-place, turned her

back on it and looked about her with a rather inane smile as though imagining the surprise of friends if they could see her now—having tea with the Warden of a prison. Then she fixed her eyes on a particularly dirty and frayed chair cover and looked pensive. In one way nothing could have been more socially assured, in another nothing more gauche than her position there, in the centre of the room.

" I suppose Gwen keeps you informed," he said.

" She does a bit," and Minty looked at him as much as to say, " I've got your dossier ! "

He asked her if she would like a drink or tea ; she said, no, she'd like coffee, a choice for which she seemed to take some obscure credit, for as she made it her face brightened self-consciously. For her, she explained, it was always coffee.

When he came back she said, " Do you paint ? "

" No—those are all by inmates."

" I like that one," she said in a tone of mockery— pointing to the stag by moonlight.

" It's funny, people always pick on that one."

" Why ? Did he become famous ? "

" Yes—he was hanged."

With a sense of loss and failure he sought uncertainly, in memory, for a face and found what might have been the right one. Then the pathos of the relic and his reasons for keeping it were sharpened to the point of making him wish it wasn't there. It was long since he had looked at it. He adjusted his glasses and stared at the carpet, seeing there a thread which after a moment he removed. Then it was Minty again, before his eyes. She was dead silent, staring up and round at the bad picture.

Suddenly she made a noise that was most like a snort and only a little like a laugh. When she again showed her face it was nauseated and incredulous. She looked at him incredulously, too: he was an object again, as he had been that night, when he talked about dancing. She said, " Got any lampshades made of human skin ? "

" Why d'you say that ? " he said calmly.

She was silent for a moment. Then she said in a bored tone: " You approve of hanging, I suppose."

" No," he said without hesitation. " On the other hand I could never get tremendously worked up about stopping it—never sign petitions and so on. It seems to me it's a very small item in the total of suffering."

She looked hostile, suddenly bored.

After a moment Ayrton said, " You're one of the nuclear disarmament people, too—one of the marchers perhaps ? "

" Of course," she said, " I believe in the future."

Although he then smiled in a tolerant and paternal fashion, he found himself affected by her tone. For some reason it threw into relief choices which he had avoided making, not so much out of laziness or impotence (though this a little) but out of indifference. To remain sensitive to all that was best in the past and still to welcome the kind of future which he saw emerging, had proved a task beyond the powers of his affections and reason. Perhaps only a chilly voice from within, assuring him that you " can't put the clock back " had obliged him to talk to the inmates, during Current Affairs, as though in favour of the future. Because how could you be " for " the inconceivable ? This child made him wish that he could feel differently . . . not about atomic weapons (because without them he was sure there would have been another war by now) but about this very " future "—as though it were desperately worth saving.

There was a silence which he attempted to fill with his

tolerant smile, which no doubt maddened her, but which concealed his attempt to come to terms with the assault she had in fact made on his indifference.

"What brought you into poultry farming?" he asked with an astringence that verged on satire.

"I wanted a job," she said.

He was silent.

"I may take a course in animal husbandry," she said. She sat down and put a hand on Peter's head and stroked his ear rather clumsily, without feeling, and then let it go.

"I see. Do your parents live near here?"

"Yes. Do yours?"

She smiled, then, intimately and provocatively while she searched his eyes as though for a response she seemed certain she could find, had always found, when she bothered to look for it. Perhaps it was just a way of changing the subject.

He said, "It was you, wasn't it, in the field last Thursday night?"

She looked bored again. "I never saw you before we met in the club."

"Perhaps you just saw a torch," he said.

Peter raised a paw to Minty's lap asking her to continue fondling his ear.

"Perhaps he recognises you," Ayrton said.

Minty said nothing, but looked down without feeling, at the dog.

"Is Mr. Liversey a friend of yours?"

"Who's Mr. Liversey?"

"One of my staff."

Minty's eyes dropped and for a moment she said nothing.

"Is that the one with the birthmark?" she said.

"You know them all then, do you?"

" I've met some of them at the George."

" That night," he said, " when Peter caught you out for a walk . . . I met Liversey a few minutes later in the road. . . . Since then I thought you'd come here to be near him."

" Thanks ! " she said, with a short laugh, blowing out smoke and still looking at the floor.

They sipped their coffee. He said, " There must be angels overhead."

Sad scorn came easily to her face. She was so beautiful.

" You like it here ? " he said at last in a tone of tribute.

" Gwen's sweet," she said.

Silence fell again. Heavily. He felt at any moment he might be going to say how beautiful she was, just academically of course.

She put her cup away as though it were empty and she herself about to leave.

And then, quite suddenly, the emptiness of the house was like a darkness in his brain and there near him was her body, under her clothes. The feeling was like an increase of weight and a furry proximation to sleep and greater strength. It took him by surprise, staggered him . . . while she looked down without speaking, at the cup she had put down; while Peter moved his paw again and the clock ticked.

He adjusted his glasses.

" I should think you find it lonely. But perhaps not."

" It's a ball," she said. " How do you find it ? "

" I ? " he said incredulously. " I'm an old gaoler."

" Well . . . not all that old."

Without looking at her, he listened to how she said it, listened to the obliqueness and the drawl and how she saved herself by a sort of scorn.

How had it happened? In the field and then again now —the invitation to anonymity, to be someone else.

Something prompted him at last to his senses. He said stickily but astringently: "You're a surprising addition to our little community, Minty."

There was another silence. She rose: "Albert says he's been waiting for me all his life. . . . Thanks for the coffee. Why don't you come round and hear some records. You said you liked jive." (She smiled provocatively, teasing him with a memory of their dance together.) "You can dance with Gwen; I'll dance with Albert."

He rose and put down his cup which was still half full.

They stood close to each other. In her stiletto heels she was as tall as he.

"My wife gets back to-morrow night," he said as though she hadn't spoken. "Then you must come and spend an evening. It's not often . . ."

He stopped and felt foolish.

"Not often what?" she said, while her eyes challenged and encouraged him.

"Nothing."

She began to smile, pityingly. He adjusted his glasses.

"Not often we have a chance of seeing such a beautiful girl," he said—academically—and with some shame, lowering his eyes to ease them.

She said, "What's the matter, Mr. Ayrton? You look unhappy."

"Which makes you look happy, for some reason. How old are you, Minty?"

"I'm a mystery, aren't I?"

"Yes—you are rather."

"Knock and it shall be opened unto you. . . ." She

smiled, and narrowed her eyes as though slightly drunk, at the same time looking down the front of his body.

"Well, come here whenever you like," he said reverently.

She remained so close, looking down, somewhere about his waist, remained smiling drunkenly. Certainty came to him, at that moment, that if he put out his arm and gently guided her back to the sofa and down on to it, she would comply. She raised her eyes and they confirmed that this was true; invited him to go ahead. He would have smiled politely—but there was something vertiginous about her stare, giddy-making as a drop right down to rocks scantily covered with liquid aquamarine. The moment passed, her expression turned first to very faint scorn and then to that enormous sadness and hostility which he thought he had seen in her face at the club.

At the front door she thanked him for the coffee and the " chance of seeing your souvenirs." Then he watched her go away with that slovenly self-conscious walk.

She has been a tart, he thought, is one. . . .

15

THERE WAS CHAPEL next morning in the main building. Jack Beasley preached a sermon on hope, and Ayrton read the lesson. Goole was there, conspicuous, because men on restricted diet always sat by themselves, at a distance from the other prisoners.

Pictures on the Wall

Gwen came in to cook his lunch and she talked a bit about Minty—said she seemed to have no people of her own. Ayrton ventured questions but Gwen had no hard information—only a few trance-like stares. "She's got some lovely clothes—really lovely. . . ." Here Gwen looked at him as much as to say, "What d'you make of that?" But Ayrton said nothing. He was expecting at any moment to hear the familiar sermon about "girls nowadays" not knowing when they were lucky nor what work meant and so on. But she said, "She's willing enough. Offered to fetch Albert's papers for him. . . ." Her eyes became dewy at the memory. Perhaps her child would have been Minty's age . . . and done the same. "She's getting a loan of my bike."

The paper shop didn't open till two on a Sunday but the queue formed early. I'd just like to see her, he thought, that's all, and he was there, parked in sight of the queue, before the doors opened. But she wasn't there. The other girl Pam was there instead and seemed to buy enough papers for twenty.

As he passed her she suddenly smiled and said, "Did you get your eggs, Mr. Ayrton?" He was puzzled. The smile had been insinuating.

When he got back he read *The Observer*, but Peter's tail thumped the floor whenever he moved. All right, he said, and Peter broke into a hymn of expectation. Before starting he stood at the door looking towards the Merridews' cottage.

It was one of those tranced late autumn days—amber, smoky, murmurous and chilled in patches. Smoke went straight up from chimneys like strands of grey wool hanging from invisible pins. Apples on the tree at the back glowed gold as myth and he knew as he looked at them he would remember them like this at the same moment of other years to come. Dahlias peered over the top of the Merridews' fence. Nothing moved. In the distance a train rattled first sharp then hollow, breaking the suspension of time, receding. Ineffable melancholy then haunted the air as though the nature of reality had come close to him, like a bride, paused, then gone, still veiled. He didn't want to meet Minty. No, he thought, not again!

Still, he would go past the cottage. . . .

There was an empty deck-chair on the tiny plot, in the hollow square of dahlias. A *Sunday Pictorial* sprawled by its legs. Albert was watching his cabbages. Ayrton waved and walked on, feeling a curious mixture of relief and disappointment. Supposing they had met each other long ago. Supposing he were younger. . . .

Beauty of a certain kind discouraged desire, by making it seem incestuous. Something about Minty was entirely familiar. He had always known her, always done without her.' How absurd, he thought, how absurd and turned his eyes outward to the trees and sky.

Edgecliffe Common is one of those enclaves of marsh and thicket which being virtually undrainable has remained wild, a pocket of England where the trees all sow themselves and where a man can stop, and sit down, look round and see not a single object except his own clothes which dates the moment. Indeed to Ayrton the swampy scrub, birch, occasional granite outcrop and families of natural oak seemed pregnant with the possibility of a sudden glimpse of some colossal vegetarian reptile dawdling in the slush, or the shattering progress of a dinosaur.

In spring the place resounded with the harsh stridence of a thousand nesting gulls, and the whole sky was a blossom of white wings. In summer, when the sun shone, smells of flowers, growth and decay steamed from the ground and insects hummed like distant London traffic. Often Ayrton had found a dry clump of heather, and just sat and watched the iridescent dragon-flies, those stylistic cousins of his own humming-birds, become grey with speed or pausing with gyroscopic steadiness suddenly glow with blue and orange fire from the sun.

It was here, too, that he went shooting, though in recent years the glamour of the chase had gradually given place to a mere enjoyment of its trappings—the scenery, the privacy, the joy of his dog, the progress of the seasons. He would simply walk or sit *savouring* with ears, nose and eyes. The relief of not seeing any sign round him of Edgecliffe Detention Centre, but of letting the ground grow up into him as though he and it were all one element, one feeling which had only to exist to have a purpose that was both personal and anonymous, ephemeral and eternal, gave him strength for another week, even a sort of general, philosophical optimism. And to think that he had once been a monk! He sometimes wondered how even then, years ago, young as he had been, he had never paused to scrutinise the singular fact that the devotees of every religion, all over the world, all through time, had been convinced that they and they only had held a monopoly of religious truth. Surely if a man had any claim of intelligence at all he must realise that only one lot of devotees could be right and if that were so, how strange that no member of the other lots, equally intelligent, should not have been struck by this fact also—and wondered. In this context he remembered the tired and melancholy wisdom of *Religio Medici*, read long ago, as an early ancestor of modern relativism, and thought it a fit gospel for the consciously

" blind " church-going of Christine and some of her contemporaries. *Credo quia absurdum est!* Who could doubt that to believe was " good ": and that to-day more than ever the art was to believe and disbelieve at the same time ! Was that the trick that had lain at the bottom of every monk's eyes, wavery, translucent, unassessable as the ocean floor just visible through clear deep water ? In the eyes of Protestant clergymen there seldom lay any trick at all. But there I Finished, all those questions : finished as youth.

He walked on, and gradually became aware of a something that was happening inside him.

How extraordinary after so long. He could no more control it than he could control a headache. Years since he had filled note-books with imitative poetry. But here was the physical urge which had made him persevere, the feeling which had thrown words into his head in series and patterns so that he would sometimes literally hurry for a bit of paper as though for a basin ; here again the increase of saliva and faint not unpleasant ache in the back of the throat which words would solve if they could be got out right. In those days he had actually *listened* to the congestion of associations in his head as though it was something entirely separate from him.

How absurd, he thought, at my age (because the feeling was growing all the time) and he felt in his pocket for a Biro and was relieved to feel the long hard shape against his ribs.

Soon, to his dog's astonishment, exposing his brilliant, hooped socks, he sat down and fumbled for an old envelope.

An hour later eight lines emerged from a battlefield of erasion.

Pictures on the Wall

MINTY

You are a maid there minding
*   her mirrored dress*
Fitting her green frills finding
*   no fault there.*

You are a bride there going
*   gold confetti*
Falling from black trees flowing
*   by silk white side.*

After a moment he crossed Minty out and wrote above
it : *The silver birch—in spring and autumn.*

Then he smiled, one of those rather grim, limited smiles,
which some people do smile when they have caught
themselves out—in merciful privacy.

If nothing else, his verses foreshadowed Minty's departure
from his life, the return of autumn after a few hours of
freak spring. He got up. It had been one of those days
which deceive even the birds and the sheathed buds on
boughs.

Why not him !

16

WHEN HE GOT BACK he had half an hour before fetching Ella and John from the station so he went out into the garden.

He had always got pleasure from a garden and there were few months of the year when he didn't spend the first and last moments of each day inspecting the minute changes of growth that had occurred in the time since he last looked. The deepest satisfactions in life, he had noticed, were in almost every case the least conscious. In this sense gardening was like sleeping, or having female company merely " around " or even like breathing. Over the years it had become a perpetual, unconsidered nourishment.

Light was failing but he went over the roses with a pair of sécateurs snipping off the dead heads, faded stubs like thrown away apple cores. He was smoking his pipe and in no hurry. He could hear the tapping of table-tennis from the recreation room. It was getting dark and a few early lights had come on in Buxton. Soon they would probably disappear because most nights mist rose out of the water-meadows in the intervening valley, finally obscuring all sign of the other community and shutting Edgecliffe up in a pearl grey world apart. There were not very many rose bushes and not very many dead heads to lop off, but he spun them out.

Pictures on the Wall

When he came to the end of the path Ayrton looked up at the eastern wall of the main block. On the top floor there were three windows smaller and set higher than the others. In one of these a faint light was burning. Ayrton knew it well—set in a deep blister in the ceiling, ten feet from the ground, protected by thick plate-glass and an iron grid. The bulb was twenty-five watts and if the glass hadn't been cleaned lately you could scarcely see to read big print underneath, which mattered very little at present because Goole couldn't read. Ayrton could imagine him sitting on the planks of his low bed, shut in all round by that cube of jaundiced whiteness, watched over by that great bleak eye, with steel lashes. He wondered who had read him the letter from his girl, Jefferies or Parks? Oh, my darling, where were you. . . .

Ayrton removed the pipe-tip from his lips serenely and packed down the bowl tighter. Seen through the spy-hole the most conspicuous thing about a prisoner in solitary, if he was awake, was his hands; if he was dozing or asleep— his head. Ayrton imagined Goole as he had seen him briefly that morning, in chapel, alert, shut away with his hands, big square hands with the spatulate fingers still yellowed from nicotine. Some of the prisoners adopted funny positions; some crouched, some lay balled up, some sprawled. In the zoo he had noticed the big cats trying to achieve relief from monotony by pitching themselves down in an uncomfortable way as though the resultant tension were preferable to the alternative blank; and then they sometimes opened their eyes or looked up quickly, although nothing had happened, and you could almost see the fantasy in their eyes, a vision of a vanishing buck perhaps, stimulating reflexes that had grown dim and slack from disuse, so that under the sleek hide a muscle tightened and a claw curved out. Goole, the gipsy, was in there, under that light, Goole who had been so free. Ayrton wondered what fantasy was passing through his head, what obsession. . . .

The telephone was ringing indoors.

He thought they must be at the station early. But it wasn't Ella, it was Minty—and she said, " How are you ? "

Her tone was justifiably tentative.

Incredulous, he said he was well, how was she ? Well, she was all right but she had expected him last night because he had said he was coming over to hear records. No, he said, she must have misunderstood : he had said he hoped she would " come *here* some day." No, she said, he had promised yesterday. Not that it mattered much. It was just that he had said he was coming and Mrs. Merridew had told her he was clever at mending gramophones and hers had gone wrong, and seeing that she had been expecting him she hadn't bothered to ask Sam, the tractor driver. So could he come over to-night ? All right, he said, Gwen was exaggerating but he would come to-night when he'd fetched his wife.

He put the receiver down, and stood for a minute by the telephone. He had a funny feeling in his stomach.

The clock in the hall chimed and he went to the garage and got the car. How extraordinary, he thought, as he drove, how incredible. . . . What does she want ?

Ella said they'd had a fine time. The Fawcetts had a nice semi-detached on the outskirts and Christine was going to tea there on Sunday. The hostel was clean. He said he'd had a nice time, too, but after supper he had to go and fix a gramophone for Gwen's lodger.

" Did she just ask ? " Ella said, amazed.

" Gwen arranged it," Ayrton said. " Well, John—did you like the zoo ? "

John said he had. Ella gave him an account. While she was speaking Ayrton found himself thinking of the mural education on packets of breakfast cereals. They got a free ride on the elephant. Minty, he thought. Even evil could be made to seem good, healthy. But why *evil*? What had evil got to do with it Minty ? Surely she was the very opposite.

17

WHEN GWEN MERRIDEW opened the door to him she looked immediately penitent. " Just impudence, I told her : I don't know where they get their ideas from nowadays, I'm sure. But go through, go through, on your left, Mr. Ayrton."

She went sorrowfully to the sink from where she had come. Albert, feet on stool before the television, removed his pipe to say, " Ai, Mr. Ayrton," but kept his eyes steady on a man putting rubber harness round a live shark.

Ayrton went through.

The Merridews' cottage belonged to the previous century and the doors fitted only roughly. Under Minty's there was a jagged clearance from which light streamed out across the coconut matting.

He knocked.

She opened the door and faced him with the same strange smile as when he had opened his own door to her. He found himself in a confined space with a bed, a few untidy clothes, some posters of pop singers pinned to the wall. When she stood back and the light fell on her he saw she was dressed for the part of the lunatic in *Jane Eyre*.

A linen nightgown with a lace collar fell to her ankles, and she had combed out her hair to its fullest spread and length. All she lacked was a candle.

" Come in."

A smile of nutty complacency and power lit her face as though she had just waved her wand and produced him here in this extraordinary place, and herself in that get-up.

" Come in," she repeated.

If she had received him naked he could scarcely have been more at a loss. Certainly he had known that her gramophone was not the main purpose of her invitation. Flirtation, badinage, a sort of adolescent sparring with words—perhaps even with Gwen for audience—would not have surprised him. But this, alone, in her nightdress . . . a scene that had some ghostly approximation to his most lurid and secret world of fantasy, this mirror, as it were, held up to the fictions of his sexual hunger—frightened speech out of his mouth and hypnotised his limbs.

Her smile expanded, became more mocking. He was relieved. It was, after all, a stunt, flirtation, so extreme as to be almost mad—but still—a stunt. She's fifteen really, he thought.

" I understood your gramophone. . . ."

" Don't worry: we all believe you."

" In the circumstances, Minty . . ."

" The least you can do is try and mend it. Come in. I'm getting cold."

Pictures on the Wall

He moved in slowly and once in stayed so near the door that she had difficulty shutting it. Everything was so close. The table, some clothes, including underclothes, a half-eaten orange, the disturbed bed. Then her naked feet, with ill-kept nails, almost touched his shoes as they passed.

"You go to bed very early . . ." he said.

"We start at six. Don't worry, I've got plenty on under this. Relax. Anyhow I thought you came to mend the gramophone, didn't you? Wasn't that why you came?"

The tables seemed to have been turned round on him. He did not quite see how. He adjusted his glasses and stayed where he was, waiting for the gramophone to be shown to him before he moved.

"Here," she said, turning away and suddenly laughing (really madly, he thought).

He went over, six feet, steering between table and chair. It was certainly a kind of pick-up they had once had themselves. And Gwen had told her right: he had once mended his own, to everyone's surprise.

With suspicions slightly lulled and interest stimulated he turned the thing on and immediately the turn-table began to rotate.

"What's wrong with it?" he said, reaching for a record.

"It's working now," she said. "How odd!"

He put on the record and lowered the arm. Immediately an electric guitar began to plonk. The notes were like immense gooey bubbles bursting in a cave. Suddenly someone began screaming. He lifted the arm. "It's all right," he said. "There's nothing wrong."

"No," she said. "That's funny. It's all right now. You must have done something."

She looked rather stupidly at the machine and as though to make sure it really was all right came closer to it, bending, so that he had to move away to avoid contact. This he did—but could not avoid smelling the sweetness and freshness of her hair, nor help staring at the seams of light in it, so close.

" Yes—how odd," she said and, straightening, looked at him, offering him as close an inspection of her eyes as she had just afforded of her hair.

" And now, Minty. . . ."

" You must go ? "

" Yes."

" I thought you said you wanted to hear some jazz."

" That specimen there," he said, dropping his eye to the sample which was still rotating, " didn't exactly whet my appetite."

" Do you like Tommy Steele ? "

" He doesn't sing jazz."

" Would you like to hear him ? . . . just one ? I'll get Gwen if you like. Shall I ? " she moved towards the door.

" I shouldn't bother. Not for one, Minty."

" Then sit down." She removed some clothes from a chair, transferring them to the bed. Then she took a dressing-gown from the back of the door and put it on. " Is that better ? "

He sat down saying, " This is most improper."

" You can always shout for help."

She offered him a cigarette and for some reason he took one, his first for years.

" It's a song about summer," she said.

Ayrton was surprised by the sound. He had expected something artificial, strained, embarrassing, such as he had heard on the *Juke Box Jury* with which Christine liked to thicken up her musical education. Instead he heard spontaneity, even the quality of innocence and joy which

characterised some of the earliest written music of Europe.
Here too was a core of celebration. Not all the time. Some
notes were sentimentalised, some spoilt by a too consciously
peppy accompaniment, but now and again the voice took
wing, celebrated, sang for singing's sake.

He said he did like it.

" It's living for something." Saying this her voice was
drab, factual.

She got off the bed where she had been lounging and
took a bottle of gin out of the old mahogany wardrobe.

" Glass or Celluloid ? " she said, holding up two tumblers.

As when she had stood centrally in his own living-room
warming her back at the fire, he was struck by her veneer
of social confidence, verging on arrogance. It consorted
so oddly, improbably, even madly with her situation.

Again that smile, pitifully vain and self-conscious, almost
as though in getting him here and making him drink she
imagined she had done something for which she would be
remembered for ever.

" No, Minty, really."

· " It's beneath you."

He made a gesture of contempt.

" I've only got gin," she said. " Gin and water. Will
that do ? "

" Just a little, Minty. Then I must fly."

She gave them each half a glass, and went to the other
seat, her bed, where she lay down propping herself on one
elbow. There she settled, smiling at him in his new
environment, smiling until her eyes dropped to his ankles.

" Look at that ! " she said in a tone of stunned surmise.
A dopy speculative look came into her face.

" Are you admiring my ankles ? "

" I thought they'd been skinned."

" You object to my socks ? "

" Yes," she said incredulously, and continued to stare at them as though every second gave them added significance.

" And now, Minty," he said, putting down his unfinished glass. " This very enjoyable visit must draw to a close."

She raised her eyes to his face with a gleam of the old mockery and hostility, took a sip and said nothing.

He hadn't yet moved.

" Minty," he said kindly and paternally, " where d'you come from ? "

" I told you," she said in a resonant theatrical sarcastic tone. " Samarkand," and she lay back and looked at the ceiling in a way that he had seen film stars lie back and look up. Still, she did it well. And the mockery faded from her face and she raised one arm almost straight above her, gracefully, opened the fingers a little and said quietly but, ranting slightly, and sounding self-conscious : " That's where I shall be

> ' *When even lovers find their peace at last*
> *And earth is but a star that once had shone.*' "

" Go on," he said.

" I've forgotten it," she said.

He adjusted his spectacles, rose. " You're a very confusing person."

" Don't you want to know why I got you here ? " she said dryly, sitting up and looking at him with mingled pity and amusement.

" I certainly do, Minty," he said.

Sadness and loneliness slowly flooded into her eyes. Then contempt swept them all away.

" What are you afraid of ? " she said.

" Afraid ? "

" Yes, you're afraid."

He laughed uneasily, tempted against his will by her familiarity. Ella had never, never at any time, even in the earliest days of their marriage, looked at him and spoken to him like that. Indeed for years she had avoided the use of his name and never shown any desire to share his thoughts. Before Minty he felt bewitched like a savage confronted for the first time by a mirror: me, he felt, is this me: what else does it show? Her interest suddenly promised significance to a whole world of thoughts and aspirations which at home it would have been waste of time to mention. Simply by making a few blunt personal remarks she seemed to have placed herself in a position to offer him a whole new lease of life, the freshness of new development. He adjusted his glasses and felt the crease of diffidence at his mouth's corners.

"Frightened..." he said. "I don't think I'm frightened."

Her silence seemed unconvinced.

"What made you become a Warden?" she said with great seriousness, as though with difficulty reserving judgment till he had answered.

"Oh, Minty—that would be a long story."

"Are you in any hurry?"

"Wouldn't it look rather odd—my staying here half an hour?"

"Then you are frightened. Of what people will think."

"A man in my position has to be careful."

She looked suddenly bored and contemptuous—disappointed, too.

It was the disappointment that got him.

"Well—I was once a monk," he said.

"*A monk...!*" It was like when he'd told her about the boy who had been hanged. She was horrified, disgusted, averted her eyes as though to spare him the transparence of her expression.

Then he tried to explain. He went right back to his childhood, just as he had in his own thoughts, not many days since. He even spoke of his marriage in terms of dispassionate objectivity; described life at Edgecliffe. She looked more friendly as he proceeded, perhaps because she had won from him a form of submission. Sometimes she interrupted with a question in a dry, astringent speculative tone as though promising no sympathy at all for his answer, and sometimes—rewarding moments—the shape of her rather sullen mouth melted into a dreamy impersonal smile. It was odd, almost uncanny, that anyone so often infantile should be transformed into . . . such a challenge, such an esteemed yardstick of experiences long ago and of life yesterday . . . to-day.

When he had finished she said nothing, absolutely nothing. He felt appeased, but also as though he had lost an advantage. Still, it was done now. He rose to his feet.

" It takes all types to make a world," he said sententiously, defensive.

" You needn't apologise," she said, grimly

" Next time it's your turn," he said.

" What do you know about anything ? " she drawled, looking somewhere in the regions of his stomach.

He put his hand on the latch.

" Did I say I knew anything ? "

Her eyes now showed smiling conviction that he was still afraid. But this time it did not work.

" Good night, Minty ! "

" Say good-bye nicely," she said.

" Good night, Minty." She laughed derisively and closed her eyes as though controlling the kind of a *fou rire* such as he had witnessed in the club. Serious again, she held out her hand, from a lounging position.

" You may kiss it."

" Good-bye and thank you, Minty," he said, taking it and pressing it.

" Full marks. But you're cold," she said quietly. " Are you a cold man . . . are you a stone, Mr. Ayrton ? "

She lay back on the pillow with her head in a raving turmoil of jet hair. Through her dressing-gown he could make out the slight prominence of a nipple held stoutly against the stuff. The position was extravagant even as film-star positions go. Poor child ! Yet . . .

Weakness suddenly sucked at the back of his legs. He had never seen such beauty so close, *so available*. " Minty," he said kindly, " what's all this in aid of ? "

She closed her eyes and said, " How square can you be? "

He stood there. She looked drawn and lonely and defeated, but defeated in what ?

" Good night," he said at last.

In the front room Albert's position hadn't changed a millimetre. Now he was watching a sting-ray.

" Ai, Mr. Ayrton," he said.

18

GOOLE CAME BACK from restricted diet, and life at home and in the Centre went on as usual.

Minty was there. Sometimes in the distance, sometimes close, within waving distance, nowadays usually accompanied by the small girl, Pam. The sight of either by herself came to look almost unnatural. Pam, of course, was the dummy and Minty so to speak, the ventriloquist. For instance, Pam took up chewing gum in sympathy and when Ayrton passed she turned towards him, which she had never done before, and said things—apparently about him—which seemed to strike Minty with all the impact of laughable originality although Ayrton would have taken a bet that Minty herself had inspired them.

He usually waved and went on his way.

Edgecliffe was the real trouble. In an effort to recover interest and find distraction at the same time, he threw himself into his lecture, convinced that if he did it well he really might be given a governorship of one of the new open Borstals. But he could not work at home so every evening he went across and settled down in his office. "Over there," he told Ella, "I've got all my things."

She didn't seem to mind.

He began making an outline, heading it ambitiously: "The Root of the Problem." But after a few days had to ask himself seriously whether what he was trying to say would increase his chances of anything but early retirement.

For, after sixty years, what was the best that anyone could recommend for the treatment of the Young Offender— nothing more nor less than what Alexander Paterson had said himself thirty years ago, and which to-day was less likely to be achieved than it was then.

Paterson, he pointed out, had condemned the then accepted method of treating juvenile delinquents in reformatories, describing it as follows:

"The lad is treated as though he were a lump of putty and an effort is made to reduce him to a certain uniform shape by the gentle and continuous pressure of authority *from without.* (Ayrton underlined the words "from without.") In course of time by perpetual repetition he forms a habit of moving smartly, keeping himself clean, obeying orders and behaving with decorum in the presence of his betters. These are in themselves very useful qualities and it is hoped by those who use this system that after some years of constant admonition and daily habit all lads will retain the same pleasing shape when no longer subjected to the pressure of those in authority." Here in brackets Ayrton wrote (Detention Centre 1960 ?).

But Paterson, having stated the case for this accepted "system," proceeded to knock it down, making a number of objections which he summarised thus: "The task is not to break or knead him into shape but rather to stimulate some power within to regulate conduct aright . . . (though) a system which seeks to work in this way must *depend first and foremost on the men who are to do the work."*

Ayrton's underlining.

Therefore as far as cure was concerned the most important people were prison staff; and as far as prevention was concerned—parents, in other words, society itself.

Taking this as his point of departure Ayrton knew that he would be chiselling at the basis of the Detention Centre system which was the very " knock-him-into-shape " principle so deplored by Paterson. *Tant pis!* Whatever the Commissioners might think, it would lead him naturally to his hobby-horse which was that the D.C. system was not so much " bad " as inevitable—made inevitable by *volume of crime*, just as electro shock-treatment was used excessively to-day because of *volume of neurosis*. In each case *our society was the villain* in that it created crime and neurosis as naturally as dung attracts flies, and on a scale which for economic reasons could only be treated quickly and collectively and therefore with an increasing tendency towards psychological violence. (Hence Detention Centres: and historical regression.)

If any Prison Commissioner should attend his lecture or read it perhaps in the *Prison Journal* they might, he hoped, conclude that he was in the wrong post : might see that his enthusiasm was for personal relations, and a fundamental approach for which there was little opportunity either in Detention Centres or big prisons.

But how would they receive all the vague generalised stuff about " our society," and anyhow what did he propose to recommend ? As a monk who had not managed to " make it " as a monk, what redeeming, fundamental or " other level " could *he* pit against the lures of " material- ism," against the sense of purposelessness which came from a world of mass commercial suggestion on one level and merely mechanical explanations on another?

People might laugh to-day at the Victorian penologists who had put a bible in every cell and thus provided a way out for thousands of men kept short of lavatory paper—a corner-stone for a pot-centred society. But in fact a vocational approach to a profession that promised neither prestige nor material rewards, was essential. His own impulse to prison work had stemmed from a blend of upper-class sense of responsibility (this admittedly, often a mere sop to a frustrated habit of—and hunger for power)— and, more positively, from the unfulfilled aspirations of his original vocation. Take away both motives and who would step forward in the future—short of bribery? Perverts? But of course not. (Ayrton could imagine the answer)—technicians; masters of this particular branch of facts. But facts by themselves were nothing. Their pattern and order of precedence required "values." But what values?

As a distraction at least the lecture was a success. He lost himself. Forgot Minty, the Centre, Jefferies. . . .

Ella complained there was something on his mind. "We don't see much of you," she said. Was he having more trouble with cigarettes or was it his lecture? Both, he said, and in a few days events gave additional substance to his excuse. Parks came in and told him there was smoking again—in the latrines at night: he had found ash on the floor and smelt tobacco. Naturally Goole was suspected and Jefferies took it upon himself " to have another word with young Hallows." Ayrton said no, he did not want that.

Pictures on the Wall

The possibility that Jefferies might make a deal with that misshapen, involuntary assassin, all in the privacy of the camp office under the portrait of the Queen, gave him feelings of apprehension as well as disgust.

The Deputy was obviously trying to make the Goole affair into a test case, and unless Ayrton was very careful would contrive a situation which would show the Jefferies approach to have been right and the Ayrton approach wrong. If that happened, Ayrton thought, my lecture won't make much difference: it will be him or me, and if the tobacco smuggling continues it could be me.

With all this in mind he decided to do some snooping on his own account. He had always made a point of being unpredictable to his staff. Once or twice he had even turned up in the small hours of the morning. Now this lecture gave him a good pretext for being in the main building late at night, not just occasionally, but often.

" We shan't see you at all now, I suppose," Ella said.

He explained. It was only for a few weeks.

One night when he was in his little room—the Warden's office—and taken out his papers, he looked round and was struck anew by the relative comfort and order which obtained here. The Government of course had paid for it. He must not blame Ella for the difference. They could never have afforded new curtains and easy-chairs—at least not without eating into those sums which they had set aside for the further education of the children. So here he was, warm, comfortable, cheerfully surrounded: and there she was with her cough and John. But what could he do about it ? All the distractions he had suggested to her seemed to interest her not half as much as her daily horoscope in the newspapers or her interminable tea drinking with Mrs. Merridew. Lately she had been dropping hints that

life—her life—might have been different if . . . if this . . .
if that. Really she was dropping crumbs to him from the
great feast of fantasy which she too had begun to enjoy on
this bleak table-land. He had had to give up the opinion
that she "never complained." Because now she did complain, not shrewishly but indirectly and all the time. Her
very appearance was a form of complaint, and so perhaps
was the condition of the house . . . her health, her cough.
Something inside her was on strike.

But what did she want? What could he give her?
Would it ever be any "better"?

Ayrton sighed and applied himself to his lecture.

The trouble at the moment was Ella had simply decided
to become old—just when he had been smitten by the fear
that he had never been young!

Such thoughts, even in the double secrecy of his head
and these four walls, dragged in their wake a load of painful
guilt. Think what he owed to Ella! Besides, whatever
urges, conscious or unconscious, had first drawn them
together were by now in the deepest sense irrelevant. Years
of affectionate relative isolation, together, had made them
a pair of rather lop-sided, psychological Siamese twins.
By now, to hurt her was to hurt himself.

At the thought of this inextricable coupling he experienced
a spasm of helpless resentment. What could he have done
to avoid his present vulnerability? Minty—or to be
realistic—the idea of Minty had only to come along and at
once, something like a prayer—from the spine to the sun—
a spine that had never thoroughly straightened to a sun
that had never fully shone, broke forth involuntarily from
his lips, craving realisation. On one level her very sluttishness and adolescent behaviour were part of her appeal.
On another youth, and life itself seemed to be offering him

a last chance." Yet he was condemned to say " No " !

He paused in his thoughts only to realise with a sudden qualm of dread how little he had really " got over " her, by working ! His very presence in this room, he decided, late at night was perhaps a tryst—not with his lecture, or with cigarettes smugglers—but with Minty.

A half-way house !

One night when he had finished his stint on his lecture and was wondering whether or not to take a look round the dormitories, he heard a thud on the ceiling above and then a muffled cry. The next moment the whole ceiling vibrated as though someone were running.

19

THE OCCURRENCE of anything unusual and sudden in a prison or a Borstal, something even quite trivial like a man running in the distance at a spot where normally men are seen walking is apt to make the blood chill. It reveals instantly the tension under which everyone is living all the time.

For prisons are always like war-time ships in convoy. The engines throb and the grey-skinned crews in their various bulkheads, sealed up, move forward across time but all around everyone knows there is a real possibility of swift unseen, destructive forces, bursting and smashing the precarious pattern of order. In every main room there is an alarm bell, and in every heart, staff as well as inmate, an equivalent, the button exposed, naked, a millimetre from the terminals.

But Ayrton had weathered enough snap crises to have developed a second or reserve reaction which almost in the same instant balanced the first by making available a condensed memory of all those other crises which after threatening to engulf everyone in a tidal wave of fear and violence had passed in a few minutes.

He stood still in the middle of his room looking up . . . waiting.

And then (that was what usually happened)—nothing did happen. Nothing more.

No . . . nothing.

But he would go up now, and have a look round. He would find nothing. Probably in the morning there would be a black eye or a cut lip, and someone would have " slipped oop and caught me 'ead on the bed like " and it would be one more insignificant question mark, one more tiny event in that other world which was as close and as obscure as a card offered, face down.

And then suddenly the alarm bell in the passage began ringing and continued. Ayrton's blood still froze at that sound and even as he moved he had time to resent the continued ringing, time to curse the persisting shrill, brazen exaggerating tongue which seemed to be releasing and encouraging the very forces it was supposed to control.

Then it stopped and the silence that followed was unnatural, as when something dislodged is falling. . . .

The officer on sleeping-in duty at the main door was

already coming down the passage, tieless, putting on his coat. He closed in behind Ayrton who made for the stair door, selecting the right key as he moved so they passed through almost as though it were a swing-door. Then on, up the stairs and in the same way through the door which led into the intercommunicating passage, where a light burned all night long.

Opposite were the reception cells and one of them was open with the light on.

Why? There had been no Receptions for more than a week.

After a moment's indecision and a glance in the direction of each dormitory, he moved quickly towards the open cell.

A small figure was lying on the high bed. Its position suggested an unwillingness or incapacity to move in any direction, as though some invisible force had awed, beaten it into cringing petrifaction. It looked like a gigantic paralysed fœtus—wrapped in a blood-stained shirt.

Hallows. On the side-table, incongruously clean and white stood an empty basin.

Checking the cuts as superficial, Ayrton turned and went out quickly, telling the Duty Officer to ring the doctor and get the hospital to send an ambulance. In the passage he heard voices from " A " dormitory.

Liversey was standing in the middle of the floor, saying, " C'mon then. Let's f——g have it. Ooo did it?" Most of the lads were awake, the rest probably pretending not to be. Liversey was pale and went on excitedly as though he hadn't noticed the arrival of the Warden.

"... Well then—go on—which of you was it—don't f——g think I'm not going to f——g find out. Let's 'ave it—which of you was it. . . ." The verbal foulness of the feeble-faced man was somehow more alarming than the bell. He didn't normally swear.

"Everyone stand at the foot of his bed," Ayrton said. "Now."

". . . You 'eard ! " Liversey said, switching with revealing readiness.

One by one the boys got out of bed and went round to the front where they stood in their coarse grey pyjamas. There was one blank—opposite an unslept-in bed. Three beds away Goole stood, prominent, with his thick-set body. Ayrton's eyes looked him over swiftly . . . his hands, the degree of wakefulness of his face. . . . No clue.

Ayrton asked Liversey if he had been to the other dormitory. Liversey said no, the assault was committed in the cell and no one in the other dormitory was likely to have known that Hallows had slept in the cell.

"Why did he ? "

"Said he was going to be sick, sir, said he'd keep everyone awake puking."

Ayrton turned to the grey lines of youths. He said, "I want to look at all your hands. Hold them out as I pass. . . ."

He walked slowly down the line of figures, examined the feet, toes splayed on the cold floor, and then, close, the pairs of hands. "Both sides," he had to say to the second man. Surely some spot must have remained on the attacker. . . .

He came to Goole, paused.

But there was nothing on him, anywhere.

At that moment the Chief Officer came in fully dressed. Parks was never more military than on occasions like this. He came to attention a few feet away and remained so until

Ayrton said, "Finish the inspection, Mr. Parks. Search the beds, everything. . . ." Then he went back to Hallows, who was still in the same position.

"Hallows," Ayrton said.

After a moment in which there was no sound but laboured breathing, Ayrton laid his hand on Hallows's head, because it alone seemed uncut.

"Who did it?" he said mechanically, aware that he was asking Hallows to repeat the crime for which he was already bleeding.

Moments of silence passed and Ayrton thought what a lot was written in serious newspapers about the futility of deterrents. Well, Hallows apparently was deterred! How? In the last resort, quite simply, *by the amount that someone had minded.* We don't mind very much so we can't deter, Ayrton thought. We cover up our lack of feeling by a lot of thinking and kid ourselves that apathy is tolerance. We bear with criminals so as not to despise ourselves, for they in their attitude to our present society, are merely extremists, not different.

Some things they at least still mind!

He felt tired.

"I'll get you out of this," he said quietly and sat down on the bed and listened to the distant sound of search, the occasional barked abuse, feet on the linoleum. The ambulance shouldn't take long.

There was a bible on the plain table at his elbow and on the wall a list of Edgecliffe rules headed READ THIS. A sort of printed shout.

Ella would have heard the alarm bell if the windows were open. It was as well she couldn't see Hallows. His pyjama-jacket was sliced obliquely in several places.

Pictures on the Wall

Through the open door Ayrton could see the linoleum gleaming in the passage and he thought how sometimes he had stood just there, in the middle of the night, equidistant from the two dormitory doors, listening. At such moments, he experienced something like intimacy with his charges, as when he visited the clothing store where all their Ted clothes hung in rows like captured tribal regalia in a colonial museum. Both in a sleeping face and the empty Italian suit he saw the pathos of a lost mask and the refuge of anonymity. When imprisoned, like Samson, they lost their long hair and their strength. Naked then they adopted a new defence, the " barrier " which, at Edgecliffe, burned steadily in their eyes all day. It became their badge, their new identity, the dearest, perhaps the last thing they possessed, dearer perhaps to them even than their expectations of liberty or their memories of happiness. As a form of *esprit de corps* it probably kept some of them going, prevented them from breaking down. But in sleep they lost even that. What could have been more defenceless than their closed eyes and open faces, more intimate than the occasional cry or mouthed rambling curse, more communicative than the unintelligible unfinished sentence? Listening to their sleep Ayrton had often felt half suffocated by an enervating sense of determinism, felt involved with them in a relationship that left neither side a margin for constructive emotion, for love. Safe it was, then at least, to indulge the facile pity which he had to spend his life concealing, and for which he knew well a corrective would soon be forthcoming when they woke up.

But when in fact were they asleep and when were they awake? Ayrton looked down at Hallows—a bloody bundle more like an earnest of nightmare left high and dry on the shores of reality than the act of a conscious person.

Did Goole do this ? And was Jefferies responsible for having persuaded Hallows to grass ; and was he himself indirectly responsible for having failed to control Jefferies ? Lately he had been thinking about other things, Minty, that lecture lying down there in his room. The " Root of the Problem ". . . . " A f——g children's nurse," a dreamer. . . .

His strange wan surroundings and company, the late hour of the night and . . . recent events amplified these questions till they achieved the resonance of dreams. Steps and voices came and went, Hallows moved and groaned. The Duty Officer brought tea and Hallows refused. Ayrton remembered the holy wine spilt on the steps and the blood on his hands : he had grassed on himself, perhaps, with the same zeal that Hallows had grassed on Goole. How much . . . or how little had he changed since then ?

The linoleum glowed red like one of those ornamental bottles in chemists' windows. He thought of Minty asleep not three hundred yards away, and at last he heard a car stop outside.

20

THAT NIGHT WAS JOINED to the day that followed.

Long after Hallows had been removed to hospital the search for the weapon went on, in the dormitories and below the windows outside. Mattresses and the heels of shoes were examined, linoleum taken up and a loose board removed from the upstairs lavatory wall. This last revealed a copy of *Lady Chatterley's Lover*—but no weapon. At four-thirty Jefferies came on and Ayrton went back to Shang-ri-la.

Earlier he had sent a message to Ella saying he had been detained. She had then walked over to Mrs. Parks in her dressing-gown and found out roughly what had happened. Now she was awake and tearful, drinking tea. She at once launched an impassioned attack on the inmates : why weren't they all put up against a wall and shot. They'd be happier dead and society better off without them. The next thing would be when they assaulted him. Perhaps then he'd see sense. All this soft handling just invited trouble.

She began weeping. She never sobbed when she wept, tears just dribbled down her cheeks, and he never knew what to do or say. His feelings seemed to dry up in proportion as hers flowed.

He soothed her as best he could and for three hours they

enjoyed some sort of a night. Before breakfast, he went back to the Centre where in the first light of day the weapon had been found near the window of " A " Dormitory—four halves of safety-razor blades slotted into a stick.

It was immediately wrapped up and taken away by the police.

Later Jack Beasley blew in from the hospital. He had seen Hallows who was much more comfortable. " Rotten luck, Phil," he said, as though the Warden, Hallows and his assailant had all three had a nasty and quite unexpected bilious attack in the middle of the night. " Is there anything I can do ? "

His pipe-angle was uncommonly high, his black eyes uncommonly warm and determined. Christianity, his manner suggested, didn't often get such a sitting pigeon. But Ayrton thanked him. He really didn't see how Beasley could help except by visiting Hallows ... " Perhaps he'll tell you who did it," Ayrton said, smiling thinly.

Beasley affected not to have heard.

Ayrton took off his spectacles and began polishing them and silence fell between the two men. Suddenly Beasley said in that tone of diverting brightness which people use with the sick or with small children on the eve of their return to boarding-school, " It's funny how things happen, Phil : I was going to come up to see you to-day anyhow ... I've been thinking the Youth Club ought to put something on this Christmas."

Ayrton hoped he managed to look diverted. In a few minutes he would be alone with Jefferies.

" A tableau," Beasley said. " Of the Nativity ! "

The pipe-angle was triumphant.

" Where do I come in," Ayrton murmured.

" Well, I've got that girl Minty Bates to be the Virgin. She'll make a ripping Virgin, Phil, don't you think ? And old Fred Reed as Joseph. And then I just wondered if you'd care to be one of the Magi . . ."

Then Ayrton was tempted to laugh like Minty did, closing his eyes and putting the back of his hand to his nose. Shortage of sleep made everything anyhow seem a bit unreal. Beasley himself was dangerously blended with dream, as he sat there under the girls watching the B.O.A.C. Comet—blended with bikinis, linoleum, Christ, the gory bundle of Hallows and the unidentified assailant.

" I know you've got a lot on your plate, Phil. . . ."

Ayrton said, " Worshipping Miss Bates would be a pleasure ! "

" Good-o. So you're on ? "

Beasley looked really pleased and a moment later went off as though the morning's work were joy, pure joy. His place was taken by Jefferies carrying an order board surmounted by a bulldog clip.

Till now they had not been alone together since the assault and Ayrton examined the face of his colleague for some sign of concern or responsibility. But there seemed to be none.

" We ditched Hallows, didn't we ? " Ayrton said dryly.

" 'Swat you get when you grass."

Jefferies sounded almost cheerful and after a moment added : " 'Allows can do the rest of his time in bed."

That was one way of looking at it. After a silence Ayrton said, " Who d'you think did it ? "

" Goole. That's who did it."

" Hallows grassed before Goole came."

" Looks like Goole to me. All the way. Proper job."

" Goole's a boxer. Personally I should have thought this looked more like the work of some twirp who depended on a weapon, someone who would scarcely come up to Goole's knee."

Jefferies shook his head, but without vehemence, as though disagreement with the Warden, who had never been a Prison Officer, never lived in a working-class street, was to be expected and in the last resort unimportant. Time would tell. As it had so far.

" Best bloke with a razor I ever knew was a boxer, middle-weight, runner-up in the A.B.A. Championship. Called himself the Exterior Decorator ... Proper queen, too. Wore silk underpants. Whenever his room was searched something silk turned up. . . . Blokes said he kept silk-worms up his arse."

After a few moments silence, Jefferies began to whistle, softly through his teeth. When he stopped, his breathing was as loud as the tune. Then they went through a few administrative points arising from the assault.

" I suppose that's all then," Ayrton said.

" Suppose so. Till we get the lab. report on the weapon." Jefferies looked at him as though inviting him to say more, about Hallows, about Detention Centres. . . .

And that was the end of the unofficial inquiry.

The official one, a few days later, furnished with a lab. report, revealed neither more nor less.

For a week the Centre resounded to words of command which sounded a little more emphatic than usual. Authority seemed to caricature itself, to rave a bit. And the barrier in the boys' faces was that much thicker ; selves that much farther back from eyes. The general ugliness took increase from fear and resentment.

Beasley called again and Ella, seeing his car from the window, asked what he had wanted.

Ayrton said: "Hallows is being moved. And that tableau I told you about. . . . We're to have a rehearsal."

"You ought to start growing a beard," she said.

21

BUT HE SAW MINTY before the rehearsal. It happened one evening, a week after the slashing episode, when he had gone into Buxton to get some things for the house. He parked opposite Cummings, the bakers, under one of the new lamps, a thing like a concrete derrick suspending a cube of violet radiance which somehow made the street look like a great tunnel full of ghosts, an underground world where there was neither day nor night but just this lofty violet light and a long shadowless vista of people and cars and little archaic houses. Ayrton did not lock the car. It was a relief to close a door without locking it. But he wound the window up to make it look as though it were locked. This done, he stepped on to the pavement and looked at the trays in the bakery, some of them empty, others littered with survivors of the day's output—sausage rolls, cakes and buns. The trays could also be overlooked from within and Mrs. Cummings was often to be seen stretching out, over them, filling bags with tongs.

While he was pocketing his key a figure appeared behind

the trays, not looking at the cakes at all but at him. It was Minty.

He felt a thrill go through his whole body like an electric shock and at once converted it to a smile of merely normal greeting. But even this modest reaction was apparently presumptuous. For she looked at him without a smile, with no friendliness at all and yet with intimacy, *with knowledge*. There must, he thought, be some mistake.

Yet there was no one else on the pavement nearby and both he and she were lit and divided as clearly as people who find themselves almost nose to nose in carriages which fortuitously halt beside each other at night in a station. He had stopped and waved. Now all that was left of that wave was the collapse of one arm—the remains and proof of a definite attempt at communication which it was too late to withdraw. Well, she did at last reply . . . she stuck out her tongue, curling in the sides so that the tip became the point of a little scroll. And she kept it out, thick, neat and gleaming with saliva in the lamplight, pointed it at him for perhaps three seconds while he experienced a feeling which petered out in his sex. It was as though he had jumped and been three seconds falling. Then she put it in and turned away.

He stood there unable to move, debating whether to go in and greet her. For surely she had suddenly caught sight of him, lit mauve all over by those fantastic lights— and mistaken him for someone else, some man who had molested her at a dance or who was for ever importuning her with stares (or thoughts!)—not someone who had perhaps been unique in treating her with deference. Or was the tongue-pulling a little message about that picture, "The Stag at Midnight," about capital punishment and nuclear weapons? If so, why should he mind or think twice about it, how at his age could he even begin to take such hostility seriously—knowing as he did perfectly well that the conscientious objections of such children seldom applied with equal force if the H-bombs and executions were Russian, or Chinese.

According to " people like Minty " it was we who made disarmament impossible—made every conference break down ; we who never had the courage to make the initial act of faith—this when the communists' record (to say nothing of their doctrinal statements) in the matter of keeping faith made nonsense of the very phrase " keeping faith," an idiom which stemmed from old concepts of individualism, free-will and personal honour, none of which had any meaning for them.

So thought Ayrton on the pavement—as a result of Marshal's girl, Minty, putting out her tongue ! He could not explain how it was that such childish rudeness and the memory of her intellectual attitudinising should increase her hold on his feelings. But they did, and in the days that followed he found it harder than ever to concentrate on anything. Once he caught Jefferies looking at him oddly and became aware he had not taken in something Jefferies had said even though he had agreed in a tone of considered judgment. No, she had not mistaken him for someone else ! He thought he understood what had happened. Previously when she brought the eggs and again when she asked him to mend the gramophone she had really been making him an offer. *Disappointed* . . . she stuck out her tongue.

Poor child, he thought. But this commendable sentiment never lasted long. Her scroll of pink flesh, bluntly pointed and varnished with saliva, fat and tight with roused intention, was scarcely an object of pity. In fact as a flagrant sample and earnest of another part of her body, the memory of it soon saddled him with an obsession which made him, rather than her, a victim. In vain he assured himself of the paternal sublimity and æsthetic remoteness of his feelings. It was no good. That neatly bulging tongue now nailed him to hopes which not long ago he would never have believed could enter his head. And when to escape his enslavement he pondered the crudeness of her behaviour and succeeded in disgusting and disappointing himself with her lack of that most sexually attractive quality, modesty—he found relief prevented by memory of her expression when " serious "—that look which went beyond modesty or immodesty, beyond self-consciousness, touching beyond words in its isolation, in its obscure claim to a reciprocal generosity on the highest, most impracticable level.

He counted the days till Beasley's first rehearsal for his tableau.

22

EVERYONE IN THE HALL, except apparently Jack Beasley, noticed the dress which she had chosen for the occasion. It looked a chic set of overalls designed to be worn over the top of another dress—except the other dress wasn't there. The amount of flesh exposed would have been extreme even at a ball, and customary only at a swimming-pool or the front row of the chorus. In an

underheated drill-hall in winter it looked cruel to the
wearer as well as absurd. True she had nothing to be
ashamed of in all she showed. The whiteness of her skin
against the dark fall of her hair was pictorially most effective,
and the fullness and accessibility of her breasts realistic
perhaps in a milking mother. Yet to Ayrton the final
effect of this public display (unlike the private message of
her suddenly exposed tongue), was now at last truly
pitiful. Beasley, Ayrton thought, was right to speak to
her with particular kindness and talk as though she were
dressed like anyone else.

"Rest it on your knee . . . support the bundle a little
lower, Minty : a real baby would be heavier than a cushion.
No, don't move your *knee*. Move the child. That's first
class. Now could we have Joseph standing a little to the
left. Now the Magi, Phil, you in front—on one knee.
You'll have a staff on the day. Stillness is the great thing.
You all want to fix your eyes on Minty's face. We can
either muster a spotlight for the day or she can hide an
ordinary torch masked with thin paper, shining up. This
will give a halo effect as well as show her features. Raise
the billiard-cues now, angels, forty-five degrees. I say,
that's coming on you know, that really is something
like it."

Suddenly Minty started one of her snort-laughs, verging
on a *fou rire* and eased up out of her position. "What's
the matter ? " Beasley said.

"Cramp," she said.

Beasley kept them at it, talking as though conscious that
if he let up for a single minute the whole precarious
enterprise would collapse and he would be left with nothing
but a chaos of madly disassociated elements, Wardens,
tarts, jivers and choir. His eyes glowed and he moved

Pictures on the Wall

about like an ice-hockey coach, in and out the groups, making it all happen, pausing to appraise, aim and relate.

What on earth am I doing here, Ayrton thought.

His knee-cap was anæsthetised by the sight of Minty looking down into her crooked arm. She could act. The experience of having everything centred the whole time on herself, seemed to have relaxed the defiance of her features and the awkwardness of her limbs. One of the cherubs fetched an electric torch. The moment the beam picked on her face a slow smile disturbed her mouth. He could just see it to one side of her hair. At first the smile was antipathetic, inanely complacent, frivolous. Then it changed, became tranquil, prophetic, and Ayrton thought he had never seen anything so beautiful.

When it was over he came up behind her in the porch where they were all getting their coats. It was frosty and breath was floating in the air like smoke. Everyone was laughing and talking like children let out of school.

" Can I run you back up the hill, Minty ? " he said.

He searched her face for some sign of embarrassment— or indeed anything at all that would relate to the extraordinary episode in the window of the baker's shop. But he found nothing, excepting a suggestion of that smile of hers which could mean anything.

She simply said she'd like a lift back but the trouble was Pam, could he fit her in too ?

Having seen Pam backstage holding a broom to her lips, he had foreseen that this might happen.

" Of course," he said.

And then Pam appeared. Close up she was a small girl with a pretty, rather boyish face and body, and a pedantic way of speaking.

Minty smiled at her and Pam smiled back. The point

made by the smiles seemed to be that Ayrton's presence needed no explanation.

They went out into the dark.

" Pam can sit in front," Minty said.

Somewhere behind him, Ayrton heard a suppressed laugh like an animal squeaking. Had Minty pinched Pam and pushed her forward ? For a moment he had visions of himself as the boys in the Borstal revue had shown him: a praying mantis in scarlet socks, touching a speck of dust with deliberation—in this context—touching a girl's arm as she got into a car. I'm old enough to be their father, he thought, and I'm only giving her a lift up the hill.

Pam sat down beside him, and as soon as the car was moving said : " Are you in the tableau every year, Mr. Ayrton ? "

Minty blew her nose in a way that might have been a disguise for laughter. And so it went on : Pam performing for Minty's benefit. " Have you ever been one of the angels ? " and so on.

" You'd better drop me first," Minty said as they passed the Merridews' cottage.

" Too late," he said.

Pam said, " He seems to have taken matters into his own hands."

The cheekiness and familiarity of this unattractive running-mate of Minty's gave him a twinge of fear, a presentiment that he was committed more than he knew.

" Here we are, Pam," he said with satisfaction.

Even then she had to delay matters by talking from outside through the window to Minty, smiling all the time as though the joke were getting better and better.

Then she said, " Thanks so much, Mr. Ayrton. You wouldn't come and mend my radio one day, would you ? "

The sarcastic, dragging dryness of her voice, her dependence for every word on Minty's appreciation. . . . He barely trusted himself to speak.

" Any time," he said.

Then they were alone, she at the back, he in front.

When the car was moving, he said coolly, paternally, " I saw you in the baker's Friday evening ? "

" Me ? Let me think. I did buy some rock-cakes on Friday. I never saw you. Were you buying rock-cakes . . . ? "

They were nearly at the Merridews'.

He said : " Why did you stick your tongue out at me ? "

" My *tongue* . . . Really I think you saw someone else."

" Perhaps, in a way, I did."

She said nothing.

" Where were you brought up, Minty ?

" Why ? "

" You don't quite fit into any of the usual pigeon-holes."

" Then perhaps you should get some new pigeon-holes."

There was a light in the Merridews' cottage. He stopped the car about twenty yards from the gate.

But she opened her door and got out. He did the same. " There's your prison against the moon," she said. " Isn't it beautiful ? "

" Night is flattering."

" Come in for a moment," she said.

He laughed : or rather made a brief nervous noise.

" Why d'you laugh ? " she said sincerely.

Her leap from sniggering schoolgirl to gravity was disconcerting.

Grave too, he said, " It's rather late, isn't it ? "

He discovered with surprise that they were both speaking low, as conspirators. Gradually then, he admitted to himself what was happening—but watched it go on as though it had nothing to do with him.

" To-morrow's Saturday, you haven't got to get up," she said.

" Indeed I have. It's Visitors' Day."

" No. Really. *Visitors!* " Something happened to her voice.

" Ella will be nearly in bed," he said. " Or we could go across."

" Could we ? " she said.

The Merridews' kitchen light was on. He thought of the dress she was wearing, and what it showed of her body.

Minty said, " It's Friday : Gwen's at her sister's. There's only Albert. Come on."

The statement about Gwen didn't make any difference of course but it gave him a funny feeling. He began to move, and it was as though he had begun to fall through a great space of air, pleasantly fast.

When she was near the cottage gate she stopped so that he bumped into her. She was looking up at the moonlit sky above the Centre. Then without a word she moved on again.

He noticed they both of them made as little noise as possible, that he walked on the grass and took it for granted she should go in by the back.

Once they were in her room she drew the blind, the curtains and switched on the bedside light.

Since his last visit there had been some small changes. An ornamental streamer made of Wrigley's chewing-gum papers hung from one end of the mantelpiece and Tommy Steele had blossomed out in colour on one wall. The chair had disappeared. She scooped things off the little table and set out the two tumblers, the bottle of gin and some cheese biscuits. Then she surveyed these preparations in terms so to speak, of him and smiled, almost to herself it seemed, as though the furniture and he too were filling positions she had already imagined.

He adjusted his spectacles, smiling. " Very cosy," he said.

She looked at him. Suddenly she began laughing, had to sit on the bed and catch her nose with one hand to stop the laugh becoming destructive of secrecy, but still had to go on with it.

" Why d'you laugh, Minty ? " He felt defenceless.

She stopped. " Oh, I don't know . . ." she said, suddenly indifferent. Then she took her coat off and hung it up. Turning she surveyed him again, this time confronting him with her pornographic dress. His eyes had been waiting for this and they did not rest on her face.

" Why did you wear that, Minty," he said, still looking, " for the Virgin ? "

" This ? What's wrong ? " Her eyes widened innocently but her mouth was uneasy.

She turned away, took a cigarette and sat down. " Have I shocked everyone ? " she said with sudden weariness. " Why don't you sit down. You can't sit on the chair because it's gone, so sit on the bed . . . I won't bite."

He made way for himself by removing a cheap edition of Coleridge's poetry and a *Junior Mirror*. " Do they go together ? " he said, holding them up.

" Perfectly," she said in a disinterested tone.

He sat as far from her as was polite.

In the subsequent silence his eye wandered, taking in the strange assortment of decorations which she had used to set her own personal seal on the room. His observation this time was more detailed, even nosy, pried, for instance, into her case, which lay open, revealing a rich chaos of objects—trophies they seemed. For some seconds the topmost object, a half-finished letter in green ink, held his attention without his realising why. Green ink, of course, consorted well with the chain of chewing-gum papers : it was another small gesture of non-conformity to the background which she so elaborately disowned but which her voice, her mannerisms, her very bone-structure and face seemed to attest. Green ink ! Hadn't he seen it quite recently . . . only a few days ago. And then . . . and then . . . his mind became dazed. Was it possible ? Goole . . . Goole's letter ! Everything seemed to stop. He, Minty, everything in time seemed to wait for him to take in what his eyes saw. She was Goole's girl.

His mind raced back to that night when he had surprised her with his torch. Liversey had been waiting nearby and next day . . . cigarettes had been found on Goole.

When he returned his eyes to her face it was no surprise to find her looking at him quizzically, mockingly.

He went back to staring at the letter and trying to reverse the writing in his head so that he could identify a word upside down. He had a vivid visual memory and it seemed to him that the handwriting was certainly the same.

Fragments of a probationer officer's letter came to mind : . . . "took up with a girl . . . who picked regularly . . . stayed with an arty family." He could see her now listening to Goole's guitar in the hop-fields, some smouldering summer evening with the gnats dancing in cones of air and people going by in open cars with appeased, reddened faces and newspapers and sweets ; glancing as they passed at that group there round the guitar and the voice and the girl who might have been an Italian film-star on location.

Something in her expression suggested that she had left the letter there on purpose.

At last he said: " Do you always write letters in green ink ? "

" Always."

" Well . . ." he said at last, " I get it now ! "

" You were slow," she said in a tone of bored criticism . . . as though the whole thing were a joke, a parlour game.

After a time he said: " Are your parents still alive ? "

" Am I one of your inmates—or whatever you call them ? "

" It's quite a normal question, isn't it ? "

" My mother is."

" Where ? "

" London."

" What does she do ? "

" She exists."

" Does she know what you do, Minty ? "

" She wouldn't care if she did. Anyhow—I'm twenty-two. . . ."

She suddenly lay back on the pillow with one hand under her head and her body askew.

" Twenty-two . . . I see." Her expression of indifference imposed silence until he said, " At any age . . . it's still a good thing to have roots, isn't it ? A place, people, a set-up . . . if things go badly . . ."

She smiled slowly as though listening to words which she thought she had heard for the last time long ago.

" Roots ! " she said contemptuously. " Tell me some roots that aren't just luggage to-day."

" You say that but . . . perhaps your presence here is

just an attempt to find roots—somehow, somewhere. Even in the most improbable soil. How can anyone exist without them—any more than a plant can ? "

She closed her eyes as though in a tube late at night, tired ; closed them against the rattle, the print everywhere.

He went on :

" Surely, Minty, a man *is* his past. He can't amputate any of it without cutting off part of what he is. Believe me : I know. . . . Apart from my own experience I see processions of young people without a milieu—or roots, worthy of the name. The result is they throw up a milieu unworthy of the name, the delinquent gang. So much of modern life is a vacuum . . . surely you know the rest by heart . . . even the bit about the seven devils coming in to sit down where one was cast out. Are you sure you aren't playing with the seven devils ? "

" I don't agree," she said in a tone of dazed, exalted obstinacy. And she blew smoke up in a great gust, with her eyes open now.

Silence fell until at last he said : " So everything's fine is it ? What you're doing here for instance. That's fine is it ? "

" Yes—that's fine."

" And what's the object of the operation ? "

She said nothing, went on smoking, smiling slightly with the portentous gravity of a child with a secret. What would be the good, her expression seemed to say, of even trying to explain to a man like you.

" Well," he said at last, " I'm honoured by your confidence. But be careful. It could put me in an awkward position."

She found this funny, so funny that she looked at him for company in her laughter. When he was unable to give it her face hardened and she stared at him coldly as though from a great distance, measuring him. To do this she had to skew her head sideways and look along the length of half her twisted body.

" Oh, dear," she said as though they had assembled to play a duet and he had forgotten his instrument. She sat up. " Let's have another drink. . . . I'm rather drunk. Are you rather drunk ? Let me see you without your spectacles. . . ."

She came close and removed them.

" Don't mock me," he said.

" On the contrary, I'm improving you. Who would have thought it ! I'm glad I took a ticket for the aquarium."

He looked at her curiously.

" But why d'you look so sad ? " she said. " Has someone escaped ? "

" Perhaps I have," he said uncertainly, looking at her throat and saying to himself, get up and go now. Instead he said : " You know you could help your Mister Goole ! "

He might not have spoken. She knelt on the bed and began to inspect him. First she touched his wrist with her forefinger gingerly as though he might bite : " Fur," she said admiringly. " Are you furry all over ? "

" In the conventional places."

" You seem to me unconventionally furry."

" And you ? "

" They tell me not. Are you drunk too, Mr. Ayrton ? You ought to get drunk sometimes. . . . Couldn't you let them all out to-morrow ? You'd never regret it, you know. Never. It would be like that time the First War almost stopped on Christmas Day. I cried when I read that story. It was so natural. Your hands are quite cold. Are you a cold person . . . ? Surely you must be."

He turned his hand over and received hers into his. She managed to bring her face close without seeming to have moved. He smiled at her. " Is this wise ? " he said.

" I always find it speaks for itself," she said, and she began examining his neck like a person looking for small caterpillars.

" Why are you doing this ? "

Her face hardened. " You can't really believe it, can you ? I'll remember that in your favour ! "

Her hair trailed past his shoulder. It smelt clean and fresh. Like the hair of a child.

" You're lonely, aren't you ? " he said. " That's all— isn't it ? "

" And you ? You've got a blackhead behind one of the flying buttresses of your nose," she said scientifically. " May I squeeze it ? "

Her expression of scholarly interest and sporting relish charmed him. She had long nails.

" It feels as if it now needed a tourniquet," he said.

" I think it may," she said objectively and added, " I hope I hurt you ! "

She stared meaningfully into his eyes.

He said, " You came here to be beside Goole. Let's talk about that."

" Goole," she said. " Who's Goole ? " and she smiled at him from a few inches. He stared and stared into her eyes but instead of being able to get into her mind and find out what was going on there he felt his own mind invaded—by a haze, an ever-increasing haze. There was no such thing as the truth under the influence of those eyes, which, now that they completed their work on his brain, turned back to his ear-lobe and his neck as though in search of more solid opposition. He thought of her tongue . . .

and suddenly felt violent against the excuses, the sublime excuses he made all his life, to avoid committing himself ever to anything risky.

Her present position afforded him a view straight down her shirt front. He could now see the rest of her pale soft breasts—even the nipples looking down into the slack, crimson-edged brassière that was more for warmth and modesty than for correcting shape. Seeing where his eyes went she stayed how she was. When at last she moved, the gap in her clothing breathed under his nostrils a faint odour of warmth and femininity which melted his thoughts.

His hand went on to her arm and up it to the elbow.

Her eyes returned to his. " Jump," they seemed to say, " you never have jumped, have you, from your high, high . . . pathetic little place, never once. Jump now . . . you'll be reborn ! "

He reminded himself that Minty was the girl-friend, perhaps the fiancée of an inmate . . . and his hand tightened on her arm.

" How has this happened ? " he said sadly, as though already foretelling consequences which neither of them would enjoy. " One never knows, does one ? I only know that I've never felt about anyone as I do about you."

" You're an original," she said, " you ought to write scripts."

" Please . . . don't mock. Not now. Perhaps this isn't love. It's more like memory . . . it's a sort of passionate regret for what might have been. Occasionally I've met someone who has revived in me the idea that we are not necessarily condemned for life to be alone. Messengers from God, I used to think them—because in their company

I felt a sense of affinity with all things, even inanimate objects. But I've forgotten what it felt like——"

She said, " You say nice things. Are you nice ? "

" Be serious . . . things are bad enough. . . ."

" Are they. Poor you ! If you knew how serious I could be ! " She was ranting.

He stroked her arm. She looked at him and said, " Serious, are you ? " Her hair touched his face. He touched her cheek, gently pulled her shoulder. She came without resistance and as she did so closed her eyes, her face devoid of expression.

Is this me, he thought, and began unbuttoning her shirt gently. She wanted it, asked for it, and now it's too late. What harm is there . . . ?

When the fifth button was undone he slipped in his hand along the soft edge of her childish cotton brassière and for a moment took the weight of her far breast in his hand, stroking the protuberance of her nipple with the inside edge of his thumb until it sprouted mysteriously like something alive. " Minty," he said, putting his lips to her ear and with sudden swiftness and force slipped off her shoulder-strap and closed her whole warm naked breast in the palm of his hand. Her face turned inwards slowly to his and they began to kiss.

He might then conceivably for once, have forgotten about himself and everything else, too—had she not straightaway surprised him, first by fondling his head as though with genuine personal tenderness and then by kissing him with of all things, innocence, and an absolutely inexperienced roughness, which by aping lust discouraged it. He had a qualm of fear, of responsibility. She, the tart, Goole's girl wanted this to be different, wanted to *mean it*. And he—what did he mean ? He took his lips away and looked at her eyes. They were closed, and as though aware of and anxious to end his investigation, she put her lips towards his like a blind animal turning towards nourishment. In her face there was relief and pain, the pain proceeding in some paradoxical way from the relief, perhaps as it might in a person who, dying of thirst, cannot drink with satisfaction or without agony. Her beauty awed him. He, too, suddenly closed his eyes and pressing his cheek to hers murmured her name, prayed it to the air as though it could not fail, armed with her beauty and the feelings he surely had for her, to deprive the future of consequences and the present of harm.

Afterwards, when he was looking at her face turned sideways on the pillow, and at her body, bare to the waist, hoarding her with his eyes against the desert of time at Edgecliffe and against old age, he became prey to grief that enjoyment could have been so one-sided. He could have understood repulse, a slap on the face, and certainly apathy if the whole thing had been bought. But that she should have solicited—clamoured—and then having yielded, well —half-yielded, lain so gently but as though a tooth were being extracted, this struck him as inexplicable and sad—not the Minty he had expected.

For the fact was she had not participated at all. She had remained separate.

The proof of this showed in her present position which suggested the archives of an atrocity. And it filled him on the one hand with pity (making him tidy her clothes and cover her bosom) and on the other mitigated the crude rush of barnyard triumph which made his blood crow. She had held back, but he had not. All his previous deference and politeness, that feeling of being her father and responsible, of being a Warden and therefore distant, all "that claim to be just," and that oversublimation and patronage masquerading (yes, sometimes) as compassion, the whole complicated burden of inhibition had suddenly been eased by being turned upside down. He had taken what he wanted, committed himself, vomited some goodness that had not been so much goodness as fear and habit. And yet . . . such a departure should have been a celebration— and should have had a partner. Instead . . . he could hardly bear to look at his liberator. It seemed to him he had never seen a face more in need of love. Was she thinking now of Goole? He found himself staring at her eyelids as though they were the flimsy covers of an intimate diary in which he was repudiated and the other preferred. The pain of already losing what he knew he had scarcely possessed turned to jealous dread that he had not really had her at all. And yet, like a person on the edge of an accident, he was glad that he was able to go.

A frown light as a left-over wraith of smoke on a windless day hung on her brows. This thickened slightly and she said faintly, " Say something nice."

He heard but was too astonished to reply. " Nice ? " he said at last but there was no invitation in his voice. In fact he wanted to stop her speaking again. Because now he felt threatened—oh, yes, of course on the threshold of emotions which might involve them both too deeply . . . " life being what it is."

Or was it simply that he felt like a burglar asked for a donation ?

No. All he wanted was that she should have a future,

a home, "someone to love," ordinary things. Not him. One had to be realistic.

He could say nothing. Not a single word would come.

For there is a limit to lack of integration and at that moment he seemed to have lost his identity, to have been broken down into a mass of disassociated elements.

After a moment of looking at her body again, he leaned over, lowered his lips to her breast, devoutly.

"Minty," he said, "I must go . . . I *must!*"

And then, because for a whole long minute she didn't move or speak, he went.

23

ELLA WAS MOVING about in the kitchen in her slippers, busying herself with those small adjustments and chores which monopolised her time even late at night. She said, "Late, aren't you?" and he said, yes, he was a bit.

It was like any other night: the teapot under the cosy, the shortbread biscuits out on the gold-rimmed plates, Ella's waistless back turned to him.

"Can I help?" he said.

"Good rehearsal?"

For a moment he was silent. Then he said: "It was uncomfortable kneeling. . . ."

Normally he would have jumped at any opportunity to tell her of some happening, however trivial, simply on the off chance of raising Edgecliffe in her esteem. As it was, he found it difficult to discuss the tableau. He had never lied consciously to Ella.

"How was your girl-friend? Did she make a good Virgin?"

"Yes, she did."

"Did the Magi get a kiss?" she said, suddenly waggish.

After a moment he said, "Ignorance is bliss, isn't that what they say?" and then, "I believe you wouldn't mind tuppence if I had an affair."

"An affair? What's that?" she laughed.

It was not a cheerful laugh. And then she said: "We'll wait till we see flames, shall we, before we ring for the fire brigade."

Stimulated by the word "affair," her gaze remained ironic.

A few moments later she must have linked Minty and all Marshal's girls with her own plight for she suddenly said, "You know, Phil, I'm sorry for those girls living in a place like this—and in digs, too!"

"They make friends in Buxton . . ." he said, and then: "I was quite happy in digs."

"When you got what you wanted," she said with complacence and a little grudge—as though she might take that time back if she could.

Another night, after a silence, he might have said, "Well, Ella, what is it *you* want—can you *tell* me?" or simply sat, weighed down with a sense of vague failure. But to-night he could not be sorry. His body still tingled with drowsy exhilaration and his mind was lit with memories of Minty. The voice of conscience did nag but he closed his ears to it. A lie was implicit now in every word and every smile. But this situation distressed him more because it was troublesome and unwieldy, than because it was wrong.

He would like to have told Ella everything and so he looked at her thinking: Shall I?

She was saying now what Gwen had told her about her sister's husband. He was doing well with a joiner in Bristol, though it meant his being away during the week. They were getting a new car.

She fetched her mending and settled near the light. A pang of affection went right through him and he almost got up, there and then, to kiss her. Instead he asked for more details of Gwen's brother-in-law and the new car. He loved everyone, everything.

" Any word from Christine to-day ? " No, there had been none.

He watched Ella rummage in the familiar basket, saw the old toffee-tin full of buttons which dated back surely to the year Christine was born. Should he tell her?

Because really it would be best—to be free of the feeling that every word, every smile was a lie. Besides what wrong had he done. He could not regret what had happened— could not. And this gave him a feeling of peace—spoilt only by the lie, and by the memory of Minty's cry, " Say something nice." In a moment he would write to Minty and remedy his omission.

There was still Ella.

She had half turned to thread a needle and the light caught her face peering, spearing at the approximate place, her eyes vivid with certainty that the eye of the needle was where it was not.

She was blind, defenceless, dedicated to one role.

He realised then—suddenly and with an apprehension of loneliness—that he could never tell her, because it would hurt her too much. She would see it as a cruel betrayal and use it as a peg on which to hang a vast increase of grievance.

Pictures on the Wall

The thing that would hurt her most would be the understanding with Minty, not the love-making. Indeed the love-making, by itself, might enable her to despise Minty as a tart or something cheaper even than that. But the truth, the fact that the love-making had only happened because of an understanding, a quite extraordinary understanding as between people who had known each other always, in another life it seemed. . . .

Say something nice. . . .

Well, that was a debt he would pay. Now. As soon as Ella went to bed. He'd write.

In the long silence he assumed the subject had been changed in Ella's mind, that she had transferred her thoughts to the patch of damp on the wall in John's room or what the postman had told her about the floods at Enstow last week.

But she suddenly said, " Marshal ought to get men to do his hens."

He said, " Did you find your ring yet ? "

Ella put a thumb over where the ring should have been as though covering a sore place.

" Yes," she said. " But it's been off that long now I can't get it on again."

He was pleased to get the value of it back but sentimentally pleased, too. He remembered the day they bought it in Liverpool and even the appearance of one or two other rings which they had looked at, too expensive to buy.

" It might be quite valuable now," he said.

She rose heavily mentioning the time. They had to get up in the morning, she said. He took her hand as she passed. " How're the legs ? " he said. She freed her hand : they were much the same. He got up, went after her and kissed her. Pursuit ! How strange, after what had happened. The years behind them both had never seemed so valuable as now. He felt like a soldier at a reunion touching a comrade of many bitter engagements long ago. Of course: nothing could go wrong. The rest was a dream.

"I've got to write a letter," he said.

When Ella had gone up he took a piece of paper headed Edgecliffe House, smiling as he thought how the euphemistic " House " would needle Minty to new heights of sarcasm. It was many years since he had written an intimate letter—excepting two or three to Christine.

Minty darling (he wrote) It's an hour since I left you.
You said, " Say something nice," but what could I have said ? Would " thank you " have done, as though you had given me a cup of tea ? Did you want me to say " I love you "—when those worn words could only have mocked the gulf in age and circumstances which divides us ? Words, you may say, cost nothing. But they do when they mean something and I respect you too much to offer you ones that mean nothing. If I had said " I love you " I would have felt bound to prove it by giving you things that are not mine to give. Besides, do you really want my love ? I doubt it, though in the last hour I have allowed myself to believe that you did—even if only a little. Darling, in fact there was absolutely nothing I could have said to do justice to the joy and gratitude I felt. I would like to have given you at that moment, as you lay in my arms, the things that would make impossible a repetition, for me, of all that had just happened—I mean happiness,

a home, someone to love and an answer to that stare which haunts your lovely eyes when you are thinking of nothing in particular. You're so young. That's something you people make so much of—yet often seem to have forgotten how to be. In all the fireworks and fun you're often a million years old.

As I write this I feel you probably have already moved far from the emotions that made you beg me to " say something nice "—so far that you'll probably be angry and humiliated when you read this. Don't be angry: I know what loneliness can make one do and say. There's no need to bite your tongue off, none at all, because I love you, Minty. There! That's why I couldn't say it: because it's true—and also impossible, a dream. Yes, I love you, Minty. What does that mean? It means you are the world, the whole world—but not for me. How can I describe what a difference you have made to Edgecliffe, what a pleasure it is to talk to you? I'm not sure that I understand what you're trying to say, or even that you yourself do. As far as I can see human beings are not a jot better than they ever were. The position is even worse because in the bright, deceptive overhead light of analytic knowledge we (in this country at least—ask Gwen who can appreciate the improvements) have all become smaller, uglier and less important to ourselves and to each other. I see you, the romantic, moving through this ubiquitous electric desert like Lear in the storm: the babbling rhymes of insanity fall from your lips. Who knows: perhaps they are the new hope. You want no atomic bombs, no gallows and no laws except your own. But in the end I expect you'll be like others, have your carrycot and insurance policy

Kleenex and Mini-Minor, pay your taxes to "Defence"
. . . I have no right to hope you won't but for my sake
don't hurry.

Could your gramophone break down again ?

Philip Ayrton

He then did something which next morning he could
not really believe he had done. He posted the letter.

24

COVER THE FACE that did " ups " next morning. Cover
at least the eyes with the thickest spectacles available. But
which face, and which eyes ? He was two people, one
of them confirmed by the usual routine, the other by the
letter which was on its way. At breakfast with John and
Ella, among the great emblazoned packets of cereals, socks
and alarm-clocks he tried to diminish the importance of all
that had happened.

Even, he argued, if Minty were the girl who had got
Goole into trouble, it was still certain that she would respect
his letter. After all her words, " Say something nice . . ."
had been a *cri du cœur* and if not a confession of love then
at least a plea for affection. He had responded by giving
her, in his letter, the very thing she asked for. . . . How
could she use it against him ? Surely she couldn't, wouldn't.

He still could not regret anything that had happened.
His eyes in the mirror were unusually bright and clear.

He felt extraordinarily well, and all the time he kept specu-
lating on how and when he would meet or see Minty next.
Much would be revealed by how she reacted. One thing
was sure, whatever she did would not be " enough." The
best would be a surreptitious wave, something secret,
intimate, unfinished, a sign such as might have linked two
spies in a foreign country; the worst—he could not bear
to think of the worst; it bore too heavily on Ella and the
children, on his whole life.

On the way home to lunch he saw Pam by herself. She
was not far from the hedge—almost within speaking
distance, and he slackened his pace while looking towards
her in case she had some message for him or could volunteer
information. But Pam in the absence of her mentor was
a different being. Even the cheekiness had gone and she
went about her work as though she had never met him.

The following day Minty was still nowhere to be seen.
By now she would have got his letter and fears which he
didn't dare explore began to nag his thoughts. She was
a neurotic. What might she not do . . . or already have
done? Seeing Gwen at lunch-time he could bear it no
longer and said, " Lost your lodger, Gwen . . . I haven't
seen her around ? "

" She's taken a cold, Mr. Ayrton."

Gwen's thoughts were never easy to gauge. Small events
she dramatised, big ones she reduced to digestible propor-
tions; in either case she hid her reactions behind an
expression of pregnant neutrality as though, judged herself
long ago, as unfit to be a mother, she would never take a
similar liberty with others. Even so, Ayrton assured
himself—as he stared at her—if Minty had told her anything
she could not have managed to look so agreeable.

" It's her head," Gwen continued, warming to a suggestion of childhood neglect and disaster. "All her life she's been troubled with the sinus. . . . She got her breakfast in bed."

Gwen made a strange little smirk as much as to say she was sure Minty cannot have believed she'd be cosseted up here at Edgecliffe—by an old woman like her.

Ayrton was relieved—though he did not like the sound of sinus. He associated the complaint by now with the most unreliable, impulsive and self-absorbed people. And in bed Gwen might mother her into confidences. He must see her himself—and soon.

The opportunity was waiting for him ready-made. It came to his mind so easily and naturally that it seemed as if some part of him had already made a plan, long ago, to visit Minty in her room, without anyone knowing.

Every Tuesday Gwen spent that night and most of the next day with her sister who had poor health, six children and an absent husband.

It would be easy—any Tuesday.

The intention was heady. Stop, a voice said, stop now, or you'll get in deeper. But he couldn't. And it wasn't just fear of what she might be cooking up. No, it was that sense of unfulfilment which addicts know. Her body, he remembered, had done its best, at the last moment, to decline what it had gone out of its way to solicit: there were, again, moments when he felt he hadn't really slept with her at all.

Remembering her now in the dress which she had worn to impersonate the Virgin, he realised how vulnerable he had been, and still was, to that sluttishness and exhibitionism, that tiresome desire to shock which common sense must condemn as neurotic in someone of her age. He could only suppose that her depravity fascinated him because it woke an echo in his own heart—an echo which was all the more powerful for being unacknowledged. He was tired of self-deception. It was not only Paterson's " claim to be just " which had become a burden—but the claim to be cultured, virtuous and worthy to rule. The personality of Minty seemed to offer an obscure possibility of escape. The fact that she was dangerous and had already damaged two men to his certain knowledge, merely made him covet her more. He loved her, with all the force of an acknowledged emptiness—as though she were a soul.

Until now he could not remember, ever before, getting up in the morning and feeling conscious of *good* health (not that he was often unwell: he just never thought of health at all). Time was now—again—anticipation. Her cold would soon be over. Even if he didn't hear from her, he would see her, and even if she was in the distance she would communicate, make some sign. . . .

It was on the third day. He was going back to the Centre after lunch and there she was, as expected with Pam, standing by one of the hen-houses near the road. Her back was turned but Pam saw him and said something, smiling and turning away. Minty put a hand to her hair but remained as she was. Only when he was level did she look over her shoulder, turning her shoulders half round, and stare.

Her expression was quite unfathomable. Pam turned round too and tried to duplicate it without success.

Going a little slower Ayrton called, " Hallo . . ."

It was then Minty shouted: " Thanks for your letter."

Pam had to turn to hide laughter and a moment later Minty turned too, laughing but making her laughter seem to do with water which Pam had spilt down her gum-boot.

He felt a physical pain run through his whole body.
Who was she? Someone else. . . . His mind exploded
into frantic rationalisation. What could it mean? It was
camouflage. She couldn't have shown the letter to Pam.
But supposing she'd even told her that she'd had such a
letter . . . No. Be calm: the other girl would have
behaved like that anyhow, in fact *had* behaved like that for
a whole week after the tableau rehearsal. A letter could
have been about anything . . . the tableau. But why did
Minty have to join in the fooling quite so wholeheartedly?
The water-spilling had been too obvious a pretext for
mirth. She could have tempered her cruelty. She could
have remembered at least that she had *asked* him to " say
something nice." But perhaps that was just what she had
remembered! Had she, after all, told Gwen as well as
Pan that she had had a letter from him? Was he surrounded
by people who knew?

Conjecture whipped on by pain and fear raced through
his brain. He tried as he shut his office door behind him to
feel as he had before he ever met Minty. His lecture was
there on the table: he put it closer. The staff leave roster
needed approval, there was to be a visit of Canadian
probation officers. These matters were real. Goole had
applied for a special visiting order. He'd give orders about
that, too. The rest was a dream: unreal. A knock on the
door and there was Jefferies with something in his face:
" Two dog-ends floating in the bogs," he said. " Like to
see 'em? "

Ayrton shook his head, trying to come back. I'd better
go, he thought.

And there they were—royal in such a place. They even
had a sentry, in the shape of Liversey. Small disintegrating
nuggets of gold—discarded. Whoever had thrown them

away must have felt there was plenty more where these came from.

Jefferies said, " All right now, Liversey. Take 'em out and put them in my office."

" We'll have lengths of cigar in the cocoa next," he added. " It's a f——g ball, that's what it is. And that's the bloke that's wanting a visit from a tart ! "

" You mean Goole ? "

" I certainly mean Goole."

It required an enormous effort to concentrate. In the past few days Goole had been on the mat twice, charged on each occasion by Jefferies.

Victimisation had always moved Ayrton to the sharpest possible reaction. But to-day he could not cope with Jefferies, could not even give him the sarcastic edge of his tongue. The Deputy's perpetual conviction that Goole was guilty of slashing Hallows (simply because he didn't like and couldn't make any impression on him) was enough to put Ayrton on Goole's side more than he anyhow was already. Or had been. Now—he didn't know.

Later he sent for Goole.

" You've applied to see your girl ? "

" Yussa."

" Where is she coming from ? "

Ayrton looked up, challenging.

Goole looked at him straight and said, " Birmingham."

" And this is the one that got you into trouble ? "

Goole paused as though objecting to the form in which the question had been put. At last he said, " Yussa."

Ayrton thought of Minty laughing with Pam, laughing at his letter, tickled pink at the behaviour she had provoked in an old Warden.

"D'you think she'll help you go straight when you get out?"

"Yussa."

For a moment there was silence. Then Ayrton said, "That's all then, Goole. You can see her on Saturday. . . I'll have a word with her when she comes."

25

TWO DAYS PASSED and he only saw Minty in the distance. Whenever letters came he went through them looking for a strange handwriting and a local postmark. But there was never anything. In the vacuum created by lack of contact he began to brood. The smallest thing was apt to take on the quality of a threat. He remembered how she had said she and Pam sometimes met members of the staff in the George. Perhaps, then, by now the whole Centre knew that he had gone to her room. In that case he hoped they also knew how often Shirley had had a drink at Shang-ri-la and how, if Shirley had boarded with Gwen, he might easily have had a drink with her in her room too, "particularly if I'd been mending her gramophone in the first place." And so on—always more childish as he became more frantic.

The only link with Minty now was Gwen. One morning affecting the tone of casual conversation he said to her as she was cleaning:

"Your lodger makes a beautiful Virgin, Gwen."

Pictures on the Wall

" So they were saying, Mr. Ayrton."

He scrutinised her: still no sign.

"I'm sure she's glad of the lift down, Mr. Ayrton," Gwen said. "They don't know how lucky they are..." she shook her head. "That girl! I don't know..."

"Yes...?" Ayrton said. "What...?"

Well, it was just the amount of coffee she drank, the cigarettes she smoked: Mrs. Merridew was sure if she had the half of it she'd never need to work again. And all them tunes, some of them almost had her dancing and others crying for mercy. But she was a lovely girl, no doubt about that. Albert was combing the tangles out of her hair the other night. Here Mrs. Merridew covered her mouth. "We had a laugh! She put a frog in his bed. I had him washing his feet and grumbling for a whole hour and me changing sheets. If there's one thing Albert won't have it's a frog."

Ayrton listened, touched his glasses, smiled dimly as though such pranks were a far cry from his responsibilities.

He went for eggs but it was Shirley in the store.

He went to see Beasley and asked the date of the next rehearsal. Beasley said clothes were the things to get on with. There was really no need to rehearse again till the beginning of December: it wasn't like a play. But he thought there could be a " clothing conference " in a week or so. Perhaps Ella would help Minty with hers—" something warm this time ! "

A week ! Ayrton knew he would not have to wait as long as a week before he saw Minty again.

Sometimes he fell into a trance at his desk trying to find some clue to her behaviour. She had seduced him, and clearly this had been her intention ever since she paid him

that visit in his home. But why? In asking himself this
he felt foolish because how often had he avoided the use
of that very word after listening to an inmate's account of
his crime. Why, for that matter (if this was indeed the same
girl as the one in the court report) had she gone off with
that farmer when she was devoted to Goole—so devoted
to him that she now did her best to share his imprisonment.
The farmer, he remembered with a twinge of imagined
affinity, had also been a middle-aged man and also at one
time at least in authority over Goole and over her too
when they were picking fruit. And rich . . . " established."
Perhaps she wished to destroy men who appeared strong,
older. Perhaps in spite of her education and background,
she had (as he had often suspected) chosen to see him,
Ayrton, as part of some mythical "establishment" and
perhaps this very attitude, and the hostility that went with
it, had constituted part of her charm—and a challenge,
too. Well—if it was a challenge—then surely he had
met it frankly, without hiding behind his age or position, and without being a stickler for archaic rules of conduct. She might therefore now forgive him for being
older and stronger, allow him membership of her obscure
élite.

He turned the matter this way and that in his mind till
it became blurred and capable of any shape he chose to
give it.

The barnyard triumph lately inspired in him by an act
of petty adultery, gradually vanished. Deprived of her
imagined love he had collapsed. But there still remained
one feeling which never changed and which gave him the
confidence to believe that everything would be all right
in the end: he loved her. Of course, she would soon
(whatever happened) be gone from his life but that made

no difference at all. He loved her and with that feeling inside him he felt protected from the possible consequences of his letter. Love was his last weapon, and with an instinct that it was in fact a weapon, he deliberately suppressed every temptation towards hatred, revenge. Now, again he believed in humility, felt sure that if he could talk to her in the right way the safety of his family and his career could be assured.

Saturday, the day for visitors, came. When he got in to his office he rang through to the front door and asked for certain ticked-off names to be shown in to his office as they arrived. Then he went on with notes for his lecture.

Peter, brought over as a treat, slept by the fire. Whenever Ayrton moved, the dog's eyes opened a crack and widened ... till the identity of this room and this bad kind of walkless Saturday sank in. Then they narrowed and almost closed.

Whether Minty came or not, work was a palliative and he was glad to be where he was and not at Shang-ri-la. Here he would be spared the long hours of leisure and the pretence of listening to what Ella or John said to him. He needed to feel useful again. Often more could be done for a boy by talking to his visitor, particularly to a girl-friend, (or so at least Ayrton imagined) than by any amount of talking to the boy himself. He had had fiancées and even wives listening to him so attentively they scarcely seemed to breathe; and sometimes there was the comedy of mothers lecturing him as though he were the headmaster of a fee-paying school which perhaps in a way he was, or even congratulating him on the physical condition of some spoilt oaf who had insisted on her spending half a week's wage to visit him a week before he was due for release. Yes, he thought, whether Minty comes or not an afternoon with the visitors will throw things a bit into perspective and take my mind off myself.

He got down to his lecture but hadn't been at it ten minutes before he looked up at the sound of footsteps outside and saw Minty coming through the gate. She was so heavily made up and smartly dressed that for a moment he had thought it was someone else. Then her characteristic slipshod gait on her fantastically high-heeled shoes removed all doubt. It was Minty all right, and a few moments later the Duty Officer knocked and announced, " Miss Roberts."

She came in and stood in the doorway as though there must be some mistake.

" Come in please, Miss Roberts," Ayrton said, and she moved another pace which enabled the officer to shut the door.

Then Ayrton said, " Minty—please sit down."

" I came to see Jim," she said.

" I know," he said.

After a moment's hesitation she came moodily into the middle of the room and began looking round—looking at his desk, the pictures and the wallpaper. Finally a trace of sardonic humour came into her eyes and she said dryly, " Well ? "

" Please do sit down. A few moments, Minty. That's all I ask."

" What is there to talk about ? "

He tried to read in her eyes some clue to her real feelings. Which Minty was it in front of him now, the one who had thrown his life for a moment into a nobler key, exalting him with the favour of her youth, her beauty and her obscure courage, or the fatuous bitch who had called out " Thank you for your letter," and then giggled, apparently at the memory of all that had passed between them.

"At one moment I thought we understood each other," he said. "I thought you meant . . . everything. As I did. And saw no harm."

She moved away and began examining the picture above the fire-place, the one of the girls in their bikinis under the B.O.A.C. Comet. No one had ever moved about this room like that, judging it.

"I believe you've got a one-track mind," she said. "These girls—and the girls at the Youth Club playing badminton, with their skirts tucked into their knickers; and the prisoners sitting here in front of you—telling you what they did to little Doris in the railway siding. It must be quite a ball, isn't it?"

He made no reply.

"The monk!" she said, stopping before the other picture, the one of the girls.

"Minty, when you've finished," he said, "I'd like to have a few words with you."

She came away from the wall.

He said, "Your contempt is perplexing. How d'you like yourself?"

"I came to see Jim!"

There might not be much time. She might simply go.

"I gather you got my letter," he said.

Her face owned it, every second; her tone was based on it. But unless he was mistaken she looked upon it not only as a weapon—but also as a wound. For a moment he imagined that his worst crime in her eyes might have been that he had tantalised her—perhaps by reviving memories of some period of her life and some early relationship that had never given her anything but pain. Had she seen him as her father? Her cry, "Say something nice" could so easily have been an appeal to someone else, long ago, the epitaph on a whole period, a disappointment that was never finished. Probably, despite the way she had talked, some part of her nature longed for the most ordinary things imaginable—security, in particular. His letter, in celebrating and praising her for a mystique of courageous insecurity, from behind the barricades of his own entrenched position (with pension to follow and wife to applaud) might have roused her to a sudden fury of resentment, which fears of self-contradiction prevented her from expressing.

He adjusted his spectacles, aware of the futility of trying to explain, doubting even at that moment the justice of the one excuse he could certainly find.

" Yes—I got your letter," she said.

" And you found it . . . amusing."

" Didn't I thank you the other morning ? "

She smiled as though at the incongruity of a punctiliousness she had once learnt in very different circumstances, and which he had now forced on her again.

" I acknowledged it verbally," she said.

" I suppose it was very funny," he said.

Soberly she said, " Yes. It was a scream."

" Minty," he said. " Will you do me a favour. Will you give it back to me ? "

She moved away, and sat down on the edge of a chair.

" Will you ? " he said.

She looked for a long moment deep into his eyes. Then she laughed—a contemptuous, almost soundless explosion of air through her nostrils. This noise somehow gave an impression of despair as though Minty had asked for a look at the very corner-stone of all creation, at God, the Father and come back, after what she had seen, laughed like this because all she had seen was a Warden asking for mercy.

"You forgot something," she drawled. "That you're thinking of your wife and children." She got up groggily. He said nothing, following her to the door. "Can I have a guide please?" she said, turning half-way.

"You could help your Jim, you know, Minty . . ."

She turned and looked at his mouth with curiosity. Then she said: "You're a record!"

She moved on towards the door. There might not be another chance of talking to her. Ever.

He felt his blood rising.

He said: "Do you want to destroy people, Minty? You had a pretty good shot at it with Jim Goole."

"What d'you mean by that?" she said slowly, stopping and turning.

"Well, I expect you seduced him, didn't you—in the hop yards—and then bitched him afterwards till he committed a crime. The princess and the gipsy! When he was gaoled you felt guilty—or frightened. I don't know what the rest means!"

She was silent for a moment, again looking at him with impersonal curiosity. She said, "I love Jim. That's something you might not understand."

"You show it in a funny way, sometimes."

She went out into the passage, and said, "Oh, God," to the gleaming linoleum.

Then Ayrton called the Duty Officer and she was taken through.

26

THE NEWS TRAVELLED QUICK and showed on every staff face within a few hours. Chief Officer Parks came in on some pretext and looked quizzically at Ayrton. Probably he knew that Minty had been to the Warden's house with eggs and that on one occasion had jived with him at the Youth Club. Ayrton helped him, said, " Goole's girl-friend right on our doorstep ! "

Parks was relieved. He said most of the disciplinary staff knew " that Minty girl," they met her at the George. But this ! This was something none of them had ever suspected. And he looked grave and expectant as though " steps " should be taken.

" We'll have to look into it," Ayrton said.

Silence followed and at last Ayrton said : " Her presence may not be unconnected with one or two things that have recently been found on the premises."

Parks's face relaxed further ; he said that was just what he had been thinking.

And how much more, Ayrton thought, will Jefferies think it—when he gets to hear.

The knowledge that Minty herself was now in danger confused his feelings more.

When he was alone again Ayrton looked round his room with new eyes. He looked at everything she had looked at, trying to see it all as she had seen it . . . " little Doris in the railway siding." No, he insisted, but felt strange. It was like when the boys in the Borstal revue had impersonated him. He was shocked by his own misgivings.

The details of ordinary living became exhausting. He inhabited a changed world. Looking back, to only a few weeks ago, everything seemed so simple. Now the simplest conversation was complicated by the need, always implicitly, often explicitly, to lie. But the trouble with the' lying was that each lie soon needed the support of ten new lies and each of those ten, in its turn, the support of yet another ten, and so on. Even silence was a strain. Every face encountered seemed a threat to the transparence of his own face, so that he felt himself almost physically retreating and sinking, deeper and deeper, behind his glasses and thickening his features into a continual blank opacity.

"You know that girl, Ella—Minty, the one who's doing the Madonna, Gwen's lodger—she got a job up here to be beside one of the inmates."

"Gwen won't be very pleased."

"Perhaps she knows. . . ."

Gwen did know. Minty had told her the day before she visited Goole.

Gwen's comment was silence, face trembling slightly, bulbous eyes lost, far out, duster hanging limp. She might have been a fisherman's or miner's wife, someone whose childhood had been steeped with the lore of disaster, living on the fringe of the breadwinning battleground.

She said, "Yes, Mr. Ayrton, she's told us now. She should have told us in the first place. I'm not saying more but that, for she's a good girl ; she's good to us."

Jefferies said, " Now we know where the cigarettes came from ! "

His breathing, like endless sighing, came and went and his little eyes looked unhappy as they attempted to speculate.

" Marshal won't want a bird with a false name workin' for 'im, will 'e ? "

" I'm thinking it over, Jefferies. I'll get the police to check on her."

" I've done that."

A stab of fear prevented Ayrton from answering as soon as would have been normal. Had Jefferies acted within his rights . . . ? Was he suspicious that Ayrton might have done nothing ? How could Minty be shielded ; how indeed could he shield himself from destruction if Minty were discovered to have been the person who introduced tobacco into the Centre ?

Ayrton felt Jefferies's eyes on him . . . till he said, " Good . . . what did you tell them ? "

" Said she could have been smuggling things. Snout, offensive weapons. . . . Been tarting around with our people, down at the George. . . ."

" Has she ? "

" Liversey ! " Jefferies said, looking at Ayrton expressively. " Never seen them together ? "

Ayrton shook his head. The ensuing silence seemed to encourage Jefferies in a feeling of superior knowledge, a belief perhaps that the Warden now admitted tacitly to having been wrong, from the start, about Goole, First Offenders . . . everything ; his breathing became more expansively laboured, more than ever eloquent and soon it achieved again the crisis of articulate speech. " It's a flippin' ball," he said, " tarts livin' all round us. They'll be dryin' their smalls on the wire soon."

Eased of this appreciation he went out and a moment later could be heard above the sound of marching boots, bawling a boy out with exuberant foulness.

In the past Ayrton had often been offended by Jefferies's swearing and had twice spoken to him about it. Now he listened to it with a sort of dread for it was ostentatiously audible—a challenge.

What will the police do, Ayrton thought. Will they visit her?

There were moments in the days that followed when the repetition of the daily round, unchanged in any respect both at home and in the Centre, lulled Ayrton into a feeling that all was well. One thing was sure : he knew she could not have told Goole. If she had, it would have showed on the man's face. Men in detention, Ayrton knew well, brood passionately over trifles concerning their loved ones : jealousy magnified by impotence becomes a fever in the brain.

No. She has not told him, Ayrton thought, as he walked past the little table for four where Goole sat with his rock-cake and tea. But she'll tell him later. Like a small child she would be drawn towards *having an effect*. Danger to herself, in so doing, might even constitute the main part of the attraction.

Days passed and nothing happened except that gradually the exacting claims of perpetual duplicity, of presenting to the world a studied and misleading face, gave him the feeling that some other person, who really was not " him " at all, had come to live with him inside the same skin.

Sometimes then, in his heart, he invoked Minty's help

against this other being, who, he felt, could "destroy us both," if things went on as at present.

At moments this sort of internal dialogue was more real to him than anything else, at others he had qualms of fear for his sanity. Because who in fact was he addressing? Surely not conceivably Minty—Goole's bird. More to the point if he wandered about muttering, "Hail Mary . . ." since the other, the sympathetic Minty had probably never existed anywhere except in his own mind.

In vain he protested: surely not: surely when she had quoted poetry (he kept returning to that) her voice had settled to a truly impersonal flatness which proclaimed her suddenly, miraculously free from the destructive and fatuous side of her self. That had been Minty and he had made it possible, just as she had made possible that long outpouring and confession of his past life. How impersonal their voices had sounded, drained of all identity, yet para-doxically, nothing quite so personal had ever happened to him before. Nor, probably, to her either. Was it sur-prising, he asked himself (becoming more cheerful,) that she had fallen, yes, just a bit—in love.

She like himself had been grateful for the sort of company she seldom got, flattered by the attention of a much older intelligence and perhaps helplessly stirred by that version of herself which she had read in his eyes and which had raised her far above the boredom, obscurity and narrowness of her lot, approximated her to the poetry she loved. Oh, Minty, he thought, we had so much in common: why this war?

But there was no answer from the emptiness all round, except her laughter in the field, her dry "Thanks for your letter " . . . That moment recurred to him like the after-taste of a nightmare, flavouring and overshadowing all rationalisation. It made him feel she had led him on with the illusion of an understanding such as he had never had from any woman and then, like one of those trick drawings, which turn from angelic to diabolic according to which way up they are held, she had suddenly become her own opposite, changed from redeemer of his middle-aged despair to destroyer of all that modest domestic happiness and professional success which he had so undervalued as to stake without a second thought, in the hope of winning—no, not something else—but something additional, something for a short time *on another level*.

In the end, after all the hair-splitting, defining and retrospection he always fetched up at the same point: she would use the letter for revenge, she would damage the good in their relationship just because it was good.

You see? said the creature who had come to live with him, inside his skin, you see—what did I tell you?

Then he looked at his new companion, talked to him—and discovered that he was as like himself as two peas—*but a criminal*—on account of what he suggested. Then—even when shaving he avoided looking in the mirror; and for the same reason avoided meeting the eyes of Ella, Gwen and John.

Could such intentions be his? They were his, but before he put them into action he would make one last attempt to talk to Minty, reason with her.

27

He rang Beasley. "Don't you think we ought to get on with the clothing conference, Jack?"

Enthusiasm from another, in any department of his work as vicar, momentarily left Beasley speechless like a man who, pushing hard against a locked door, suddenly falls flat.

"Right-o, Phil. Say the word: when shall it be? Tuesday as ever. Will you tell Minty up your end and I'll do the Buxtonians."

That was all Ayrton wanted: an authentic pretext. He sent a message by Mrs. Merridew that he would pick Minty up at seven on the day if she wanted a lift down. And at seven he was there.

Mrs. Merridew opened the door and Ayrton saw Albert pipe in hand, feet in slippers and old railwayman's waistcoat gaping over his paunch.

"Ai, Mr. Ayrton."

Mrs. Merridew said, "Didn't she tell you, Mr. Ayrton, she can't manage the tableau."

Albert opened the *Mirror* again and shut it in a new place. "Turning cold again."

"Was that all the message she left?" Ayrton asked, unable to move away.

"Well . . . I'm sure she'd be sorry there was a misunderstanding. I said to her, Albert heard me, be sure to tell Mr. Ayrton you can't go because he's bringing the car specially."

He should of course leave; he shouldn't stand there with Mrs. Merridew's sharp eyes at work on him. She had a taste for emergency, even when there was none.

She said, " Is there anything I can do, Mr. Ayrton ? "

He began to move away saying it was just that he was surprised: Mr. Beasley had set his heart on her for the Virgin. He wondered if the whole thing might not be called off now. Had she given any reason ?

" Well, I think . . ." Mrs. Merridew looked conscientiously over her shoulder as though for once, since the subject was Minty, information might come from the engrossed and impervious figure of her mate. " Didn't she say something about pluckin' late near Christmas with them machines ? " The question had to be repeated and then explained. When it got through Albert let out one high husky note of derisive laughter, apparently for Minty, machines and Christmas. Then, unplugging his pipe he said: " She was near pluckin' me last night."

" Those two ! " Mrs. Merridew said archly, making a wry mouth.

Ayrton went.

Minty was not at the conference, nor had she told the vicar of her intention not to take part. Beasley took the news as another challenge but his concern was touching.

" Phil," he said. " You're neighbours—couldn't you make her change her mind ? "

Ayrton said he could have a go at her to-morrow.

And he did.

" Vicar's orders ! " he said to Gwen at the door. He knew Minty was in because he'd seen her light streaming out at the back. Merridew was reading the *Mirror* in exactly the same clothes, attitude, and place. " Ai, Mr. Ayrton," he said. " Better day. Sharp wind."

Gwen said to Albert, " Mr. Ayrton's come to make Minty change her mind about the tableau."

Merridew gave his squeal laugh and some seconds later said, " Brought a crowbar ? "

" Vicar's orders," Ayrton repeated.

Albert whinnied sceptically without shifting his eyes.

Ayrton went through and knocked on her door. She must have heard his voice because her tone was strange, unnatural, " Who is it ? "

" Philip Ayrton."

There was a long silence. Then the latch moved hesitantly. She opened the door about ten degrees, and stood there looking at him. It was only seven o'clock but she was in her long green dressing-gown, holding it closed across the bosom with one hand. Her hair was down in a great black cascade. For a moment he felt that all he had wanted for days and days was merely to see her again close alone.

" What d'you want," she said, pretending surprise.

Mrs. Merridew had sharp and interested ears and the sound of her brisk better-thing-to-do movements at the sink increased rather than lessened his fears.

Loud, he said : " About the tableau, Minty. . . ."

" I saw Mr. Beasley to-day."

" We thought you might have second thoughts. . . ."

She knew what he was really talking about. He could see it in her face, in her whole position, in her hand on the half-opened door.

" For everyone's sake," he said, lower.

Seconds passed and they stood there looking at each other. The sound of Mrs. Merridew's rinsing paused and even her feet kept still for a moment though there was a floppy sound of something being shaken out carefully and quietly.

Then slowly Minty opened the door and turning her back, walked away, in.

He followed. To-day there was a papier mâché tray of eggs on the little table, a half-eaten apple, envelopes, and a letter. He knew that handwriting, even upside down from six feet. . . . How absurd to feel pain.

" You've got your chair back ! "

" Yes."

" How convenient ! May I sit down a moment ? "

" If you think there's any point."

The chair was relatively clear. He sat in it and she sat on the edge of the bed.

She lit a cigarette and looked at the floor with boredom.

" I'm not going to be blackmailed, Minty," he said quietly. " Get that straight."

He had never said, " Get that straight " to anyone before and it felt odd, pretentious, particularly in the gangster tone he had used.

She smiled sardonically as though detecting this departure from character.

" You needn't be blackmailed," she said.

" What d'you mean ? "

" Give Jim his remission back. And I'll give you the letter."

After a moment's astonishment he said, " I told you : I'm not going to be blackmailed."

There was silence while she smiled through the smoke at the floor.

He said, "It's part of your repertoire, is it, Minty, blackmail?"

She snorted quietly. "My repertoire!" After a moment's silence she said, "Does it interest you to know blackmail never occurred to me till you gave me the idea, that day, in your office—by asking for your letter back. Then I thought: What a good idea. I'll get Jim back earlier."

She had thought that up. He could see it in her face.

He said quietly as though talking to an unruly child, "Even if I was prepared to be blackmailed—I couldn't restore remission once it's taken away. It's against the rules."

"The rules! Do tell me the rules."

"You love your Jim, don't you?"

Her face hardened and she looked as though she hadn't spoken.

"Of course you love him," he went on, glancing towards the letter. "Part of my job, is to . . . censor the mail. I've read your letters, Minty. If you want to know, they made me wish I'd ever had such letters. Ever!"

Still she said nothing but she did look at him, warily.

Why could they not be friends? An absurd desire came over him to convince her of " all he had done for Goole," to tell her how he had taken a personal interest in the man's reading lessons, how he had resisted other members of the staff in their efforts to prevent Goole receiving her letters or her visit, how from the first he had believed he was innocent—or at least innocent in the sense that he had been provoked, to an action that was in its own way and in a certain milieu just and even courageous, and to him admirable perhaps enviable. . . .

But for some reason he could not speak of Goole.

" Well ? " she said dryly.

At last he did say, in an impersonal, technical tone, " We did our best for Goole, Minty, we respected him. We believed that he might have been convicted, as I said to you before . . . through very little fault of his own."

She looked at him.

He went on, " You like to own things, don't you, Minty, people too. You owned Goole and now you own Pam. You'd also probably like to own me. You've made a beginning. But I wouldn't like to be owned by you, Minty, because I think that you destroy whatever you own, even though perhaps you don't mean to. You're destroying your Goole probably. Why not let us all go ? "

She put her cigarette to her lips, inhaled and blew it out as though everything in the world were foul. She looked suddenly forlorn and unconfident. Her beauty sapped his strength and deflected him. She was weak, defenceless, isolated . . . yet her face made everything wise seem suddenly trivial and irrelevant ; there it was again that face, quite close after so long, so long. . . .

" Minty—I meant what I wrote to you," he said.

The pressure of some inner reaction induced a curious movement of her head and cigarette then an expulsion of smoke through her nostrils. She looked up at him rather theatrically as though she were still learning him, and still discovering new vistas of doubt in that experience.

" I meant it," he went on quietly, " as one does mean these things." . . . After a pause he went on : " I meant it more than anything . . . for years. Perhaps ever. At the same time . . . I realise . . ."

One of her slippers had fallen from the foot that was crossed over the other and her solid bare foot was showing, the toes moulded together gracefully like something budding, fresh from a sheath of promise and immaturity. The skin, pale and smooth, suddenly reminded him of all her body, so that a sudden ebbing feeling, a divine weakness emptied his head of thought. Once again he could not believe in all the impediments, in the shame or the danger, or the wrong, could not even believe in Goole. He could only give in to the conviction that the feeling he had had was by its very nature answered, just as the sun was met by the response of flowers. Believing created truth. He had made it true. And she, hadn't she cried out : Say something nice.

She said, " What is it you realise ? I'd like to know. . . ."

" The impossibility," he said.

" Why ? " she said, veiling her eyes. " It might be possible. Where there's a will, there's a way . . .! "

He looked at her suspiciously.

She said nothing. He got up and she looked somewhere about his middle with her eyes out of focus. He walked towards her . . . she looked up but she didn't move.

Then she put the cigarette to her lips and looked at the chair as though he were still sitting in it, although by then he was beside her knees. Then he lowered himself to the bed. When he touched her hand she still didn't move.

He heard himself say, " Minty, please. . . ."

She smiled sideways, away from him, as though for a congenial witness. " Oh, God," she said.

Her shoulder was quite close and the fall of her hair. Former familiarity with her body gave him the feeling that it was his when he wanted it, any time . . . now : love of her " inmost self " encouraged him to believe she could never refuse him, nor ever, in the last resort, injure him. Look : she couldn't move away from him . . . couldn't say or do anything. . . . She was his ! He put out a hand. . . .

Steps sounded outside and a door opened and closed. He got up, adjusting his spectacles punctiliously, and moved with a sense of folly towards the door, wishing to be near it if Mrs. Merridew came and asked if they wanted tea. But she didn't come and Minty laughed. Nevertheless he stopped in safety, moved sideways a bit as though merely taking a turn. He was grateful to the sound of that door: it had brought him back to his senses.

" Sit down," she said, still smiling at his precaution.

He said, " Minty, I know you wouldn't do anything with that letter but someone else might. If you give it back to me I'll do nothing about you. . . ."

He let this drop calmly but with complete assurance.

She said, " Me ? What have I done ? "

" Smuggled cigarettes in to Goole."

She turned away and was completely silent.

Then she started laughing, in irregular convulsions, like someone trying to stop hiccups. The message seemed to be that in a thousand years he would never learn the extent of his own awfulness.

Blood rose in his head. He wanted a whip and to use it on her, again and again. He had to stand there waiting for reasons to take the place of the blood. The bowed white nape of her neck jerked with this mad laughter. She was having hysteria. She needed a slap, several. The Merridews would hear. Goole, he remembered, Goole hit her, again and again. Oh, he could see why, he could see why. But he—he stood there, watching. . . .

" Minty," he managed, in a voice that seemed to belong to someone else, " believe it or not, I loved you but I also love my family."

" Ah ! At last. Here it comes ! "

Then she sat up straight-faced and looked at him. " Well,

if you love your family, you won't think twice about giving Jim his full remission, will you? Because if you do think twice about it I won't think twice about giving your letter to Jim and everyone else, too! Now you've got it, Mr. Ayrton, 'straight,' if I may quote you. You see, I owe him something. (She was acting to herself, he suddenly saw it: Minty the heroine.) More than someone like you could ever understand." Her voice dropped and she said with intensity, " But about one thing you were right. It's my fault he's where he is. I was doing the usual, if you want to know, doing what I always do, see? —what I'd do with Liversey, a leper or a Warden when I feel like it—doing that when I belonged to him, when I was his, only his and only wanting him."

She was trying to convince herself. Tears, built-in perpetually to her voice, now for the first time showed in her eyes. After a moment, she turned, to escape his eyes it seemed, and he heard what might have been another person say calmly, " Oh, go away . . . you needn't worry about your letter. Or the remission."

The suddenness of the switch was too bewildering. He waited.

" Then give it to me, Minty," he said at last.

" I said you needn't worry."

He thought—and doubted. Finally, doubted. " Well, Minty, we've got evidence. You can be sent to prison for smuggling things into a Detention Centre. I've got to have that letter."

She turned and stared at him then through her tears, incredulous and dazed to the verge of indifference.

" You poor thing," she said. " Would Ella leave you? Would your little flattering empire collapse? "

He hated her then.

He said, "You're the great anti-nuclear pacifist, aren't you? But as a result of you and your cigarettes a boy got slashed almost to death. Was that Jim Goole's handiwork as well as yours?"

She blenched, never moved but remained staring at him. He went on, "Hadn't you better go back where you came from?"

The purpose in her eyes was worn indeed now. But something like a scab of stone was forming to protect it. Go back, he had said, but where to? He had mocked her to the core.

"Why torture each other, Minty," he said miserably. "You have only to give me my letter. So . . . quick!"

He stood there, staring at her. Suddenly he realised that he had lost.

At last he said, "Very well. But remember what your Mr. Goole did to you last time! If you value your pretty face I should keep quiet about that letter, damn' quiet!"

"Get out," she whispered.

28

ELLA WAS SEWING when he got in.

"Phil," she said with a slight tone of grudge, "have you got the 'flu—you look as white as a sheet . . . ?"

He said he was all right and sat down near the fire with the *Daily Telegraph*.

Later she said: "There's a letter from Christine. . . .

She was over at the Fawcetts' last Sunday. Jack has asked her to go to the hospital ball with him. Phil dear, are you sure you're all right? It's years since I've seen you like this."

" Like what? "

" Well, you look awful. Have you seen yourself? "

" I may have a chill," he said.

" Well, why don't you go up then. I can ring the Centre in the morning."

No, he said, he was all right.

" Frankly I'll be glad when they give you that change, Phil." She went out to the kitchen where she could be heard getting the tea ready.

He thought, she's right about the change. Things started going wrong as soon as we came here.

Minty, he thought, would die for Goole. And Ella would die for me.

" Tea's ready, Dad."

It was John, standing in the doorway.

Ayrton adjusted his spectacles and rose. He managed to touch his son: " Well, John . . ." The very precariousness of everything made him keep his hand on John's shoulder. " How're things? " he said. " Tell me what you did to-day."

He longed to hear about the most ordinary and dull events imaginable. Yet he did not take them in when John began to murmur.

" That's fine," he said, thinking, my family!—as though he had suddenly had a vision of it, himself included, all frozen, poised like the moment before an accident, all fated but still unharmed. The familiarity of the scene, the time on the clock, the vacancy that came into Ella's eyes as she picked up the *Daily Mirror* all added up to what he supposed was a norm of family happiness, an example of the one and only world which a man to-day could hope to influence and bring to as good a fruition as possible; just this—Ella and he, and the children. Indeed he had read somewhere that the family had become the largest meaningful unit and that this was why everyone loved the Queen and the Duke of Edinburgh, two ordinary family people, without power or glamour.

It had not been easy for him to construct a similar little unity from the confusion of his adolescence. In its way his achievement, which might pass unnoticed if not scorned by many, was not unlike those triumphs in follow-up reports which showed that X had gone straight for two years now, and held the same job for six months, and had a wife and child. The comparison was not absurd. When he had shed the identity of a professional Christian, of a monk, he had faced a world quite as strange as the one that greeted a man in the early morning at the prison gate; perhaps stranger because there are many ex-prisoners outside prisons but almost no ex-monks. In his case, of course, after-care had been exceptional, Ella had given him " a second wind "; he had made good—up to a point. Well, he was not prepared to risk losing what he had achieved with such difficulty merely because of a letter. He could see how silly he had been but not that he had done much wrong, except possibly in the last hour (already he could not bear to think of what he had said to Minty in her room). He held no objection to adultery as such: it usually made at least one person unhappier than before, often everyone. But there were " special situations " . . . when the unnatural condition of marriage had to be balanced . . . in the name of sanity and health. Anyhow, all this was academic because on another level, and he would always insist that it had been essentially " on another level," he could never regret what had happened, come what may. He had loved Minty—enjoyed a beautiful girl naked, yes, that for the first time—but loved her and still did—in spite of (perhaps all the more because of) what had just happened. But even this consideration did not alter the legal fact that a letter belonged to the person who wrote it. He had no alternative, therefore, but to recover his at once.

Ella turned the page. John left his baked beans unfinished and went to the telly. Ayrton sat there immured in himself, spreading butter thinly and precisely. Without the letter Minty would be powerless. Who would believe " Goole's bird " ? Or Goole ? No one in the world. Goole and Minty would scarcely believe themselves when they told people. People's faces would say to them . . . " We know your kind."

So he would " fetch " the letter . . . one Tuesday when Gwen went to her sister's ; about eight in the evening when Minty was out.

It was a funny feeling. Heady.

29

THE MOON WAS FULL that first Tuesday night. He told Ella he was taking Peter for a walk but when he got to the garage he shut the dog in the car. Amazed, the animal followed his movements with cocked ears, waiting for him to come round and get into the driving-seat. But Ayrton put out the light and shut the garage doors thinking Peter's expectation of an outing in the car would die slowly: he wouldn't bark for some time.

Ayrton hadn't gone a hundred yards before he heard a muffled yelp more like a hoot than a bark. He paused and tried to weigh how much it would matter, if Ella or anyone, later, were to remember hearing Peter bark. He stood there, listening and thinking. In his lecture notes was this phrase: "the superficial Rubicon which divides the ordinary citizen from the criminal." Not since boyhood had he had a view, so to speak, from the other side. How different everything seemed! How vast every detail—a dog's single bark loaded with portent. Should he go back ... take no chances? But what could he do with Peter? Letters of course belonged to the people who wrote them. Better to see it that way, feel it that way all the time, simply walk in and take back the thing that belonged to him—having first, of course, made sure she was out. The feeling of innocence would create its own rhythm of plausibility. He must keep things simple, be confident though not of course to the extent of going in by the front door—or being accompanied by a dog.

It was frosty. Light shone sparkling on the road from the Merridew front window and faintly on the field at the back from Minty's room. Muffled explosions and rifle-fire laced with violins proclaimed Albert in position. Ayrton found a tree opposite and stood behind it in shadow. The ground was like a great sheet under the sky, from hoar frost. His vigil started. Stars bored into his skull diamond sharp and rotating, dripping light or if resented, if pursued, sucked his senses upwards and drowned them in the dark outer shallows of infinity. He tried not to let himself think anything except that the letter belonged to him.

Peter yelped again, sounding faint from here. He'd say he had put him in there while he went over to the office to sign something. Peter's paws on the linoleum had made trouble in the past. . . . Peter's paws on cherry floors, Peter's flaws made cherry chores. . . .

An owl hooted ; the explosions gave place to voices.

Suddenly her shadow crossed the curtains. She had her hair down and was brushing it. He could see the long sweeping tugging movements and the upward straining of her neck almost as though she were looking up into rain and wind and drinking them. He could swear she was laughing and talking at the same time. Ayrton felt a pang. Hadn't they almost been like that together once ? It was all he had wanted. Minty's arms shot up with drooping hands like a child pretending to be a ghost, she whirled, recoiled and went back to her brushing. Albert and Minty ! The strange relationship magnified her in his eyes although it added another contradiction to her nature. For now she looked so natural and unneurotic. Her movements denoted freedom, confidence and strength. She might have been a happy daughter flirting harmlessly with her father before going out, confident of a close and legitimate guinea pig on which to practise wiles. Was it that Gwen and Albert had given her love or that she needed a retired porter and adulation before she could feel a grain of confidence. It's true, he thought, she has to be queen!

Her shadow moved and sank, distorted down the curtain. He heard Peter again, pained and incredulous in the distance. Then a muted pop record could be heard yearning at the back.

Again her shadow drifted past the curtain, arms high and curved this time, apparently in the attitude of a hula girl and then she vanished again. The record finished and the faint pallor of electric light on the back field suddenly gave place to instantaneous darkness. He heard a door bang and then the sound of her slipshod steps.

She passed quite close, leaning a little forward and looking at the ground with one hand at her throat, clasping the edges of her collar. Even there in the dark, almost invisible, her form gave the impression of slightly crazy fanaticism. She *blundered* forward—like a slap-happy paratrooper into action, Minty obstinate, bigoted, relentless in the execution of her extraordinary loyalty. For a moment he had an impulse to step out and make himself known, as though his feelings for her gave him certain rights, even powers which she could never resist. But he had sampled that fallacy once already. And he watched her pass, saw her features momentarily flash under the moon into a sudden, silvery mask of austere and bewildered sadness.

She was not carrying a handbag, and she was heading for Marshal's.

Marshal's farm and Pam's lodging were half a mile away.

He gave her five minutes and then crossed the road, keeping to shadows. The gate wheezed. On grass again, he heard lovers murmur throatily while battle raged. Explosions, violins and shouting. Then it all went faint as he turned into the black darkness of the side and back. An acrid smell of a dustbin. Now thumb on the latch. The door swung and the lovers and the battle surged up against his ears, streaming from under a broad, ragged line of white light ten foot ahead. He slid in, closing the door, and in darkness, looked to his left where Minty's door was ajar. He could smell her room without seeing it—her clothes, her scent and powder, the whole musky bouquet of her recent presence. Then he crossed the threshold . . . closed her door without a sound and switched on his torch. . . .

There was the usual untidyness. Garment after garment showed in the moving beam: orange peel, disordered make-up, the stained edition of Coleridge, the absurd magenta chain of Wrigley's wrappers, her writing-case, a new spirit lamp and an open tin of Nescafé. For a moment he was disconcerted by the familiarity of all these objects. They made her seem suddenly present but defenceless. Had she been lying there asleep under his eyes he would not have been so suddenly struck by pity. She had so little, in the way of weapons, with which to fight her extra-ordinary cause: a single letter to defend her illiterate and imprisoned champion. And now he must take it.

Quickly, too !

Having found the door open at the back he had strolled in and picked up what belonged to him.

Her bag was by her bed. . . .

He opened it and a smell of scent emerged evoking her presence almost tangibly. His fingers turned fast from a hard edge of mirror to crumpled handkerchief, chewing gum, purse, lipstick, nail file and orange stick. A frayed fringe of letters and papers packed tight into a compartment gave him a feeling of success imminent. First some Italianate handwriting, a sonnet, a picture postcard of Picasso's " Travelling Tumblers " and another of a woman sitting on sands with a little boy, " Blue period," (he began to hurry)—more letters, one faded, decades old, handwritings, then a photograph—herself and a young man like a Spaniard, yes, Goole leaning against a shabby lorry, he holding a guitar, she with her arm round him. Ayrton put this out on the table, wanting to look at it again and then raised another photograph of what might have been a triumphant banker, a man with a leonine beard, pince-nez and flashing eyes and unpleasant mouth. For some reason a crude halo, with rays spearing outwards, had been drawn roughly round his head in green ink. Photo Nerino: Florence. Her father? Ayrton hurried . . . keys, envelope addressed to Miss Heidi Roberts, Birmingham address, registered envelope with four £1 notes in it addressed to " Miss Aminta Villiers," and provisional driving licence issued in Hereford, same name . . . but no sign of his letter. He put the bag down and began searching, drawers, pockets, the cupboard and then under things . . . her pillow, mattress, folds of clothes.

And then—suddenly—he heard steps . . . outside the window, coming round the corner of the house outside, *clip clip* down the concrete path. Minty! He put out his torch. The steps paused.

They came on again then—slower. He could not move. He heard the back door opening. Then she paused again. But not for long. Suddenly she clicked the latch, pushed the door and smothered on the light, all in one movement.

One of his hands was still buried in scarves and handkerchiefs. But what did it matter where his hand was?

She loitered in looking at the mess he had made and at the photo of herself and Goole which he had put on one side for inspection; then, stopping beside the bed, she considered him with an expression of morose triumph and mockery.

"Couldn't you find it?" she said as calmly as if she had asked him to look for it.

He couldn't speak.

After a moment she said: "Did you think I might have left it out for you?"

She smiled then, quite normally, as though the situation in which they found themselves was commonplace and his behaviour, in the circumstances, conventional. He heard his voice with a slight shock, as though he had never expected to hear it again: "Well, Minty, since you put it like that . . ." and he stared at her incredulously searching for further confirmation that . . . that she found it possible to be fair, quite fair . . . level-headed.

She smiled encouragingly. He thought: it's true: we were lovers, intimates. There must always be limits to the hostility that either of us could feel for the other.

"Yes," he said at last, "I'm sure you *might* have considered leaving the letter out for me—since it belongs to me."

He forced the ghost of a smile, offered some charm.

Then she (it was like when she thanked him for his letter in the field) turned away, stifling a snort-laugh with her wrist and bending over a bit to ease the violence of the paroxysm, accepted the support of the bed, from where finally she stared up at him, out of her great black eye-shadows, stared and stared as though now at last she did give up, communication being impossible.

She was acting of course, she always was . . . up to a point.

But she went on looking at him like this, went on and on till she said: " Burglary's lawful when it's done by you, is it ? "

He saw then how her recent calmness had tricked him into parading his self-justification. He saw, too, now what she must think of his attempt to " act freely "—meet people like Goole and herself on what he imagined to be an equal footing. Moments passed.

" Do you keep it on you ? " he said suddenly, meeting her eyes.

She must have noticed a change in his voice, because of the way she looked when she said " Yes " after the strangest hesitation.

" Give it to me then——" he said, and approached her.

She made the mistake of laughing again even though on this occasion it was done instinctively to master her fear. Afterwards he remembered her adam's-apple, the swelling in the middle of her round throat as she leant back, coiling up her knees and raising a hand, and then the increase of fear in her face, the closeness of her struggling body, the sudden convulsion of effort as his hands knit on throat. He heard a scream—like suddenly rent material and felt a sense of freedom, terrible, full of destruction and love, too, and with every second that passed, less consciousness, less knowledge of what he was doing, where . . . who he was. . . .

A searing pain along his cheek and in his knee-cap and the sight of somebody he didn't recognise, a face that called to him, through noise, confusion, pain and disappointment to remember what he was doing brought him round; woke him in a strange place, beside an overturned table and scattered clothes and letters—wherever he looked, letters and picture postcards spread over the floor.

He was near the window. She was still on the bed, leaning right forward, feeling her neck with her eyes closed, groaning.

Surely not. . . . Not him.

How long after, he never knew, when she was still there, very slowly moving her hands up and down on either side of her neck, he had the impression he tried to explain.

" Go away," she whispered. " Don't you know *yet*— you're *mad*."

She pronounced these words frantically as though trying to get through in an emergency, or an impossible trunk wire. They got through. They felt like the last words ever to get through. And in particular he remembered the word *yet*.

He went cold with dread, with a sense of absolute loneliness.

Because the proof of what she said seemed to leap at him from the overturned table and from her scattered belongings. He hadn't heard the table go over: so what else hadn't he heard—all his life ? He got up and bent down picking things up one after the other. She might scream any moment. Indeed, why hadn't she ? *Why ?* (He could still hope.) " I'm going," he whispered. At the door he looked back. She was still feeling her neck and leaning forward. A sudden gust of crowd laughter like a switch turned on and then off came from under the living-room door. He wanted to say something. He heard a tiny " *plap* " like the first drop of a thunderstorm falling in vegetation, and he saw a newspaper lying below her face : a tear must have fallen on it. He remembered that, because he had never been able to imagine her crying. He had wanted to stay and felt he had a right to. Instead, a moment later, he was under the stars, wanting the day of their changed pattern to be now.

30

THE FOLLOWING DAY he conducted a party of Commonwealth officials round Edgecliffe and while they had biscuits and coffee in the chapel he told them his methods.

Then a day passed and another day.

What he " was " and what Minty might have already done with his letter he relegated by an act of will to that category of remote concern which included such matters as whether or not atomic weapons would ever again be used.

Life must go on. For the occasion he developed another mask, a children's party one this time perhaps, thin with cheap elastic round the ears. But it was better than nothing and in it he functioned—and waited.

On the fourth day Ella rang through to the office in the morning and said, " There's a man to see you, Phil."

This was how he had expected it to come : discreetly at first. Even courteously.

" I've got my rounds now, dear. Can he wait ? "

" He's from the school."

" What school ? " Ayrton murmured.

" John's, of course."

" John's . . ."

" I'd like you to come, Phil," Ella said, sounding suddenly tearful.

" Who is the man, what is he ? "

" Oh, I don't know I'm sure," she said irritably. " It's about John. I'm sure I don't know what he's talking about." She didn't ring off but nor did she say anything more, she remained at the telephone as though expecting him to say something that would explain matters or even take the man away. She said, " He's here, Phil, now."

" I'll come," he said.

There was a Mini-Minor in front of Shang-ri-la with a new raincoat, a Tyrolean-type gent's hat and a number of typed papers lying on the front seat. The whole effect was all too familiar : bureaucracy, medium level.

From the hall he heard Ella in the kitchen. He called to her but she didn't answer.

The visitor was by himself in the living-room on his feet and looking, apparently, at the pictures. He was a cheerful, balding, paunchy thirty with rimless spectacles and bright bow-tie. Gold propelling pencil and ballpen peeped from the waistcoat of his new check suit. An atmosphere of prosperity, extroversion and superficial efficiency emanated from his person, but there was something flabby and over-soaped about his skin which for some reason made the cheerfulness seem cynical. He might have been a salesman for a firm of electric gadgets. Only his eyes were different. They were soft, Jewish, " deep." They gave to the first impression of slickness a slightly disturbing other dimension which might be good, might be bad.

As they shook hands he said, " Benson, from the Children's Office—indirectly," then in a tone that had something disturbingly encouraging about it, he explained Mrs. Ayrton was just making a cup of tea and this might perhaps " be an opportunity " because really he had wanted a few moments to talk to Ayrton alone.

Ayrton motioned him to a chair and sat on the sofa facing him. Well, said Benson, as he had already explained to Mrs. Ayrton, John's headmaster had got in touch with the Education Authority, " as is now the practice in cases like this." The Education Authority then asked " us " . . .

" But who are you ? "

" I'm the psychological worker with the Children's Office."

Benson smiled agreeably and then looked serious, an expression which did not suit his face at all. He even adjusted his pince-nez with finger and thumb, spanned wide. " This may come as rather a shock to you, Mr. Ayrton," he said. " But not to worry. Your son is suspected of stealing some things that had been missed and were found in his locker yesterday ; with them was a diamond ring." (Here Benson paused, looking at Ayrton.) " He refused to say where he got the ring but I get the impression from your wife that it is hers. . . . She tells me she has always let him have it when he wanted it . . . to play with. . . ."

At last Ayrton said, " She knew where it was."

" With John ? " said Benson.

" I don't know . . . she told me she knew."

A face was all that was needed. No : he didn't mind Benson asking questions. Let him go ahead. And Benson did. Ella brought in tea and he squeezed her hand. She was crying.

And half an hour later, when the questions were over, he said, No, neither he nor his wife would object to John attending the clinic. He doubted if Ella would go; and he doubted if he would have the time. But he would try, yes, he would try, if it would help. And he appreciated the headmaster's agreement to do nothing—meanwhile.

The humiliation of letting his child be put under the care, possibly of young Mr. Benson himself, left him speechless.

How had it happened? Well, it had happened.

Why fight any more? This was no place for a family; perhaps no era for a family. Christine had been glad to go. And why struggle to get John a private education. Benson's world would win in the end. By resisting one was merely prolonging John's pain and loading him with a dilemma that had better die with his father.

Plunged in silence, Ayrton sat thinking that he knew this man whom he had never met before, very well indeed. Benson, he decided, was " representative." Like that news-caster, chick who had never suffered, out of a Cellophane shell-less egg, he should have been a historian and a poet and above all *a native* before he should presume to psycho-logise. All the same he would win. There was, in the future, no alternative to Benson's world—that world which at best had faith in so-called facts and " social sciences," at worst, and most usually, faith in nothing. As he had loved Minty on sight, so now he despised Mr. Benson with the same immediacy. And now with bowed head, he felt how his clothes, his room, his whole family situation must appear " wrong," ruined, dated to a man whom he despised yet who, with the full support of the national atmosphere and all contemporary trends, was in a position to despise him. Minty and some of the inmates, yes, they at least had seemed to make a faith out of the absence of faith, made roots out of a cult of having no roots. But this man here had no nationality, no creed, no past, no culture in the sense of *echo* : he was like the man in the television set who read the news—newborn at thirty. Facts ! What were facts by themselves ? Nothing ! Worse, chaos. Benson was a ball of unrelated facts congealed with varnish. Compared to an aboriginee the dullness of this New Man had cataclysmic significance.

Soon Benson would hear that Ayrton had once been a monk. Ah ! he would think—ah ; failed—couldn't settle down and make a good honest life's work out of a decent honest-to-God systematic neurosis. Well—it was Benson's world now. A new Creation. Matter was making man in its own image and the priests would be merely statisticians and mechanics of the mind. All values relative. All actions determined. Efficiency would dictate all shapes, all functions. In time boredom would raise nuclear war to the level of a salvation, prayed for but undeserved. But before it came, as it would, just to while away the years the Bensons would be priest-entertainers because in dealing with neurotics, that is to say everyone, they would restore some of the interest and drama which once belonged to religion.

Carried away by the passion of his resentment Ayrton lost the thread of what Benson was saying. He rose—asked to be forgiven : he had to return. He hoped Benson would arrange times and so on with his wife.

Then he went through to the kitchen and pressed Ella's hand, asking her to go through again. He'd come back, he said, as soon as he could.

He tried to control his rage, his grief, his impotence. He pictured John. How long since he had talked to him, played with him ? Tenderness and guilt surged chaotically in his breast.

31

WHEN AYRTON RETURNED to the house Gwen was in the hall putting on her coat. She averted her eyes but her face was eloquent. She knew.

"He's just a boy, Mr. Ayrton, just a child!"

She put a knuckle to one eye and smeared a tear into extinction. It had probably been a man rather like Ayrton who had once assured her that her child would have a better chance in life if it was put to a home for adoption. But she forgave. It's Benson's job, Ayrton thought, he's got to do it.

"How's my wife . . . ?" Ayrton said.

Gwen eyed him, "D'you know what I think, Mr. Ayrton . . . it hasn't come to her yet."

He knew too well what she meant.

Ella was at the sink. She didn't turn as he entered.

"How did you get on with Benson?" he said.

"We didn't," she said tearfully. "If that school of John's supervised the children as much as it did the parents they wouldn't miss things. Took my ring indeed, I said, didn't you ever take your mother's ring, you must have been unnatural."

"John's eight now, dear."

"Don't *you* start, Phil."

"A boy of eight doesn't usually go in for playing with jewellery, Ella."

" He was playing me up for all they know."

" Ella dear, why did you tell me you'd found the ring ? "

" Well, I had found it, hadn't I ? I knew where it was. . . ."

He didn't dare corner her—or anyone, not now.

She said: " Anyhow . . . he's to go to some clinic. I don't know ! The address is on the humming-birds."

He gave her shoulders a squeeze as much as to say they were all in the pie together and it would pass, but she said, " Oh, I'm not worrying."

" What d'you mean . . . ? "

" They give him milk he doesn't need at eleven so they can give him clinic too for all I care."

" Let's hope it helps."

" I might have guessed you'd fall for it, Phil. Why don't you put him inside with yours ? "

" Ella—it's mad to talk like this."

" Mad ! " she laughed. " It would be a wonder if we weren't, wouldn't it, up here. I don't know. . . ." She was going to cry properly now. Perhaps break down completely. He felt fear, astringence, guilt, a desire for order. He adjusted his glasses.

She turned away and merely raised the corner of the oven cloth to one eye.

" Mad ! " she repeated. " I like that."

" You told Gwen," he said easily.

" What's the harm ? "

Looking at her inturned eyes he saw that her own private version of what had happened remained intact. She was picturing a toddler, a two-year-old, walking away on one of those uncertain, tottering journeys with some new find, something bright, pleasing to touch and valued by other people ; she saw him sensitively prod and pull it about, finally forgetting its separate existence, raise it to its mouth. . . . "Little scamp, so that's where you are . . . and my ring, too ! "

Everything was dissolving. The patterns were too wrong. They were turning to their opposite—chaos. Ella said, " Christine can't manage the concert. She's spending the day with the Fawcetts."

" I'm glad she's making friends. Ella—what are we going to say to John ? "

" Well, you'd better have it out with him, hadn't you ? Aren't you used to that sort of thing ? "

When he came in that evening, he found John at his homework copying a picture of a Norman soldier. The child's chalks bit deeper into the paper when he sensed his father behind him. " What's been happening at school, John ? " Ayrton said kindly. " Can you tell me all about it ? "

After a moment's silence, John said, " Joey Spencer broke a window."

" But what's all this about a ring ? . . . Did you take Mummy's ring, John ? "

Minutes passed during which there was nothing but the sound of the boy's chalks on the paper, and the bowed position of his body. Ayrton questioned him again. Gradually the silence changed in quality. It became intimidating because it revealed what surely he should have noticed long, long ago, that his son *was somewhere else.*

And he . . . where had he been ?

32

GOOLE DID THE MILE in 6 minutes 20 seconds three months ago and in 4 minutes 40 seconds his last week. He got a blue ribbon. Some did better at Edgecliffe than Goole. Childersley, for instance, in 1960 did well at Edgecliffe. He did the mile in 4 minutes 30 seconds and lost no remission. He got a red ribbon and now wrote from Liverpool to his probation officer (who forwarded a carbon of the letter) that he was earning £15 a week and engaged to be married. So perhaps the mile mattered. Ayrton pinned the carbon of the letter on the notice board under the timings for the mile and the lengths for the long-jump.

And there was the towel-horse. In the joiner's shop Goole had finished a towel-horse and was to be allowed, under Home Office dispensation which came through only last month, to take it away with him. Ayrton heard the instructor say: "You're lucky, Goole: not everyone goes away with a towel-horse."

Things were moving, the great world moving all the time and over Edgecliffe the sky was moving, full of heavy grey clouds. In fact the weather closed in that week; for days on end there was a sharp wind that jumped round corners promising snow. Wild geese, evoking previous winters at Edgecliffe, began to work the big fields behind Marshal's. Dawn and dusk they straggled over the Centre, talking purposefully to each other and in the distance the tips of their wings flickered like the fringe of a multi-footed insect.

He saw Minty sometimes—in the distance going about her tasks; Jefferies said he had again seen her in the George and had told all officers they were not to have anything to do with her. Gwen sometimes mentioned her, quite naturally, proving with every look and syllable that she, too, still knew nothing. Even Pam, whom he met one day in Buxton, showed no sign of special knowledge.

The day came when he took John seventeen miles into Eardsley to see Benson. On arrival his son was taken away by a Miss Vaughan to the " play therapy " room while Ayrton waited on a long wooden bench.

Beside him a distraught and untidy-looking woman pestered a child that looked as if it had been born before the days of National Dried Milk and free orange juice. The mothers had that self-conscious and guilty look which working-class mothers (who still have that kind of child) do have. Now and again she looked apprehensively at Ayrton as though he might be an inspector of some kind sent out into the waiting-room to get advance information. She adjured her child to leave him alone on pain of a slap. Soon Benson came outside with a man who immediately tried to look as if he hadn't been with Benson inside. " Hallo there—with you in a minute," Benson said in a gaily *entre nous* tone which promoted Ayrton a little. " Now, Mrs. Clayton and Cathy—how's Cathy ! " Cathy stared up through tangled hair and grime like a pygmy looking at a quite unusual parrot in a top bough. She seemed taken out of herself for a moment by sheer surprise. The door closed and Ayrton read a recipe for stuffed tomatoes and a description of braking tests in the Monte Carlo Rally.

Then it was his turn.

There was a calendar with Margot Fonteyn in colour dancing Petrochka besides Benson's tyrolean hat and curtains in which red sea-horses in black squares faced green sea-horses in red squares.

Cheer up, Ayrton told himself, you are not alone. The popular press seldom has difficulty in finding clergymen whose joy it is to walk round Woolworth's with a mirror fixed to the end of a walking-stick, a mirror which, when suitably placed, gives a worm's eye view, upwards, of underclothes filled with sturdy thighs, of stockings that swell towards the top till they give up, burst into a cornucopia of white mottled flesh, ambrosial warmth, flounces, fancy borders where the eye can nest at last in privy darkness; or in finding a doctor whose stethoscope finally becomes a stalking horse round the most congenial breasts in the practice, or a schoolmaster who accommodates himself at last for one brief fatal corridor minute to the ruling passion of a fifteen-year-old in C stream handicraft. Far from alone, he thought, as he sat down in the indicated chair and watched Benson press the release button on top of his gold Biro and smile downwards at paper in a way that was no doubt meant to be encouraging, kindly and philosophic, but even so could not escape conveying irony shot with indifference, the whole flavoured with fatigue. (He glanced at his wonderful watch.) Supposing, Ayrton thought, I told him about Minty. Would he ask for extra time, another period, a week, say half an hour? And about my spell as a monk? Another hour at least for that too?

The first week Benson merely asked more questions but at the second session he addressed his blotter in quite a fussy fashion, smiling slightly as though this psychology lark needed a sense of humour just like all the other larks. Indeed at moments he reminded Ayrton of Minty being polite : self-control precarious.

" Miss Vaughan and I had a talk about John, Mr. Ayrton, and we're quite agreed on the basic issue. If you'll allow me to speak frankly : we think John is stuck—probably near the age where his mother would unconsciously like him to be stuck. Three or four years back, at an age that is, when she was useful to him, when he provided her with a purpose in life. Now what's holding him there ? . . . " (Mr. Benson made another fussy arrangement of a pen and again his mouth drifted into a smile like something coming unmoored.) He went on, " By now he should be identifying with you and the world of men, the father's world. For some reason he can't. While it's certainly true that his mother's holding him back, (the theft of one of her most intimate belongings suggests a violent desire to break her hold) that seems to us not the whole problem. You see, we very much wonder whether he isn't prevented from identifying with you mainly *by you yourself*. The fact is we've had cases like this before—sons of policemen, judges, schoolmasters—of people whose professional lives consist a good deal in wearing a mask of authority, if you follow me. Now does it sometimes happen you come home tired and, having adopted a certain authoritarian manner with prisoners all day and got in a rut, you stay that way with your wife and child ? You see, that might make you seem unapproachable to your son and prevent him from identifying. It might even be enough to bind your wife and son against you, unconsciously of course."

" Of course," Ayrton said.

" Does any of that make sense to you ? "

" You're suggesting I'm a tyrant. . . ."

" Why put it so strongly ? Look. You can do the trick yourself. Try to make a point of doing something every evening with him, perhaps even put on different clothes, an old sports jacket—anything—so that you don't look like the chap who runs a D.C. ; know the sort of thing ?—relax, be yourself. . . . We all have to wear masks of various kinds but it gets serious when we can't occasionally take the mask off. Try throwing the mask right away, Mr. Ayrton, when you get back from work. . . . Why d'you smile ? I assure you it's worth considering."

" The mask ? . . . I see. Do you think . . . throw it *right* away ? "

Benson looked puzzled.

Ayrton smiled, dismissing his own question and thanked Benson. How could he embark ? Besides, with Benson, where to ?

Later, back at home, he put on a sports shirt after tea and got down on the floor. It was difficult to have faith in the kind of attentions which he believed he had never neglected and which he thought should come naturally or not at all. However he had to admit that, whatever may have been the reason, John seemed to improve, became less like a spy with a bomb.

Then Goole came up for Last Interview.

A month ago Ayrton would have spent himself in trying to prise a chink in that armour but to-day he could only go through the motions of attempted contact. He told Goole to sit down but scarcely met his eyes. Would Goole go straight ? Yes. Would he keep up his reading lessons with the help of the After-Care Associations ? Yes. Would he marry this girl who had stood by him? Yes, he thought he would. And was she the right kind of girl for him? Yes, he thought she was.

Once he paused as though hypnotised by the link of which Goole was still unconscious. There was much he would have liked to know: how Goole and Minty had come together and which of them had made the running; liked also to have known if Goole had been responsible for the slashing of Hallows. The name " Miss Roberts " hung at the parted threshold of his lips. Why not? Goole knew that he had met her, read her letters . . . so why not mention her in more detail, recommend her to him as someone who could keep him straight, praise her to him and confide her to his protection. Somehow the words would not come.

Instead Ayrton found himself returning to questions about Goole's plans for the future. As long as the man was standing there in front of him, he felt he had some contact, however vicarious, with Minty—which was what he had now lacked for weeks on end.

When at last he came to the end of all the things he could feasibly say the thought occurred to him that if Minty did nothing about the letter, simply went away with Goole in a few days' time then he would never see her again and that therefore, in a sense, this moment, here with Goole, was his last opportunity of having anything to do with her. It was then he heard himself say: " Would you like us to ask Miss Roberts to the concert? "

Goole looked suspicious as though there must be a trap. Ayrton explained the special circumstances. Relatives and girl-friends were normally not invited only because they lived so far away. Miss Roberts had become a local person.

Goole agreed then—without enthusiasm.

" All right, that's all, Goole."

Afterwards he wasn't sure why he had done it. There might have been better ways of seeing Minty again. At the concert he would probably only see her in the distance and certainly have no chance of talking to her. No. He decided it had been the result of a feeling which he had had now for years, getting stronger and stronger, that people convicted of crimes, far from being deprived of contact with society, should be given as much of it as possible—should have women and meaningful work and all things likely to nourish a more positive attitude to life. In the world as it is to-day, a penal settlement run on these lines had a chance of becoming the ideal place to live. Of course, he could not, as he would have liked to, pull up all the wire round Edgecliffe and invite the girl-friends of all the inmates. But he could obey an impulse—and invite Minty to the concert so that she could hear Goole sing. A small beginning indeed for his idea. Perhaps. But it did not feel small. When Ayrton gave instructions to the part-time civilian secretary to send Miss Bates an invitation to the concert, he felt almost the God of a new Genesis, putting Minty and Goole down together to make what the outside world usually was not—a community.

The following day Jefferies brought in a police report on Minty. It gave her real name as Aminta Mary Villiers, daughter of Colonel Ivo Villiers believed to be living in France and Georgina Thorpe of Iverneagh Court, Kensington. She had been on probation for shoplifting in the Birmingham area two years ago. In the last twelve months she had worked as an occasional traveller for Horton's Toys, demonstrating puppets to shops in the Midlands. There was a likelihood she had supplemented her income by immoral earnings in which activity she was alleged to have been associated with Goole at the time of the latter's arrest. . . .

Ayrton heard Jefferies's breathing as he read it through a second time.

Goole a ponce . . . Minty a tart?

No one knew better than Ayrton that the world of crime has none of the glamour and excitement which is often imputed to it by the public which spends millions of pounds a year reading about it. The criminal's commonest characteristics—he knew to be—an almost unspeakable unhappiness, confusion that bordered on madness, loneliness that rivalled the grave, without the grave's anæsthesia, and sometimes an ugliness, which like Keats's "Beauty," deserved the big U of a spiritual concept.

And yet when he read this factual assessment of Goole and Minty as two of the sadder, more squalid type of criminal, his opinion of them did not change.

33

THE MOTTLED SKY at last yielded snow, covering the scruffy cinder paths and the mangy football pitch, muffling the boots of the squads and making congenial work for parties with shovels. Shang-ri-la looked almost pretty when the sun came out. Diamonds gleamed in the contraption that hung above the porch and long purple shadows slanted away to the pillow-like rise which yesterday had been the fence. Round the Centre familiar shapes of ugly poles and wire became unrecognisably thick, like bandaged limbs, and from the boiler-house gutter xylophones of ice hung, brilliant with many-coloured light. Wherever the eye turned there seemed to be a covering of cheerful artifice for all that was drab, utilitarian and penal. Edgecliffe, by this white miracle, looked, for once, a fit place for celebration.

The concert was the one relaxation of the year and was held more to bring the neighbourhood into some sympathy with the Centre than to give pleasure to the inmates. As entertainment it was poor. Smallness of numbers, shortness of sentences and the strict limits on intercommunication in daily life (to say nothing of the " tempo ") prevented inmates from even discovering let alone rehearsing the talent that might be available. Yet strangely enough there was always someone who for a few minutes stood out and made the surroundings seem small-minded if not actually mad. Last year it had been a man whistling, this year it might be Goole. Even so Ayrton doubted if Minty would come. She always looked so haunted when alone . . . had to have someone with her *she owned*. Well, he could not and would not invite Pam.

Ella did not want to attend this year but Benson had thought she should, and take John with her. So Ayrton took them across. By then the news of John's trouble at school had spread. Furtive glances were stolen in his direction and Beasley, already in his seat, made a point of speaking to the boy heartily and affectionately. Ella reacted by asking after Mrs. Beasley in a candidly pessimistic tone which the vicar was able to refute by the spirit but not by the substance of his reply. " It's a shame, for her : one thing after another," said Ella, as though ill-health was similar to delinquency—in every respect.

The alderman arrived and the Hon. Mrs. Cunliffe who had been on the board when Edgecliffe was an orphanage.

Ayrton stood at the door, welcoming.

Minty was the last guest to come, and with her was Pam. Both were chewing and you could not have got a knife between them, even as they walked. Seeing him from a distance, Minty looked down and put up a hand to her hair as though to protect herself from some kind of extreme reaction. For fifteen feet she used Pam as guidance. Only when within a foot of him, did she raise her eyes, liquid with suppressed emotion, and look him in the face.

"I brought Pam," she said.

"So I see."

His tone did nothing to quench the liquid look. (Was it laughter—or just " nerves " ?)

She said, "I hope you don't mind. We heard in the village you like to get as many respectable citizens as possible."

Whatever may have been his motives in asking her to come they had probably included a desire to placate. Perhaps Minty suspected this for she contrived to look unusually implacable. If her expression communicated anything specific it was simply defiance of any objection he might make to Pam or indeed to anything she chose to do on these premises. She had stopped, conspicuously, in front of him. A death-grey strand of slimy rubber suddenly appeared, extended, between her front teeth and then vanished as it was squashed flat in a stony, close-lipped smile. Her heels were so high she could look down on him, which she did with a certain pleasure. The moment seemed long for it had to deal with so much that could not be said. It was not only his letter which she held over him, it was her bruised throat . . . and this penal dining-room with its fifteen-foot coloured diagram of how to hold your knife and fork " The right way " . . . " The wrong way."

" You'll find seats over there," he said.

They sat behind Jefferies and were hardly settled before a hush fell. Something like thunder, or was it a train in a tunnel, then broke upon everyone's ears. From level inarticulate vibration it emerged into rhythm and became recognisable as the tread of many gym shoes marching in step. Cut by a sharp shout the noise ceased. Another shout and it started again, lighter this time as the sections of eight inmates at a time were marched in.

Ayrton saw Minty looking round as the boys in their dyed battledress tunics marched with arms swinging shoulder high to their places. As soon as they were seated, they immediately folded their arms and kept them like that so they looked like rows of people in strait-jackets. This position was routine (to keep hands out of mischief) but at the annual concert it was always dropped. Jefferies, Ayrton thought, must have given orders to the contrary.

Going out in front to welcome the guests, he said, " All right, lads—sit at ease. . . ."

At first the boys looked uncertainly at each other to see if they had not been mistaken in what they had heard, then one and gradually others loosened their arms and let them go to their laps, their thighs and chair edges clumsily, like superfluous attachments.

Minty was still looking round, trying to spot Goole.

Jefferies, judging by his face, had seen her and was looking at Ayrton almost peacefully as though now he knew he was mad. Ayrton met the Deputy's eyes briefly and indifferently, then said a few words of welcome, wishing everyone a happy Christmas.

Ayrton stood down and at once a man came out of the

" stage," that is, the kitchen door and sat down at the upright grand under the diagram of the knife and fork. Looking sideways he sang in the manner of Cliff Richards. Then he was replaced and there was a story about an Irishman, a Scotsman and an Englishman, then the "Mountains of Mourne," then a brisk take-off of a drunk being copped for speeding. The clapping was thin, the joy meagre as a ration of margarine. Then suddenly Goole came on with a guitar, borrowed presumably for him by one of the staff.

He moved with assurance, positioned himself easily and professionally on the edge of a table, one leg on the ground, one leg up under his half-extended elbow. Shufflings, snifflings and creaks died out. The atmosphere in the room changed absolutely before a note was heard. Goole frowned at the instrument as though it were alive and holding out against him. His fat fingers suddenly seemed to pinch all the strings at once and then to fan out immediately into an apologetic caress, these movements being answered by a staccato explosion of sound and an exquisitely articulated run in a tight, minor chord. Then smothering the resonance, his head shook slightly as though denying what had happened and challenging what was to come. Now he suddenly lifted his head and cried out one harsh word that seemed to be several notes at once, like the chord he struck with it. " *Aiiee-oh* " and then another cry and more chords. The effect was startling in that place : North African and the very anthem of unrestrained emotion. Full of feeling but *what* feeling ? It was the raw material of all feeling, unrefined, undifferentiated and violent. And then incredibly it was followed by the air of " Waltzing Matilda " picked out on one string . . . as though a man singing the tune in the distance was coming nearer and nearer ... till suddenly Goole's voice emerged, alone, calm, full of the casualness of the vagabond. Then suddenly that cry again like an interruption from fate, followed by wild premonitory, thrumming chords.

Ayrton was reminded a little of the narrative songs of the Hungarian gipsies recounting the legendary exploits of heroes in battles against the Turks. The harsh cry wavered on the semitones of the east and seemed about to break into recitative describing battle but then, like a gull abandoning the invisible unaccountable wind, went on into the wingbeat of the often-heard tune. It was astonishing. Goole was an artist and Ayrton felt addressed by him, also taken out of himself for the first time for weeks. In the first verse, in the vagabond's song he experienced some of the pleasures of his days off on Edgecliffe Common, the distance shimmering in the amber heat, poplar and birch leaves cool as the sound of a girl's cotton dress, ponds speckled with insects.

" *Under the shade of a Koolibar tree.*"

No time, only existence; only the path and the prey " *and he sang as he put that Jumbuk in his tucker bag. . . .*"

The second verse was more liberally interrupted with explosive interruptions heralding the approach of misfortune. " *Down came a Squire mounted on his thoroughbred.*"

Squire ! Someone laughed and Ayrton smiled. Then the troopers " *one . . . two . . . three* " Goole sang this slowly, raising his eyes to the far wall, with fractional pauses between each word as though he had seen first one, finally three policemen, men without names or significance except in their personification of all that was antipathetic. After the word " one " there was still hope and even pleasure and defiance; then " two " was stiffened with terrible premonition. " Three " was over the worst—faint and clear, on another level from the other words. Acceptant.

Then the cry and explosion of chords which followed seemed to assimilate the room and the whole world as part of the instrument. Bitter laughter at one moment floated on this extraordinary storm of sound. It was the imaginary destruction of the enemy, all the enemies. But only imaginary. Reality was now intolerable but even the shout, " *You'll never catch me alive* " was not enough. Enraged apparently by the inadequacy and futility of the single statement and the limitations of the lyrical form, Goole went on as though he were his own chorus coming in, determined to make an epic of a single line. " *You'll never catch me alive you'll never catch me alive alive, said he* " until suddenly with a thump of a flat hand on the strings he amputated the resonance. The man in the song was dead, crushed at the bottom of the chasm.

Goole made the return of the voice a thrilling surprise. Its peacefulness was mocking, tender, haunting, beautiful as the vast virgin country which in time had swallowed the one bagman and then the Squire and the other of the three human specks. Only the voice remained, reiterating the irresistible invitation to all who did not wish to be dead in life : to freedom :

> " *Waltzing Matilda, waltzing Matilda, who'll go*
> *a-waltzing Matilda with me.*"

The applause could not wait and had to sweep away the last note. Ella had mobile tears on her cheeks but a look of apprehension. She had been destroyed, who hadn't been ? Except Goole, who after a vestige of a bow, only one, looked down at his instrument, and stayed still.

While clapping Ayrton cast a glance over his shoulder. Minty was hardly clapping at all. Her face was private, religious and Pam, deprived of her *raison d'être*, had no courage to meet Ayrton's eyes, simply looked past him self-consciously and uneasily : she was alone now.

Goole stepped down and disappeared in the crowd.

Ayrton hardly noticed the rest of the show, or Jack Beasley summing up. As people rose he turned round to look at Minty for what he must hope would be the last time, turned with a smile of remote congratulation, friendliness and diffident farewell. He was prepared to find her expression unattractive, possessive, aggressive and contemptuous, prepared to find her enjoying vicarious prestige and limelight, really rolling in ownership.

Instead—she wasn't there . . . wasn't anywhere. She must have gone before anyone.

Why ? To avoid him ?

He adjusted his glasses.

A few minutes later with Ella's arm through his and holding John's hand, he was tramping through the snow.

" That last one would make a fortune with a barrel organ," Ella said. " He had me quite upset."

" He'll be free Wednesday week," Ayrton said.

" Wasn't that the Bates girl sitting behind us. . . . How did she get there ?."

" I asked her."

" You do do funny things sometimes, Phil."

That's all then, Ayrton thought. Now I shall probably never see her again. But Goole I shall see, when he goes and then again when he asks for money. Some rendezvous at night. Or I shall hear his voice on the telephone. . . .

34

AYRTON ALWAYS SAW INMATES OFF from the front door, like a good host. Goole was to be no exception.

When the Centre's blue Dormobile swooshed past his window he opened the big note-book marked Interviews and at the bottom of Goole's page wrote, "Went out 20th December."

There was not much on the page, not at least below the words "Care not to provoke," written three months ago.

"Last Interview" stood as a mere heading over a blank. Ayrton closed the book.

Goole was standing at the main door beside a cardboard box with string round it and a towel-horse roughly swaddled in paper, a different Goole in tight trousers and short jacket and a fancy shirt with a sort of ruffle down the front. He looked a little like a Regency beau or highwayman.

Ayrton asked him if he thought he would be warm enough. Goole muttered a dour affirmative.

"Good-bye then, Goole . . ." Ayrton said and put out his hand.

He put it out in a take-it-or-leave-it manner as though to protect himself from a feeling of utter falsity, or the possibility of a snub.

But Goole took his hand. Their flesh touched.

"Good-bye, sir," Goole said.

Pictures on the Wall

How different probably was this Goole here in front of him to the Goole of his imagination. Ayrton took comfort for the future. This stocky twenty-year-old who could not read or write, this modern waif would soon return to a milieu as remote almost as a Polynesian island! Surely he would be unlikely to blackmail even if put up to it by Minty. For such a person an atmosphere of authority and impregnability would always attach to a Warden's person.

Ayrton tried to look stern, formidable and tough.

"You ought to be able to make a living with your voice, Goole."

"I might try," Goole said.

"Miss Roberts could help. She ought to write round for you. To agents . . ."

Goole cocked his head noncommittally and lowered his eyes. The Dormobile driver peered down sideways to see when he was coming. The engine was revving and the towel-horse was in.

Goole was free. As though knowing it he suddenly nodded and turned in a way that was final, valedictory and marginally polite. A few moments later the Dormobile was out of sight.

Minty . . . Goole! Three months ago the little daily drama of family life and professional promotion in the service had seemed too small, ego-centred and dreary to be endurable. The tail-end of life (it had seemed the world's life, too!) had unfolded before him as a depressing cul-de-sac while the early years of his youth had depreciated in the light of an older more honest vision. There had followed a sort of Flood in his mind, but on it as always an Ark. The animals went in two by two. Minty and Goole . . . Into them, perhaps he had projected a merely normal determination to believe in the future, but in the process

seen them as they were not: Goole as the good criminal
—the secret hero which his life had never dared acclaim,
and Minty as the redeemer, the " soul " he had looked for
often enough.

It was necessary to know very little about the people
concerned if you were to indulge such dreams. He did not
know Goole or Minty. But then neither did he know Ella
or Christine or John. He, like every other individual, was
enclosed. There were windows in the walls but on closer
inspection these usually turned out to be mirrors or, if
windows at all, then windows as it were of a train going
one way only, and showing a view never to be repeated
and never the same for a single moment. Truth changed
even as you observed it. And then, he thought, when a
man does not think, which is most of the time, there are
no windows—just pictures on the wall—the ones desired,
feared, thrown up by dim chains of association and feeling:
Minty . . . and Goole. Himself as Goole, Goole as himself.

His office seemed empty when he returned to it. At lunch he
heard Gwen talking to his wife: " That Minty, she up and
left—just like that. Never a word to Marshal she were
going, never even collected her money. We knew of course.
Albert got bedsocks and a kiss," Gwen laughed. " ' What'll
you do now ? ' I said to him. ' You'll miss her, too,' he
said, ' so don't give me that ! ' And d'you know I will,
too ! She said to me, ' Gwen, I'll always remember you,'
as though she was going to the wars or something. Well,
I said, ' Come back and see us, Minty. Get that boy of yours
to take a proper job and quit meddling with other folks—
and then come back and see us if we're still here.' She
was a nice clean-living type of girl. I never could see how

she ever got mixed up in bad company. I just hope nothing happens to her." Well might Gwen stare as she did then, into space, after Minty.

Ayrton found it hard to believe in his new condition. The habit of seeing the field outside and the roof of Gwen's cottage in terms of Minty lingered and affirmed her presence; so too did his conviction that her sense of theatre would never let her vanish without taking—or making—a last curtain. Besides, he believed she wanted revenge, not so much for what he done, as for what he had not done and this nagged him with the peculiar pain that attaches to unfulfilment on a level of development higher than the one normally lived. *Higher?* Yes. That power remained to her, and reason could do nothing to lessen it. At moments only death seemed ever likely to cure him of Minty and then he felt some ease in regarding her as life, appearing to him perhaps for the last time in certain guise.

That evening he was reading the *Telegraph* and beside him Ella was sewing. He had Receptions at six. Suddenly the telephone rang, "I'll go," he said at once, as Ella began to move and he went, closing the door behind him. It was no surprise to hear Minty's voice and although he dreaded what she might say, he was relieved. "We want to see you," she said—with her drawl more pronounced and rougher than he had ever known it. Was she drunk? "Who's *we*?" he said.

Complete silence followed as though he were connected not to a kiosk but to a coffin; then he heard movement and sudden sound, breathing as though a hand had been removed from the mouthpiece. Goole must be standing there beside her.

"I've got something you want," she said. "It's Minty."

" Where are you ? "

" Up the lane beside the George."

" I'll come now," he said.

He heard breathing again and the clonk of the receiver. Then he went through and told Ella that X (a local police officer) had asked if he could come down to the George for a drink—something he wanted to discuss.

She said she was going to ring Christine. " Give her my love," he said.

" You'll be seeing her Saturday."

" Saturday ? "

" The pantomime."

" Oh, yes—I forgot."

" You mean you never heard. I'm sure I don't know where you've been lately, Phil."

He went out leaving her by the fire, under the " Stag at Midnight," beside the frayed Penguins.

" Take your coat," she called and he did, from above the humming-birds—his duffel-coat with the hood.

And so he set out.

He did not know what he would do. He might pay them money, he might try to frighten them ; if Goole was looking not for money but for physical revenge then again he did not know what he would do. . . . That, too, would be a new experience. It would be new. The whole thing was new.

Peter got into the car as he opened the door and Ayrton let him stay.

Fine rain began specking the windscreen as he drove into Buxton. It was a dark night and no stars showed.

He passed the bakery where he had seen Minty in the window. The lights were off inside but he could see the huge white trays, empty and gleaming.

Pictures on the Wall

Familiar places conjured up images of the past as though he were going away for ever. There was the Y.W.C.A. where he had addressed the Women's Institute on Juvenile Delinquency when he first came, and there on the hill was the modern school, like some sort of breeding cage, with a raised bit like the cenotaph made of concrete and glass at one end and a swooping roof, like the penguin house in the London Zoo; and then the new slaughter-house and bus-shelter, and the lane running off to the Pole who did Ella's feet once a month, and the old Victorian station.

Victorian! . . . When it came to a scandal things hadn't changed much. It could kill Ella, he thought.

In spite of these premonitions Ayrton felt relieved, even stimulated. He was meeting Goole as an equal, unprotected.

He stopped about fifty yards up from the corner and switched off his headlights and lit his pipe. While the flame was alternately bending and leaping at the rim of the bowl he saw headlights coming from behind in his driving mirror. They were close together and high suggesting a small old-fashioned car, perhaps a Baby Austin. The slowness of its approach held his attention—and then the fact that it was preparing not to pass him but to halt behind. This it did, whereupon its lights went out altogether.

There were no street-lights here, only the porch-light of the hotel fifty yards away, so for a moment it was as though the car had vanished. Then he picked up its outline, surely a Baby Austin.

She must have kept it here, he thought, somewhere in the village.

Would it be just the two of them or would Goole have got help? The important thing, Ayrton remembered, is to keep your kidneys covered, curl up tight like a ball. He heard a door slam and he got out.

The outline was unmistakable—Minty—by herself.

"You came," she said, mildly sardonic, faintly incredulous.

Then her stiletto heels came on, sounding sharp and groggy on the pavement.

"Did you think I wouldn't?"

"I wondered."

"Are you alone?" he said.

"Well, there's you," she said, "I suppose I ought to have a bodyguard."

"Won't you get in? It's damp."

"I think I'll just get damp." And she stood there.

"Well?" he said.

She could still try to tease—tease him with his own fears, with her purpose, with the question marks that would always stand against the way she had behaved. But he was past teasing. Perhaps she sensed this for she said: "I've just got something to give you—that's all. . . ."

Something white in her hand rose up in the darkness towards his face—sulphuric acid—a demand for payment by a certain date? It stopped somewhere level with her waist.

"Aren't you going to take it?" she said.

His hand closed on a package.

"What is it?" he said.

"Your letter—and a present."

"My letter . . ."

"Wasn't that what you wanted?"

"Well, what's the price, Minty?"

"Price? . . . you said you wanted it back. . . ."

He was silent for a time holding the package awkwardly.

"But why now . . . suddenly. And why all this . . . here . . . at night. I don't understand."

" I wanted to see if you'd come."

He heard the vestige of her tease laugh, her inane school-girl snigger which usually preceded her " old soul " look, as closely and paradoxically as a clown going before a king.

" Was that the only reason ? " he said.

He never forgot her hesitation.

" Yes," she said.

Then he understood: she was there without Goole's knowledge.

" No one knows you're here, do they ? " he said.

Another hesitation—and that was enough. In case he had misinterpreted everything yet again, he changed the subject, choosing to fix impressions as they now stood, for ever.

" What's in the parcel, Minty ? "

" Socks . . . I gave Albert a pair."

" Albert . . ." he said involuntarily.

" He earned a souvenir, too ! "

" Minty, is there anything I can do ? "

" Such as ? "

" Can I help—either of you ? " She hesitated again—less agreeably.

" You want to feel good, don't you . . . approved of . . . by everyone, the fathers, even God still ? But don't worry, you're perfect, all round, surely you've proved it, haven't you . . . ? "

" Minty ! "

" What ? "

" Don't go on. . . . I know . . . my letter was false."

" Was it ? " A silence fell. What was the good of trying to explain.

" Take some money, Minty," he said at last, in a low voice that verged on bitterness.

" You mean for that visit you paid me ? "

" Don't say that."

" Then why ? "

" Because it would give me pleasure."

" In that case give yourself a real kick . . ." and she put out her hand.

He gave her what he had on him which was a few pounds.

" Thanks," she laughed, and then stood there without moving or speaking.

" Good-bye, Minty."

" Good-bye."

But she still stood there.

Amazed and influenced slowly like something beginning to float he took a step forward and kissed her cheek, paused with his lips on the flesh. " Good-bye," he whispered, as though speaking to her for the first and only time. She never moved or spoke and that, for some reason, was an answer, the only answer, possible.

Then it finished like a trick or an optical delusion—and things were themselves again, the roads and the two cars and the separate lives and the inexorable identities: she walking back to her car and he following. When she was in and the window wound down she said:

" He can sing, can't he ? " He saw two gleams, like blades or dew. There were tears in her eyes.

" Yes . . . he can sing," he said. He thought, I never loved anyone, not till now. It was always just myself, extensions of myself. But now . . .

" Good-bye, Minty," he said.

Then the starter groaned, the engine burst into feeble life, and the ancient upright shape of the Baby Austin turned sharply towards a gate and after two reverses went off back the way it had come, pausing for a moment on the verge of the main street where the bright background cast by its own lamps on the far verge showed the little box in silhouette, brilliant red all over, with Minty's head a blob in the rear window and the exposed wheels turned acutely and in full view like the castors of a table.

Suddenly he wished she had kept the letter.

The inside light of the car was broken so he did not open the package till he got back to the hall of the house. There, by the humming-birds, and barometer, he uncovered his letter—and a pair of violent electric-blue socks striped with marigold and cherry zigzags. There was something else in the parcel: a cutting from *Reveille*—a girl on the ground turning sideways to avoid the lick of a white poodle. She was laughing in a bikini. You could see into her mouth but not much between her breasts because they were so full and constricted that they touched. Minty had written underneath in green ink, " For your office."

Ella was sewing, in the same position as before and *The Telegraph* lay sprawled where he had left it.

" You weren't long, dear."

" No. He had to get on."

" Was it nasty out ? "

" No," he said vaguely. " It wasn't bad at all."

He unfolded *The Telegraph* and turned to the letter column.

" Guess what," she said, beginning to smile in a way that made him lower the paper, and look at her. " Christine rang when you were out: she's engaged ! "

Ella's eyes were liquid. " After the hospital ball," she said, " Tom Fawcett saw her home. They don't want to wait, though it will mean her giving up her music. You won't stop her, will you, Phil? She's so happy."

" But how are they going to live ? "

" She's taking a job with Welsh and Peabody till he gets his diploma."

He felt the silence in the house grow as though far away a keyboard had been shut with a bang, a humming bang, a vast unresolved chord, the raw material of all feeling, undifferentiated like the single wild cry of Goole in his song; then he felt a sense of defeat that was oddly pain-less. Christine, his daughter, was happy. The reflected glory of that single fact shone now on Ella's face, making her look happy too. It was as though the two women had escaped from something. But from what . . . what else but the tyranny of his aspirations and of his own point of view? Well, he too was glad. With love he pictured Christine's face, her awkward piano-playing, thought of the pressures he had put upon her and of his undervaluation of what she clearly valued most, basic, simple things far removed from the exceptional and the ' sublime '. In remorse he felt delivered. But by whom? Paradoxically it was Minty who seemed like some sort of optical illusion, to have lured him not, as hoped, to herself, but to where he was better off; and to have demoralised him only to strengthen him.

" That's fine, dear," he said. " I'm so glad."

The movement he had made in putting down the paper had given Peter the idea that a walk was impending. The dogs tail thumped the ground. Ayrton said he hoped Christine would be happy both with Tom Fawcett and at Welsh and Peabody, and then after a few second; staring into the fire he said " Yes, that's great news, dear. I'll ring her up."

Pictures on the Wall

Ayrton gathered together the edges of the paper and Peter's head subsided. Christine's news deserved more celebration than he seemed able to give it. Ella smiled with confidence but he knew she could tell him nothing about Tom Fawcett or Welsh and Peabody or how much they were likely to see Christine in the future. Nevertheless for Ella it was enough: posterity was assured.

Turning his thoughts from family happiness to the reprieve, unknown to Ella or Christine, which made that happiness possible, he wondered if he would ever tell anyone of the life he had led in recent weeks or whether memory would soon affect a suitable censorship. The explosive socks which Minty had given him and her ringing question—Don't you know you're mad?—should help him not to forget, but they did not help him to understand.

Awed suddenly by a primitive sense of gratiude which sought some Power outside himself to thank for his narrow escape, his eyes settled on that part of the sofa where Minty had sat only a few weeks ago, and from there lifted to the picture of the stag at midnight by which she had been so shocked.

He remember her expression and his eyes turned inwards in search of some half-forgotten association. Wasn't it in the Buxton stationers last week, near the bakery, he had seen a reproduction in a plane-wood frame of an early French Madonna and Child. . . . The expression was something like Minty's rarest, unless he had imagined that to: impervious calm, bearing hope and love even in the most hopeless circumstances . . . and in the light of foreknowledge.

Ayrton decided he would change the pictures in his office, and get the reproduction from the stationers for a start.